PRAISE FOR
THE CREATIVITY PROJECT

An Amazon Best Book of the Year So Far

★ "Anyone reading this book will discover the joy
and wonder in each and every prompt and response."
—*School Library Connection*, starred review

"Packed with ideas and inspiration, this volume
provides fodder for the imagination...."
—*School Library Journal*

"There's plenty here to ignite kids' imaginations
and provide both laughs and food for thought." —*Booklist*

"This is a must-have resource for creative writing classes
and clubs, or for anyone seeking to launch or hone their
own imaginative capabilities." —*The Bulletin*

"An end section includes 44 additional prompts from
the participants for readers, which further emphasizes
the collection's celebration of 'the way ideas can be story
seeds that take root and blossom.'"
—*Publishers Weekly*

"Demonstrating the anarchic nature of creativity might
be the most powerful message of this inviting project...."
—*The Horn Book*

The CREATIVITY Project

Edited by
COLBY SHARP

Little, Brown and Company
New York   Boston

FOR THE STUDENTS OF PARMA ELEMENTARY. DREAM BIG!

———————————————

Compilation copyright © 2018 by Colby Sharp
Additional copyright/credits information is on page 278.

Cover art © 2018 by Javier Pérez; color pencils © BarvArt/Shutterstock.com; tape © schab/Shutterstock.com; sticky note © Kindlena/Shutterstock.com; pencil shavings © Dokmaihaeng/Shutterstock.com; sharpeners © ziviani/Shutterstock.com; paintbrush © revenaif/Shutterstock.com; marker © vandame/Shutterstock.com; hand lettering by Margaret Kimball. Cover design by David Caplan and Nicole Brown. Cover copyright © 2018 by Hachette Book Group, Inc.
Interior design by Nicole Brown

Little, Brown and Company
Hachette Book Group
1290 Avenue of the Americas, New York, NY 10104
Visit us at LBYR.com

Originally published in hardcover and ebook by Little, Brown and Company in March 2018
First Paperback Edition: September 2019

Little, Brown and Company is a division of Hachette Book Group, Inc. The Little, Brown name and logo are trademarks of Hachette Book Group, Inc.

The publisher is not responsible for websites (or their content) that are not owned by the publisher.

The Library of Congress has cataloged the hardcover edition as follows:
Names: Sharp, Colby, editor.
Title: The creativity project : an awesometastic
story collection / edited by Colby Sharp.
Description: First edition. | New York : Little, Brown and Company, 2018.
Identifiers: LCCN 2017028849| ISBN 9780316507813 (hardback) |
ISBN 9780316507806 (ebook library edition) |
ISBN 9780316507783 (ebook fixed edition)
Subjects: LCSH: American literature—21st century. | Creative writing. | Fiction—Authorship. | Creation (Literary, artistic, etc.) |
Classification: LCC PS536.3 .C74 2018 | DDC 810.8/006—dc23
LC record available at https://lccn.loc.gov/2017028849

ISBNs: 978-0-316-50779-0 (pbk.), 978-0-316-50778-3 (ebook)

Printed in the United States of America

LSC-C

10 9 8 7 6 5 4 3 2

CONTENTS

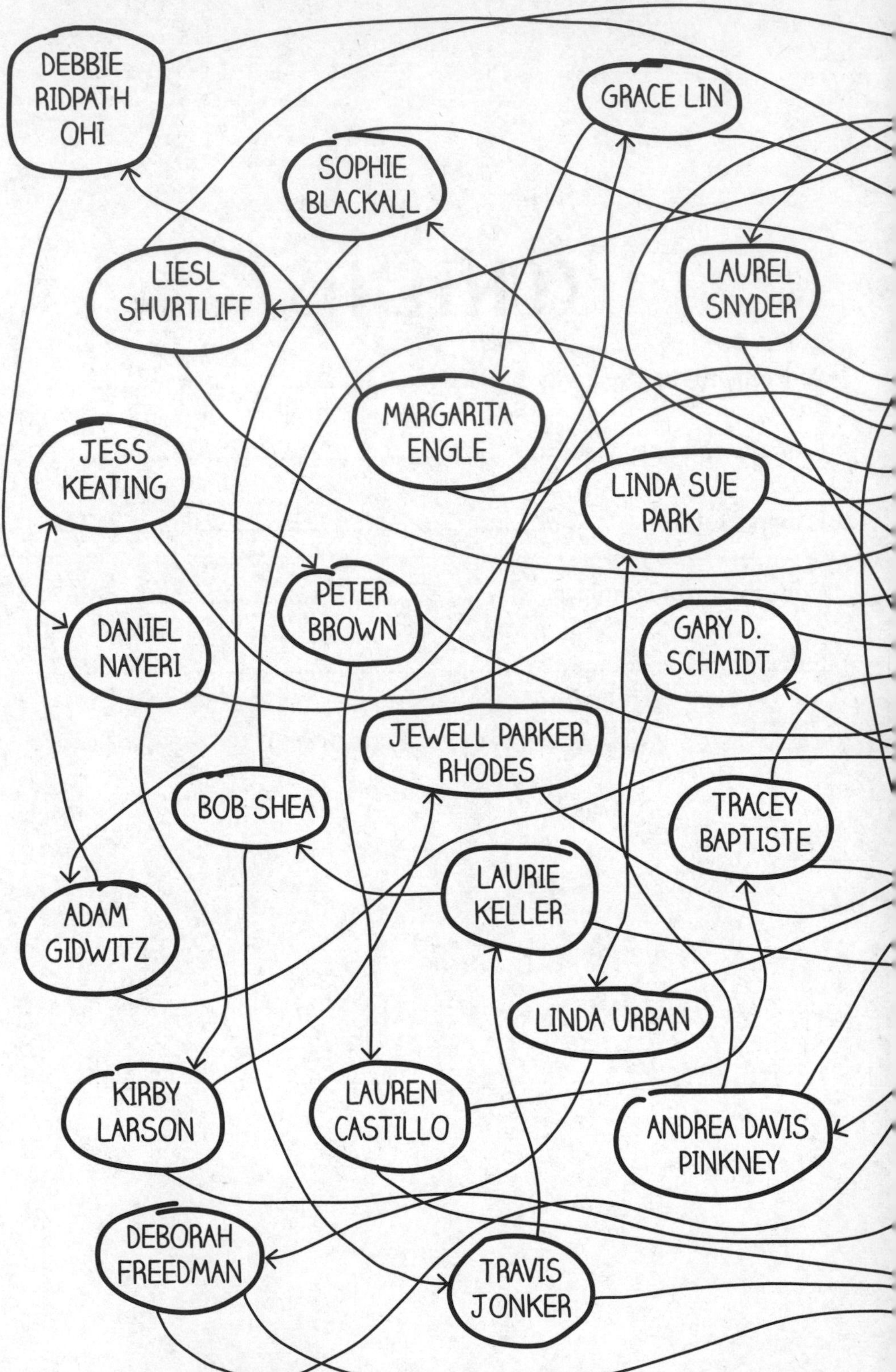
DEBBIE RIDPATH OHI
GRACE LIN
SOPHIE BLACKALL
LIESL SHURTLIFF
LAUREL SNYDER
MARGARITA ENGLE
JESS KEATING
LINDA SUE PARK
PETER BROWN
DANIEL NAYERI
GARY D. SCHMIDT
JEWELL PARKER RHODES
BOB SHEA
TRACEY BAPTISTE
LAURIE KELLER
ADAM GIDWITZ
LINDA URBAN
KIRBY LARSON
LAUREN CASTILLO
ANDREA DAVIS PINKNEY
DEBORAH FREEDMAN
TRAVIS JONKER

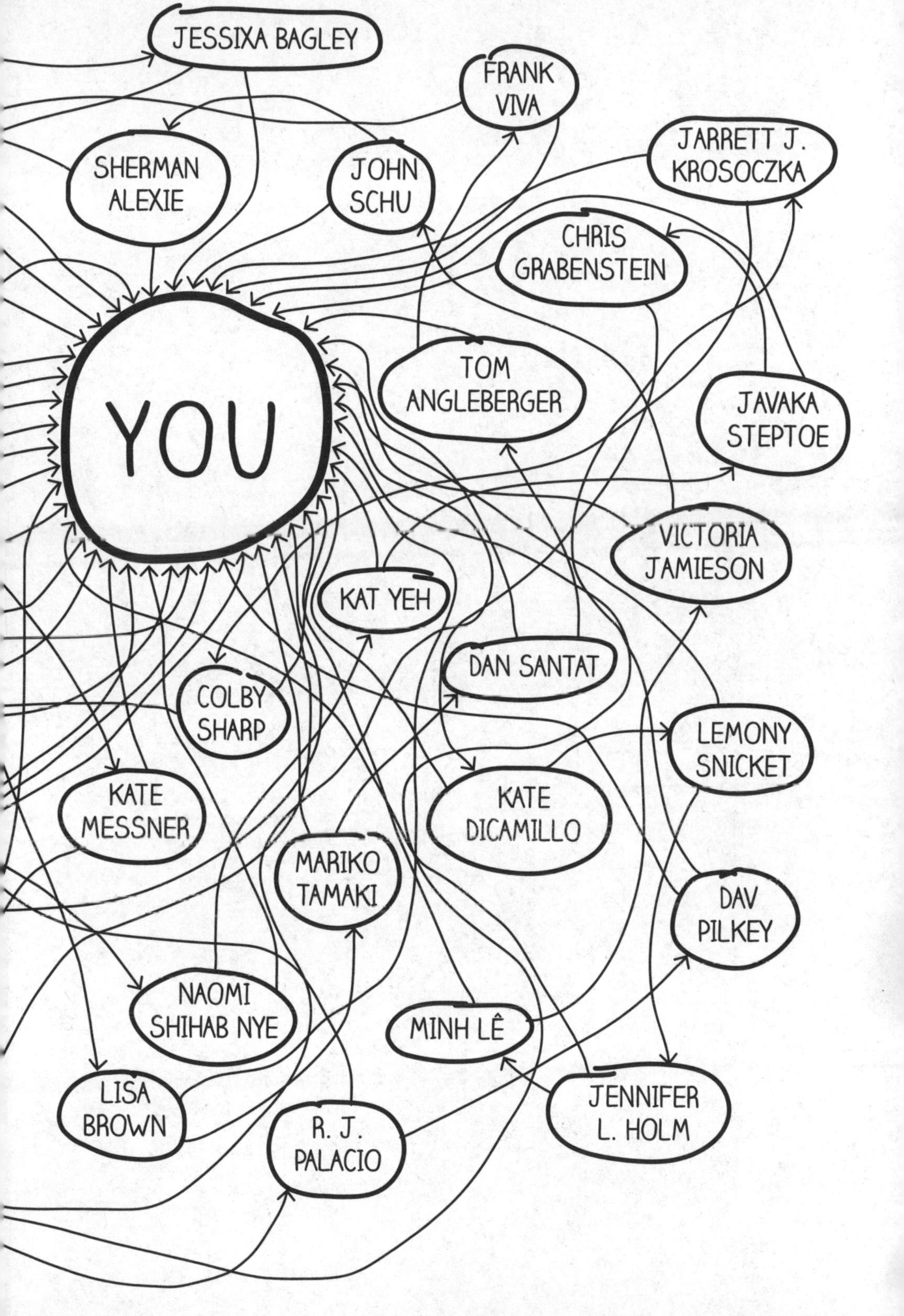
JESSIXA BAGLEY
FRANK VIVA
JARRETT J. KROSOCZKA
SHERMAN ALEXIE
JOHN SCHU
CHRIS GRABENSTEIN
YOU
TOM ANGLEBERGER
JAVAKA STEPTOE
VICTORIA JAMIESON
KAT YEH
DAN SANTAT
COLBY SHARP
LEMONY SNICKET
KATE MESSNER
KATE DICAMILLO
MARIKO TAMAKI
DAV PILKEY
NAOMI SHIHAB NYE
MINH LÊ
LISA BROWN
R. J. PALACIO
JENNIFER L. HOLM

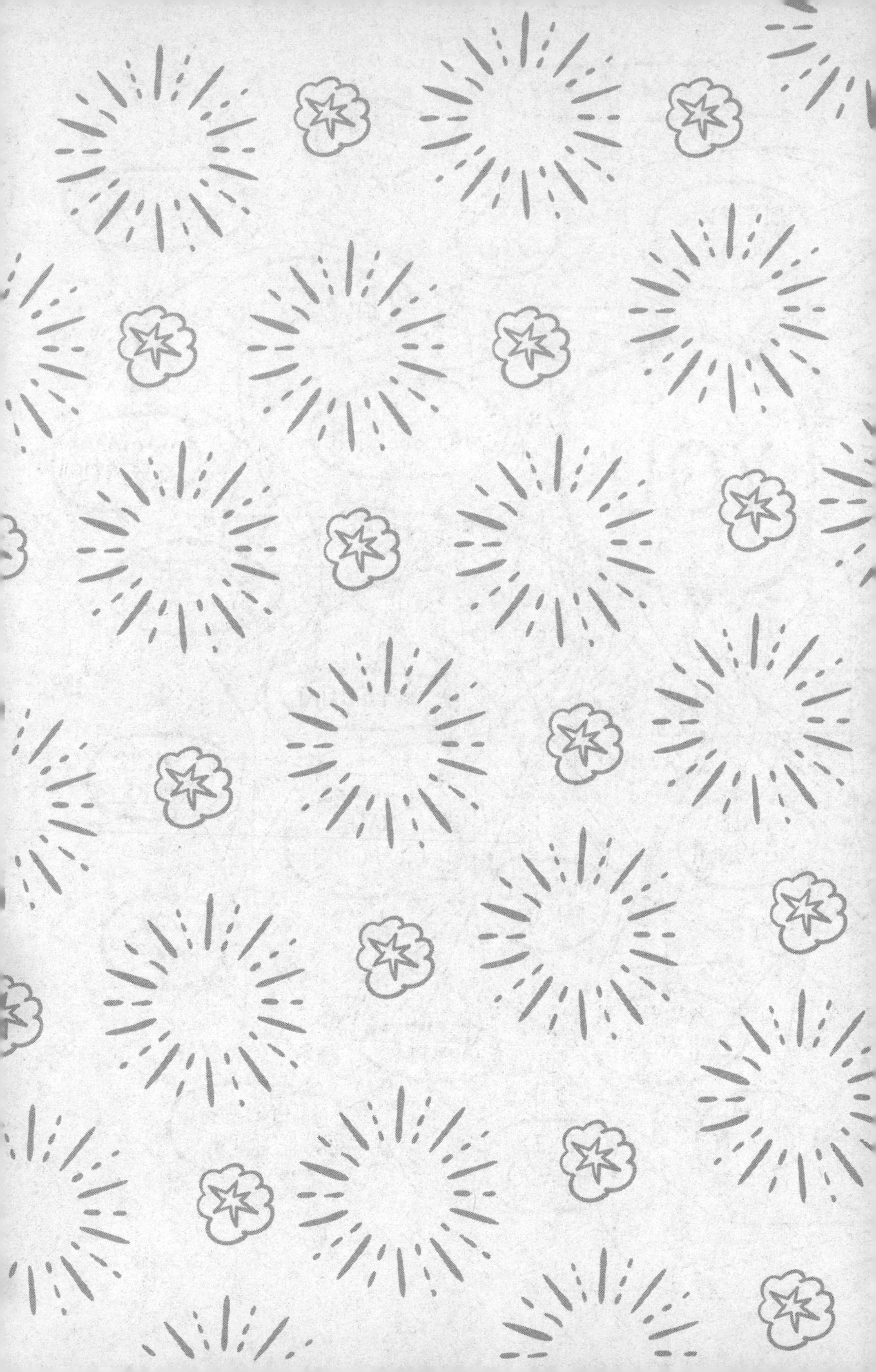

WELCOME TO THE CREATIVITY PROJECT!

The book you hold in your hands is filled with ideas and stories created by some of my favorite authors and illustrators. Here you will find talking hats, a magic elevator, a hefty cat, and advice from beyond the grave. Each time I read through the collection, my mind is blown.

This project began with an idea: I wanted to celebrate the way ideas can be story seeds that take root and blossom. I decided to embark on an experiment and observe the way that creativity works. So I challenged forty-four children's book creators to a crazy game of creativity. It made my heart sing when they all said yes.

Here's how the project works: First, I asked each contributor to send me two creative prompts—seeds that could get the wheels of their fellow creative friends' minds turning. Prompts could be poems, photographs, drawings, *anything*.

Then, I mailed off a mysterious package to everyone containing the two prompts that I picked for that person. They were asked to choose one and use it to inspire an awesome creation. A few weeks later, the pieces started coming in, and HOLY SMOKES! I was completely blown away. We received all sorts of fantastic contributions: short stories, comics, poems, and illustrations. Experiencing them caused me to laugh, cry, think, wonder— and one even made the hairs on my arms stand up.

On the following pages, you will find all these prompts and the pieces they inspired. You will also discover a section at the end containing forty-four fresh new prompts, one from each contributor, intended for you, to inspire your own creations.

More than anything, I hope that you enjoy the Creativity Project as much as I have. But here is a warning before you go any further in this book! Chances are that while you are reading, your arm will start to wiggle. Your fingers will search for something to write with, and your brain will start thinking of what you would do if I sent the prompts in the mail to you. Don't fight the urge. Pick up a pencil, a crayon, or a marker, and create something awesome.

Colby Sharp

PROMPT

BY KATE DICAMILLO

Get on any method of public transport (bus, subway, school bus, train, plane) with a notebook and a pen. Write down five overheard sentences from five different people. Take one of those sentences and use it as the opening line of dialogue in a very short story (five hundred words max) that is told entirely in dialogue.

RESPONSE

BY LEMONY SNICKET

"I want to make myself perfectly clear. Do you understand?"

"Yes."

"I'm not sure you do. I want to make myself perfectly clear."

"I understand."

"I want my entire body and all of my clothing to be completely transparent. Do you understand?"

"What?"

"Look at my shoes. You can hardly see them. Do you see?"

"Yes, your shoes are the same color and texture as the floor of this bus, so I can hardly see them."

"No, you can hardly see them because I'm making myself clear."

"I don't understand."

"I want to make myself perfectly clear. My toes and my ankles, my socks and my shoes, even the few specks of dirt under my toenails are completely transparent."

"Why are you talking about dirty toenails? You're not making yourself clear."

"Yes, I am. Look at my knees. Do you see?"

"No."

"Exactly! You can hardly see them."

"That's because you're wearing pants that are the exact same color as the seats of this bus."

"No, it's because I'm making myself clear."

"You're not making yourself clear."

"Yes, I am. You just don't understand."

"That's what I mean."

"My pants and my entire leg, including bones and muscles and skin and little hairs, are becoming entirely transparent."

"Now you're talking about little hairs? I don't understand you."

"Why don't you understand? I'm making myself clear."

"No, you're not."

"Yes, I am. Now it's my entire body. I'm tired of being stared at. I don't want anyone to look at me because of my clothing, or the shape of my body, or the color of my skin, or my hat."

"The hat is pretty ridiculous."

"Well, I'm making it clear."

"You are?"

"Yes. In just a few seconds I'm going to be entirely transparent. No one will stare at me ever again for any reason. I'll even stop talking, so I can make myself perfectly clear."

"Why would you stop talking in order to make yourself perfectly clear?"

...

"I don't understand."

...

"Where did you go?"

PROMPT

BY MARGARITA ENGLE

road trip with puppies
just one whiff of forest air
delivers wildness

ROAD TRIP

by Debbie Ridpath Ohi

WE'LL BE AT YOUR UNCLE JOEY'S SOON, EVAN. CAN'T WAIT FOR YOU TO FINALLY MEET HIM!

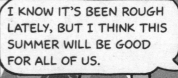

I KNOW IT'S BEEN ROUGH LATELY, BUT I THINK THIS SUMMER WILL BE GOOD FOR ALL OF US.

AH, JUST BREATHE IN THAT FRESH COUNTRY AIR! SMELLS LIKE A CHANCE FOR A NEW BEGINNING, DON'T YOU THINK?

EVAN? ARE YOU LISTENING?

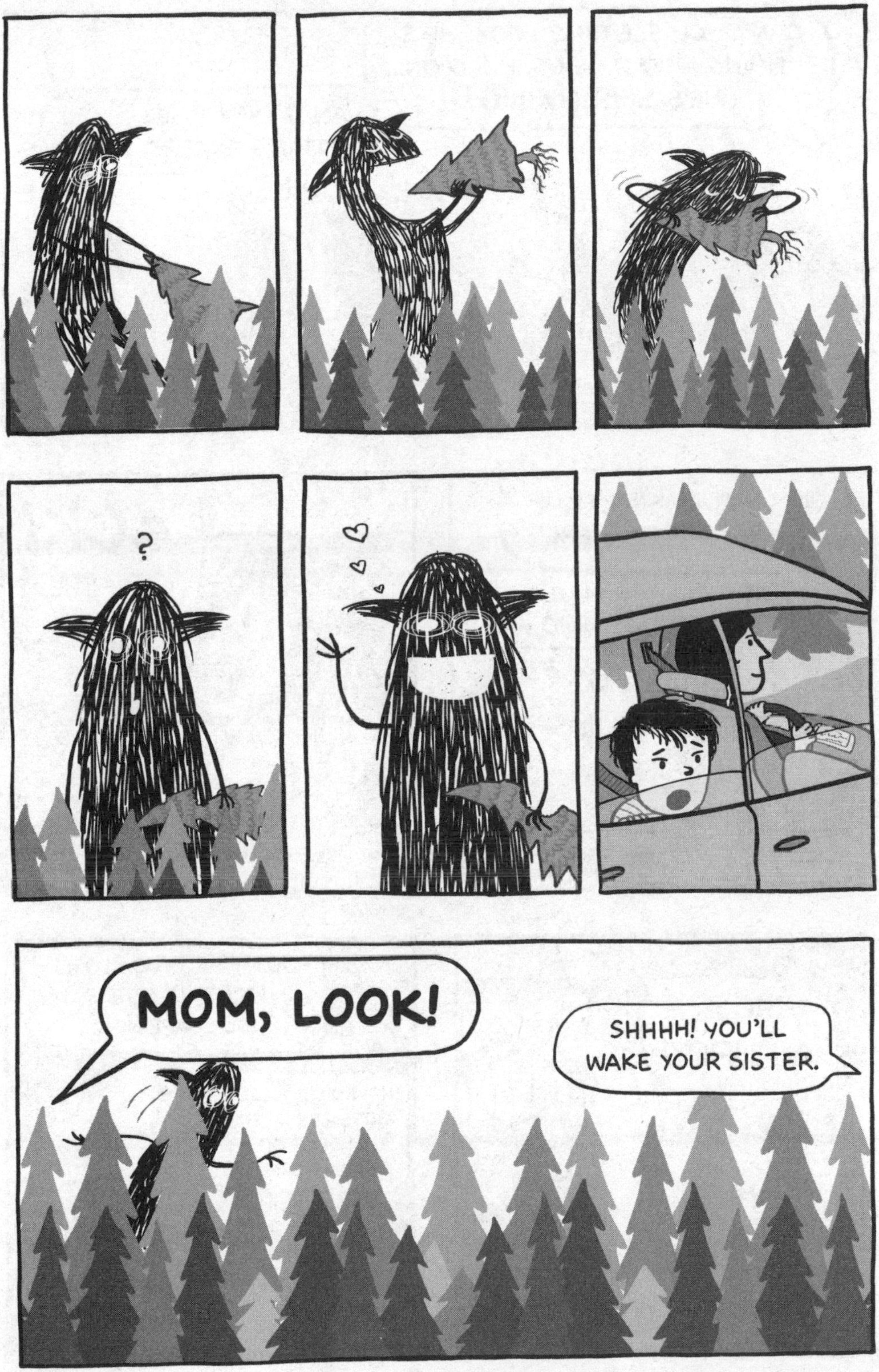
?
MOM, LOOK!
SHHHH! YOU'LL WAKE YOUR SISTER.

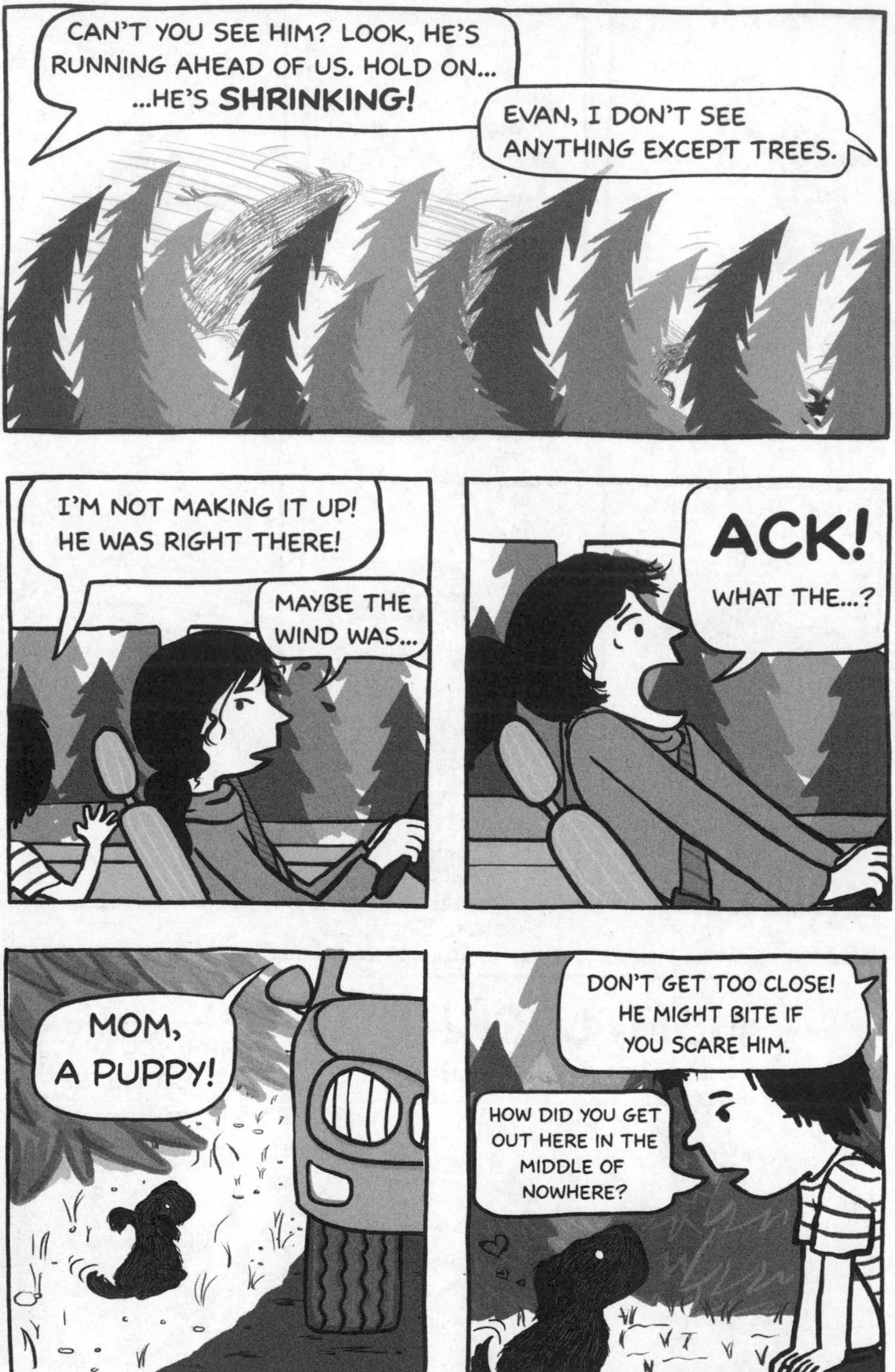
CAN'T YOU SEE HIM? LOOK, HE'S RUNNING AHEAD OF US. HOLD ON... ...HE'S **SHRINKING!**
EVAN, I DON'T SEE ANYTHING EXCEPT TREES.
I'M NOT MAKING IT UP! HE WAS RIGHT THERE!
MAYBE THE WIND WAS...
ACK!
WHAT THE...?
MOM, A PUPPY!
DON'T GET TOO CLOSE! HE MIGHT BITE IF YOU SCARE HIM.
HOW DID YOU GET OUT HERE IN THE MIDDLE OF NOWHERE?

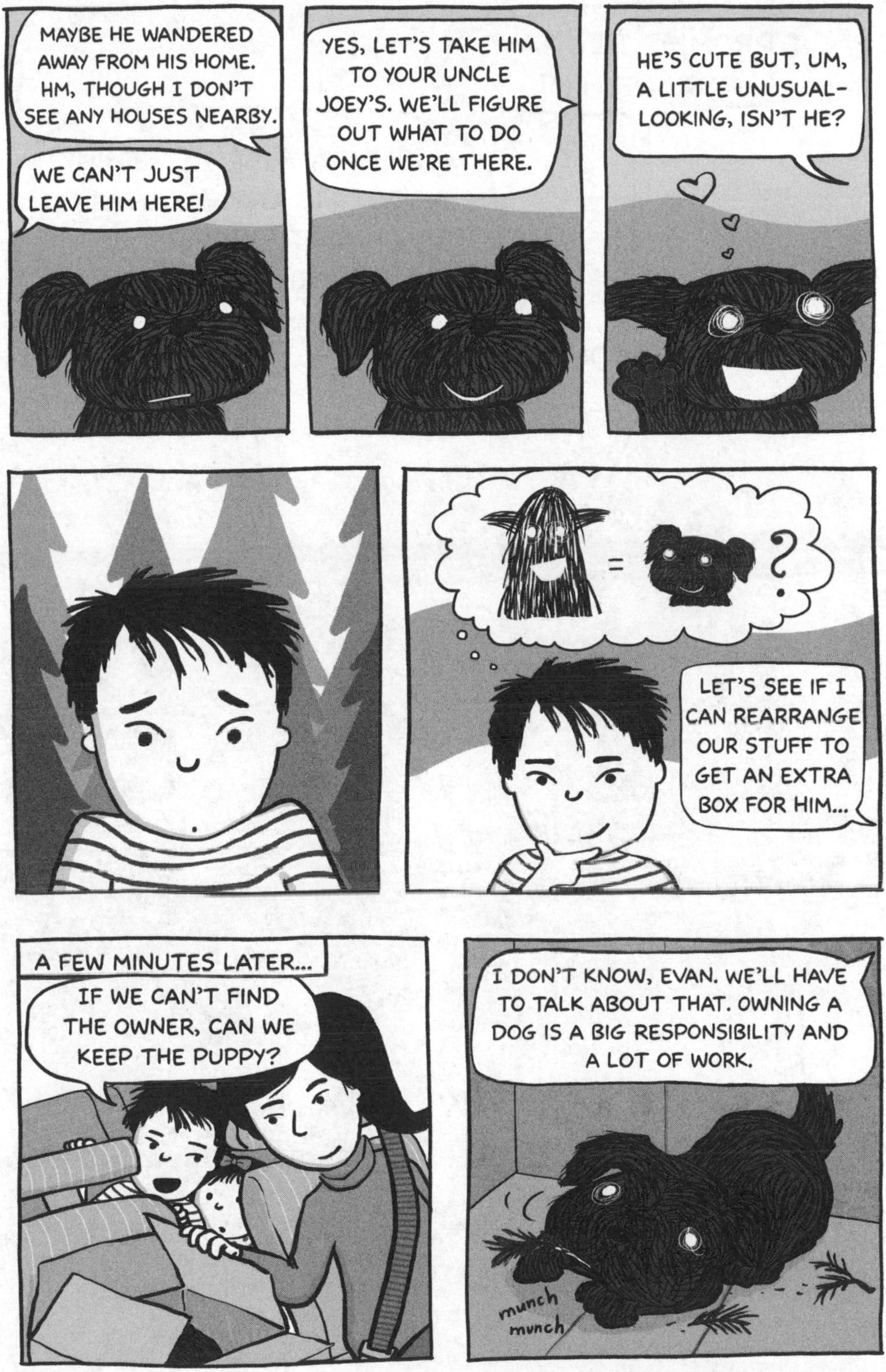
MAYBE HE WANDERED AWAY FROM HIS HOME. HM, THOUGH I DON'T SEE ANY HOUSES NEARBY.
WE CAN'T JUST LEAVE HIM HERE!
YES, LET'S TAKE HIM TO YOUR UNCLE JOEY'S. WE'LL FIGURE OUT WHAT TO DO ONCE WE'RE THERE.
HE'S CUTE BUT, UM, A LITTLE UNUSUAL-LOOKING, ISN'T HE?
LET'S SEE IF I CAN REARRANGE OUR STUFF TO GET AN EXTRA BOX FOR HIM...
A FEW MINUTES LATER...
IF WE CAN'T FIND THE OWNER, CAN WE KEEP THE PUPPY?
I DON'T KNOW, EVAN. WE'LL HAVE TO TALK ABOUT THAT. OWNING A DOG IS A BIG RESPONSIBILITY AND A LOT OF WORK.
munch munch

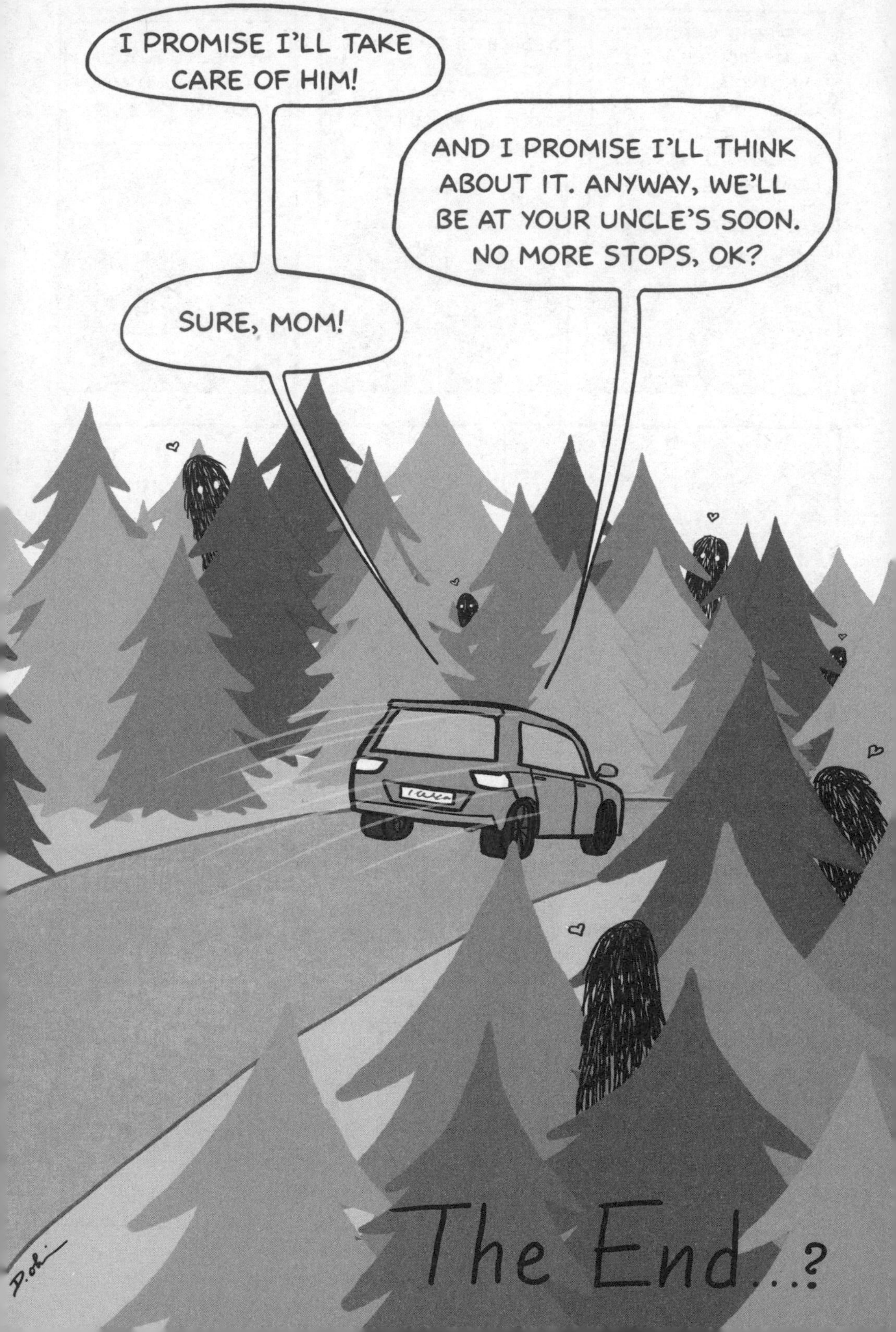
I PROMISE I'LL TAKE CARE OF HIM!
AND I PROMISE I'LL THINK ABOUT IT. ANYWAY, WE'LL BE AT YOUR UNCLE'S SOON. NO MORE STOPS, OK?
SURE, MOM!
The End...?

BY JEWELL PARKER RHODES

You've been dead for a long time. Someone who just passed away asks you what to expect.

RESPONSE

BY GRACE LIN

He never thought he would actually die. Even with all the plastic tubes the doctors had put in his arms and when his skin had turned mottled and blue. Even when his coarse breathing was the only sound he could make, the electronic beeping of the machines keeping tempo with his air-scraping solo. Death was not for him, he believed. Other people, other times, yes. But not him and not now.

"He's in denial," I heard the two women next to his bed whispering. "Should we make him see the truth? He's"—and the woman choked on her words—"he's not going to make it. I don't want him to go the wrong way."

Even though they couldn't see me, I shook my head at them. Perhaps it was only a lesson one can learn after being dead as long as I had, but there was no wrong way to die. Nor was there a right way. Dying is like a stone being dropped from a mountain: The stone can do nothing but fall.

Which is what he did. As his last breath left, I saw him fall right out of his body and tumble onto the floor. He sat up in a daze. The machines began their electronic wail, like a screeching train, as the women gasped and clutched at each other.

"Flo?" he said, looking up at one of the women. "I'm right here, I'm okay. Look."

"She can't see you," I said.

His eyes searched and found me. "Who are you?" he asked. "Why can't she see me?"

"Because you're dead," I told him, answering the second question.

He finally turned his head to see his own lifeless body above him on the bed. Then he swore.

"So are you an angel or something to bring me to heaven?" he asked. "I thought they wore white and wings and things. I didn't think they'd wear sweatshirts that said DITCHED THE BOYFRIEND, KEPT THE SHIRT."

"I'm just a dead person like you," I told him. The room had filled with chaos and wailing, but all of it was barely an echo to us.

"Oh," he said and looked at me again. "Were you hit by a car going to school or something?"

"No," I said. "When you die, the appearance you take is how you looked when you were the most beautiful."

The man glanced at his withered arms, touched his creased face, and snorted. "Yeah, right," he said. "I look just like I did ten minutes ago, and I know I look like an ugly dog."

I tried not to sigh. The newly dead always had so much to learn. "You don't look like you did ten minutes ago," I said, patiently. "You look like you did last week."

"Last week?" he asked. "I was beautiful last week?"

"Yes," I said. "When you told your wife how you realized you didn't tell her enough how much you loved her, but you hoped she knew that you did even if you didn't say it."

His eyes began to water and he quickly looked down, brushing his tears away.

"So, what happens now?" he asked. "Do I get to go to the good place or the bad one?"

I thought for a second. "Both," I said.

"Whaddya mean?" he asked, his words slurring in his rush of sudden fear.

"When you die," I said, "you revisit your ugliest moments the way you are now. You revisit your ugliest moments at your most beautiful."

"That sounds like hell to me," he muttered.

"It is," I said, "but it isn't. Because now you can relive them as the

13

person you should've been. You can change what you did or what you said or make amends. And after you do that, you'll see that it's really heaven."

The beeps and sobs had ended, and without our noticing, his loved ones had left. The room was empty except for one lone orderly unhooking the dead body from the now-silent machines.

"I don't think I wanna go back there," he muttered to himself. "It was a long time ago. I was angry at everyone. I should never have gotten on a train...."

"So you remember?" I asked. "Some people don't even know when they were at their worst."

"Maybe," he said, looking downward, his pale face starting to darken. Then he looked up at me, a curious expression on his face. "How did you die?" he asked.

"Cancer," I told him. "It's true what they say about cigarettes. They'll kill you."

"And this is you at your most beautiful?" he said, looking me over.

"I know," I said, "I would've guessed my wedding day or when they had that surprise party for me at my fiftieth, but nope, this is it."

"You were fifty?" he asked, in surprise. "You look like a kid."

"I was in high school," I told him, indignantly.

"Yeah," he said, "a kid."

The orderly had finished with the machines. Now he was unfurling a white sheet, the ends of it flapping a gentle breeze.

"Well, tell me, then," the dead man said, "why is this when you were most beautiful? What were you doing?"

"Nothing much," I said. "I was just riding the subway, late one night. I had met some friends for something and was on my way home and worried I was going to get in trouble because I was getting in late—past my curfew—and I knew my parents would have a fit. Then I heard this shouting in the front of the car. I was curious—I never was one who could mind their own business, so I got up to see what was going on."

The orderly straightened the folds of the white sheet, hiding the outstretched fingers of the lifeless body.

"Then what?" the dead man pressed me.

14

"Well, there was this guy, completely drunk, yelling at this woman in one of those scarf things—what do they call them again? To cover their hair because they're Muslim? That's right, hijabs. Anyway, he was calling her all these horrible things, like a terrorist and calling her hijab a rag—"

"A rag?" the man interrupted. The orderly had left, and now only a shrouded form lay on the bed.

"Uh-huh." I nodded. "I could see that the woman was really scared and everyone else in the subway was just standing there, staring."

He swallowed and looked at me. "And then what did you do?" he asked.

"Well, I don't know why, but I just barged through everyone and sat down right next to her," I continued, "and I said, 'Hey, do you know my friend Saba? You look like one of the ladies that came to her birthday party.' Which was kind of true, even though I knew it wasn't her."

"That woman looked at me with such big eyes, I remember thinking how shiny they were—like black nail polish...." I began to drift off, remembering.

"What did that drunk guy do?" the man cut in, gaping at me.

"Oh, he yelled a bit more," I said, "but we ignored him. We talked—I don't even remember what we said, I think I blabbered about Saba's party. But he kind of lost steam when we started talking. We got off at the next stop, and then I was really late," I said. "Yeah, did I get it when I got home."

"You didn't tell your parents?" he asked me.

"No, I didn't think it seemed like anything to tell," I said. "But now, I guess it was, since...well, look at me."

He looked at me and I met his gaze. His haunted eyes burned into mine, and his mouth dropped open. He did remember.

"Come," I said, reaching my hand out to him. "The train is waiting for us."

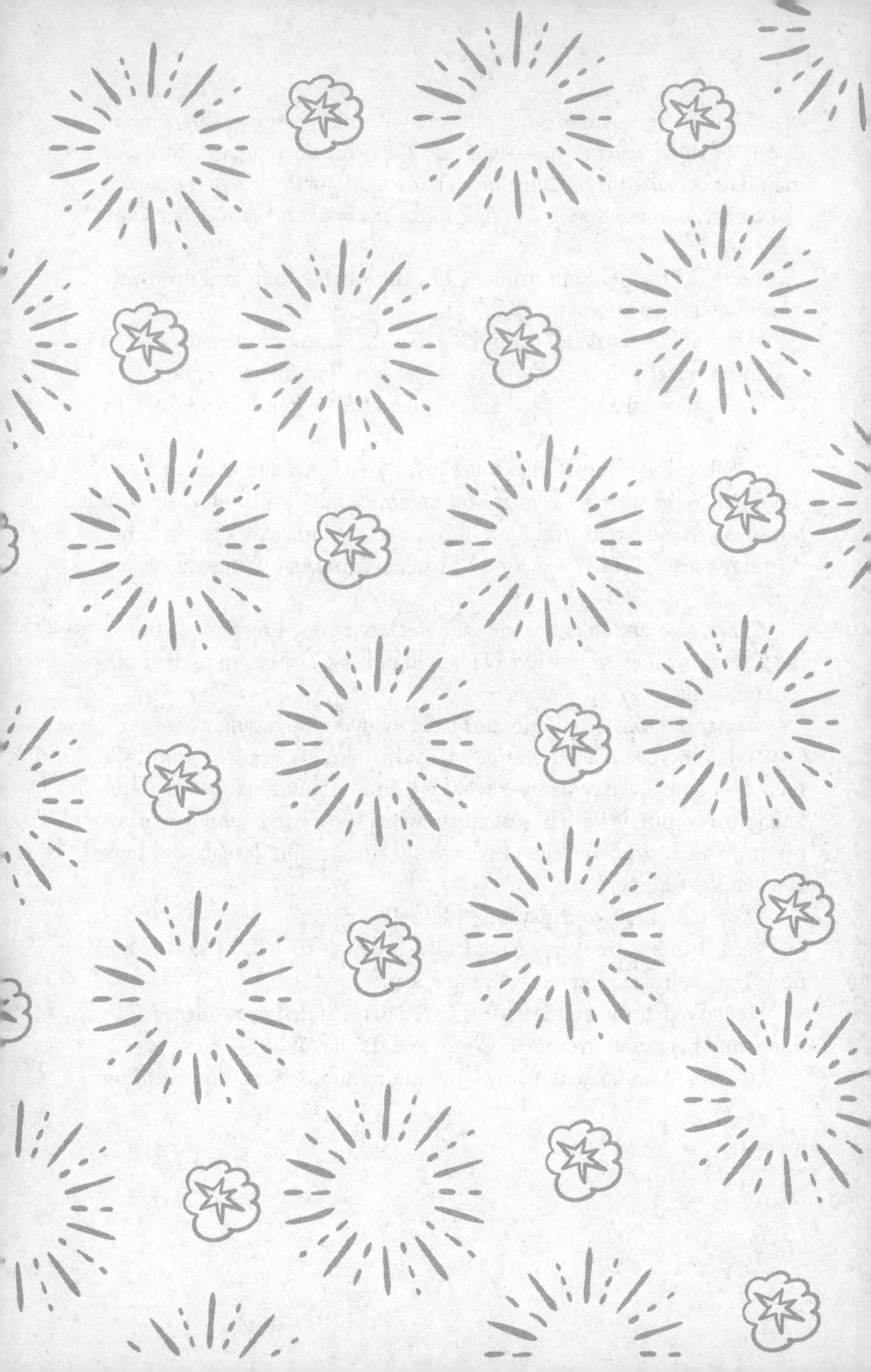

PROMPT

BY LISA BROWN

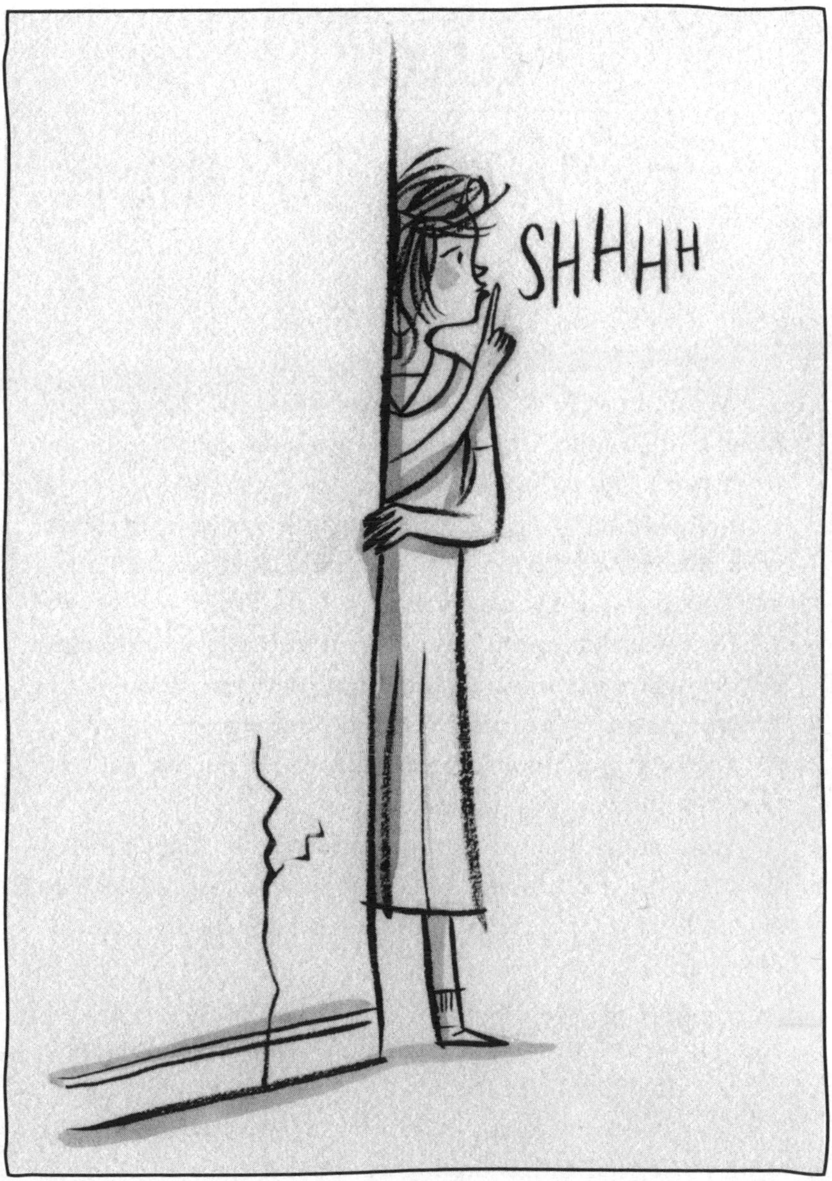
SHHHH

RESPONSE

BY MARIKO TAMAKI

To the lady who lives at 425 Briar Hill Avenue:

My name is Angela and I am ten years old. I live at 459 Briar Hill Avenue. It is the house with the oak tree in the front yard. I go to St. Clements school.

I am writing because three days ago ~~I was in your house broke into your house~~ I was in your house and I was not invited into your house and you did not know I was there.

I was not alone ~~but it is not my job to write for the other person who also was in your house with me. I was with another person whose name I am not telling you.~~

I was in your house because another person and me were working on being spies.

Spies are people who are paid to watch things around them. Spies are looking for people who are suspicious and following up on that to see what happens so they can report it.

To be a spy one thing is you have to be able to access and gain entry into a house without someone inviting you in or knowing you are there.

This is because a spy is looking at people who do not want to be seen and so do not want to let spies in.

So because your house is kind of busted up and the side door doesn't work we decided to do your house.

Also because it seems like you don't want to let people in.

Also my friend said maybe you are doing some secret things because you wear big sweaters all the time and you have lots of papers all around your house and you don't have a job. Also my dad says your car has a trunk big enough to fit a body in.

I was in your house three times.

The first time was just to see if the door was open and it was. I stepped inside your house with both feet then we left. The radio was on.

The second time we went up the stairs into your kitchen and looked at your fridge and we went through your garbage to see if there were any files in there.

There were no files and you have a lot of yogurt in your fridge.

And we saw your cat. Does your cat have one eye or is it just closing one eye all the time?

And the third time we went through the kitchen into the room with the dining table and into your living room. My friend thought your living room looked like a haunted house because you have the painting of the guy on the wall. I thought the guy on the wall looked like Dracula. Maybe it is your dad. We were looking at the painting when you came home in your car with the trunk big enough for a body.

My friend and I lied behind the couch while you had tea and watched soap operas.

We lay there as still as a person can possibly lay for a whole hour. My friend had to cough the whole time.

You have a lot of cat hair behind your couch.

You talked to your cat and it sounded like you were eating yogurt. Or something. Or maybe you weren't talking to your cat, maybe you were talking to the painting of the old guy.

Maybe that's why you kept saying, "Who's a grumpy face now, smart guy?"

Then we heard you get up and go to the kitchen and we decided to make a run for it. So it was me and my friend that knocked over the lamp when we made a run for it because we were afraid maybe we would never get out.

I do not know if you saw us on the way out.

I thought maybe you did.

I thought maybe you had one eye closed as well when I saw you but maybe that's not true.

I am still wondering but my mom said whatever is happening with your eye or eyes it is none of my business.

My dad also said that you should know I am a minor and that I have my whole life ahead of me.

If I stop committing crimes like breaking into houses.

So I am sorry. I hope the lamp was not broken and next time maybe you should clean up your house a bit more.

Yours truly,

Angela

PROMPT

BY TRAVIS JONKER

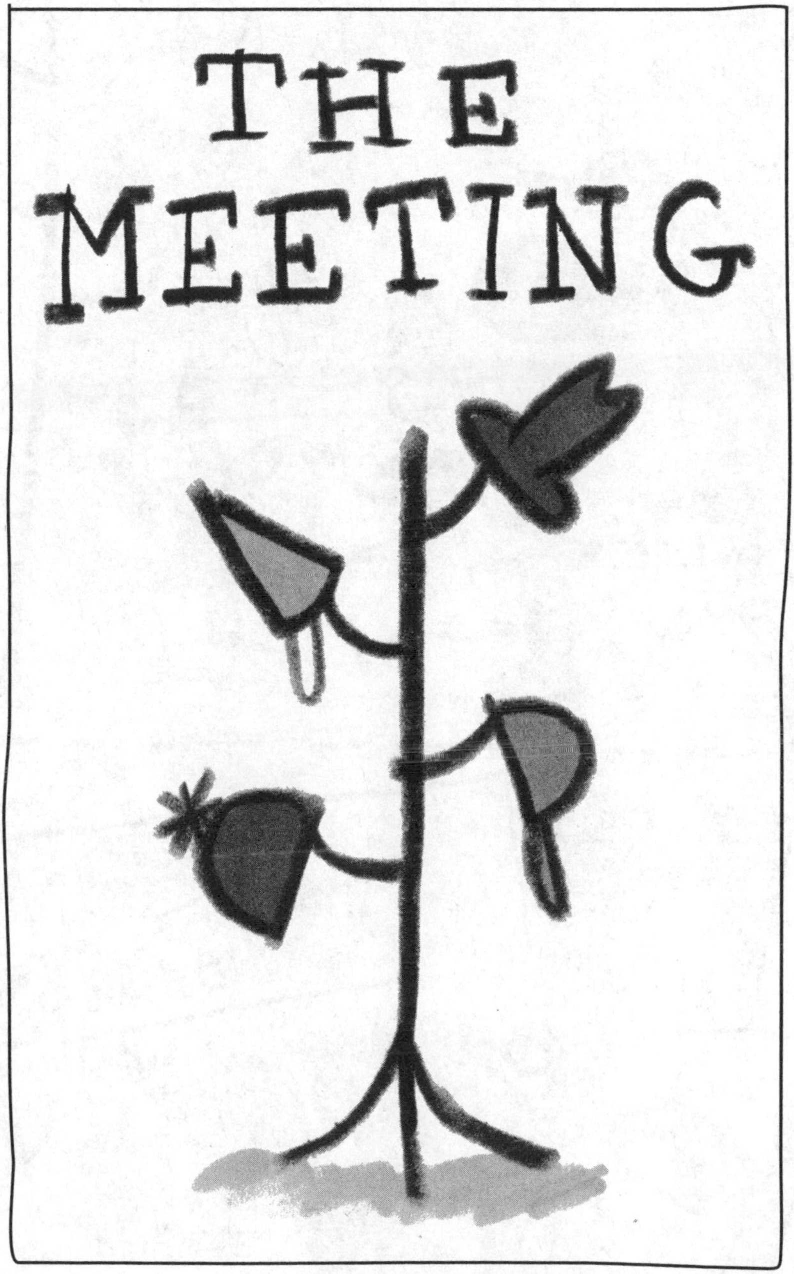
THE MEETING

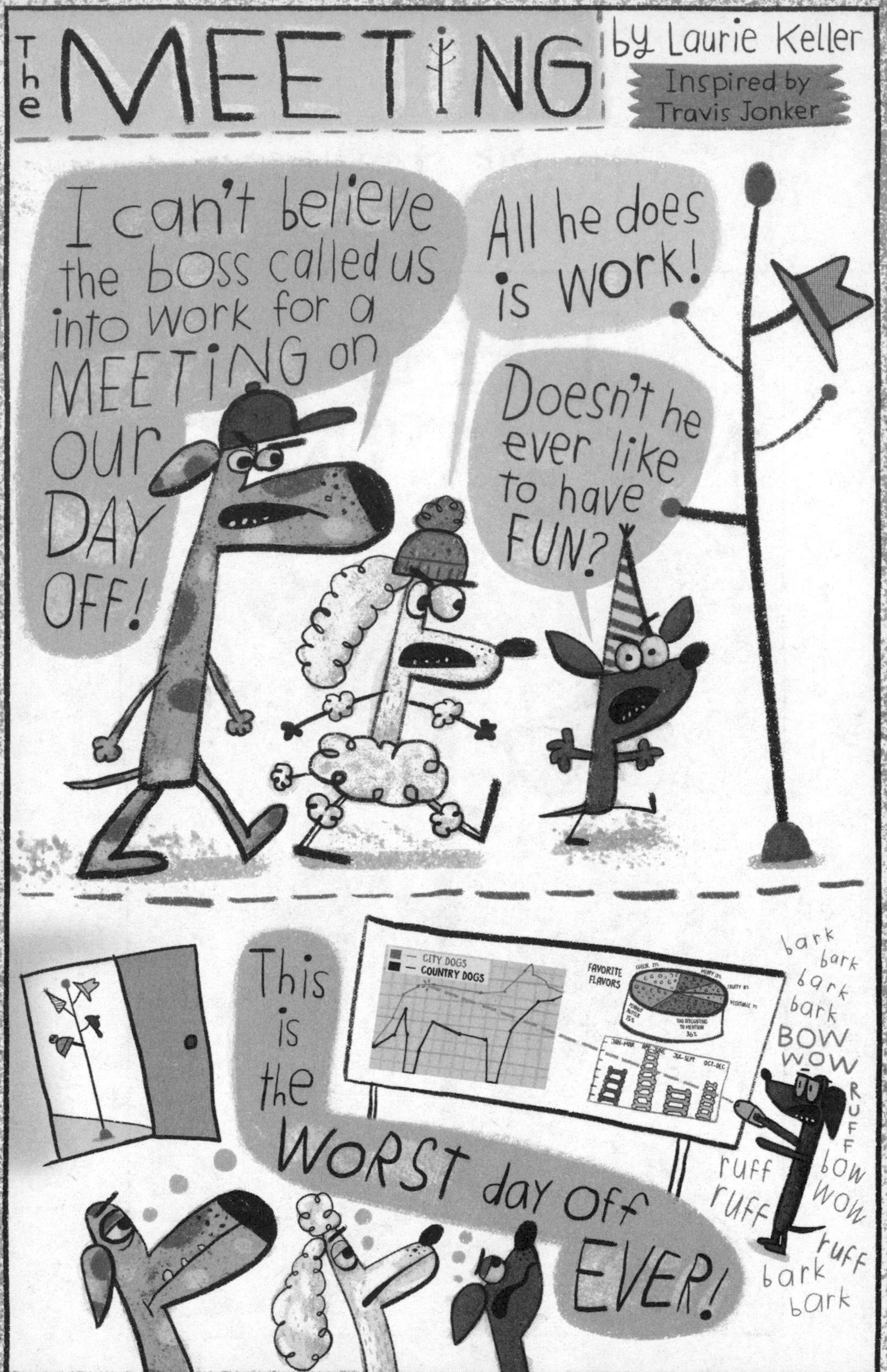
The MEETING
by Laurie Keller
Inspired by Travis Jonker
I can't believe the boss called us into work for a MEETING on our DAY OFF!
All he does is work!
Doesn't he ever like to have FUN?
This is the WORST day off EVER!
CITY DOGS
COUNTRY DOGS
FAVORITE FLAVORS
PEANUT BUTTER 15%
TOO DISGUSTING TO MENTION 36%
JAN-MAR
JUL-SEPT
OCT-DEC
bark bark bark bark BOW WOW RUFF bow wow ruff ruff ruff bark bark

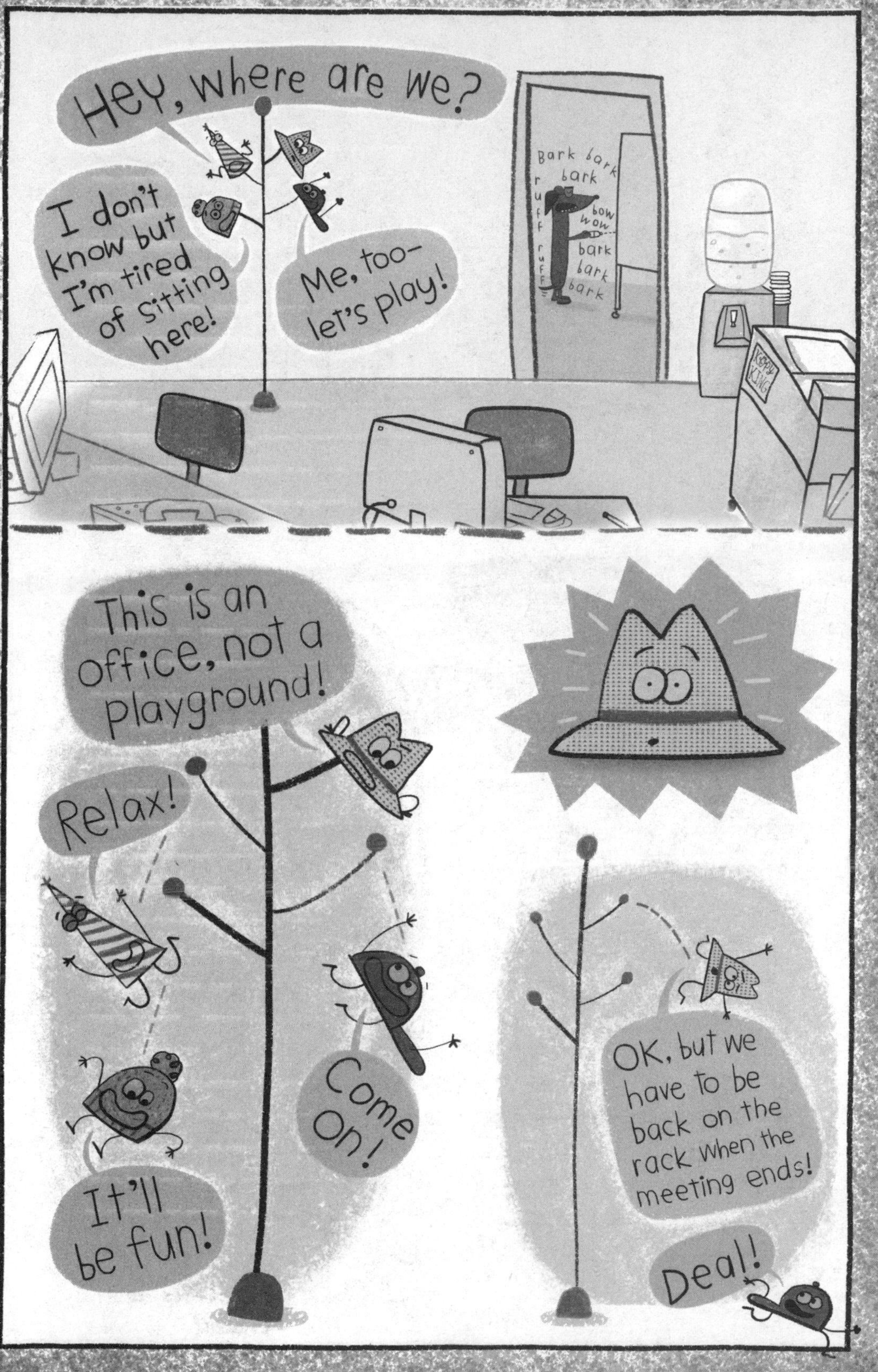
Hey, where are we?
I don't know but I'm tired of sitting here!
Me, too— let's play!
Bark bark bark
ruff ruff
bow wow
bark bark bark
KOPY KING
This is an office, not a playground!
Relax!
Come On!
It'll be fun!
OK, but we have to be back on the rack when the meeting ends!
Deal!

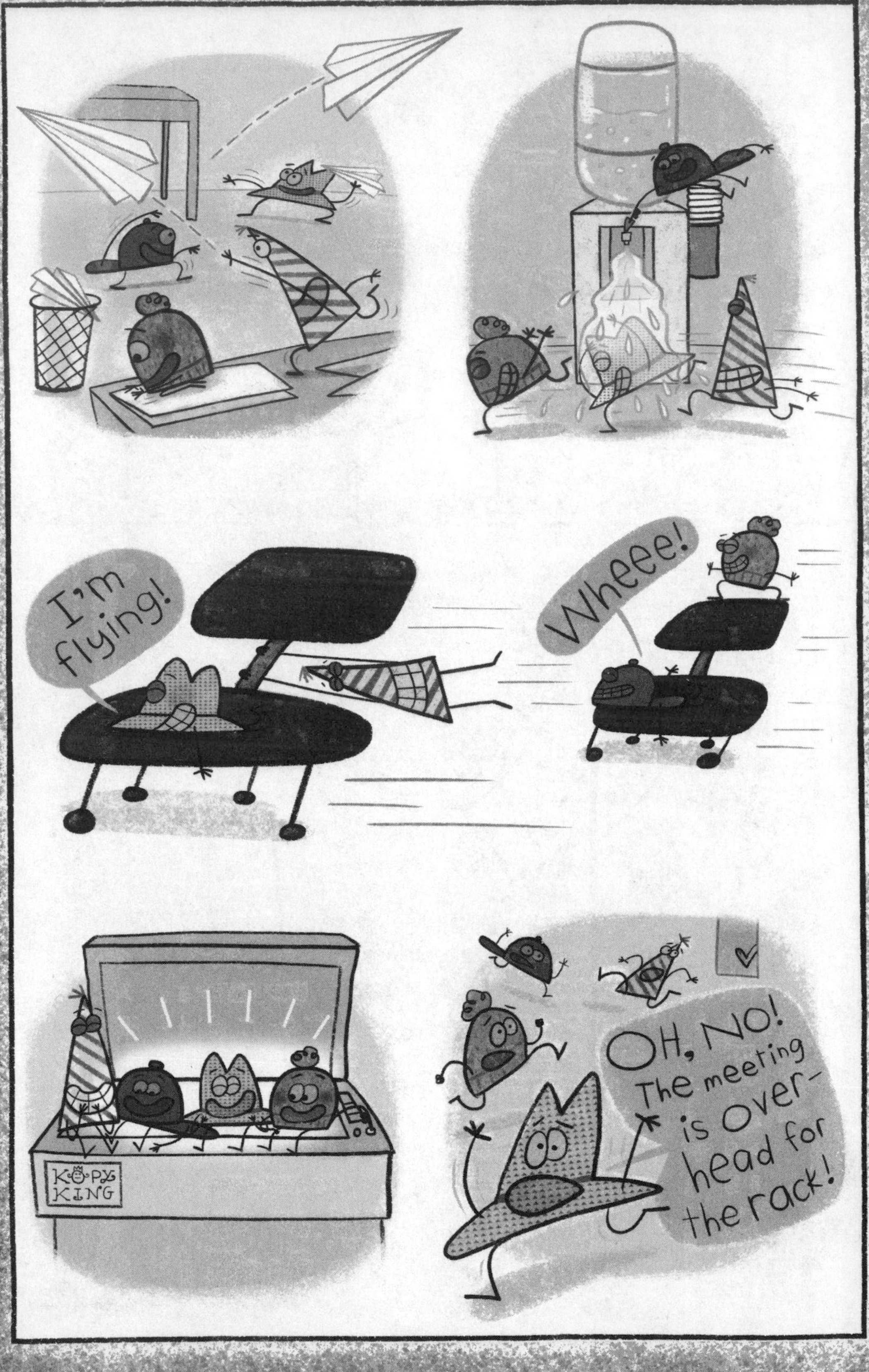
I'm flying!
Wheee!
KOPY KING
OH, NO! The meeting is over-head for the rack!

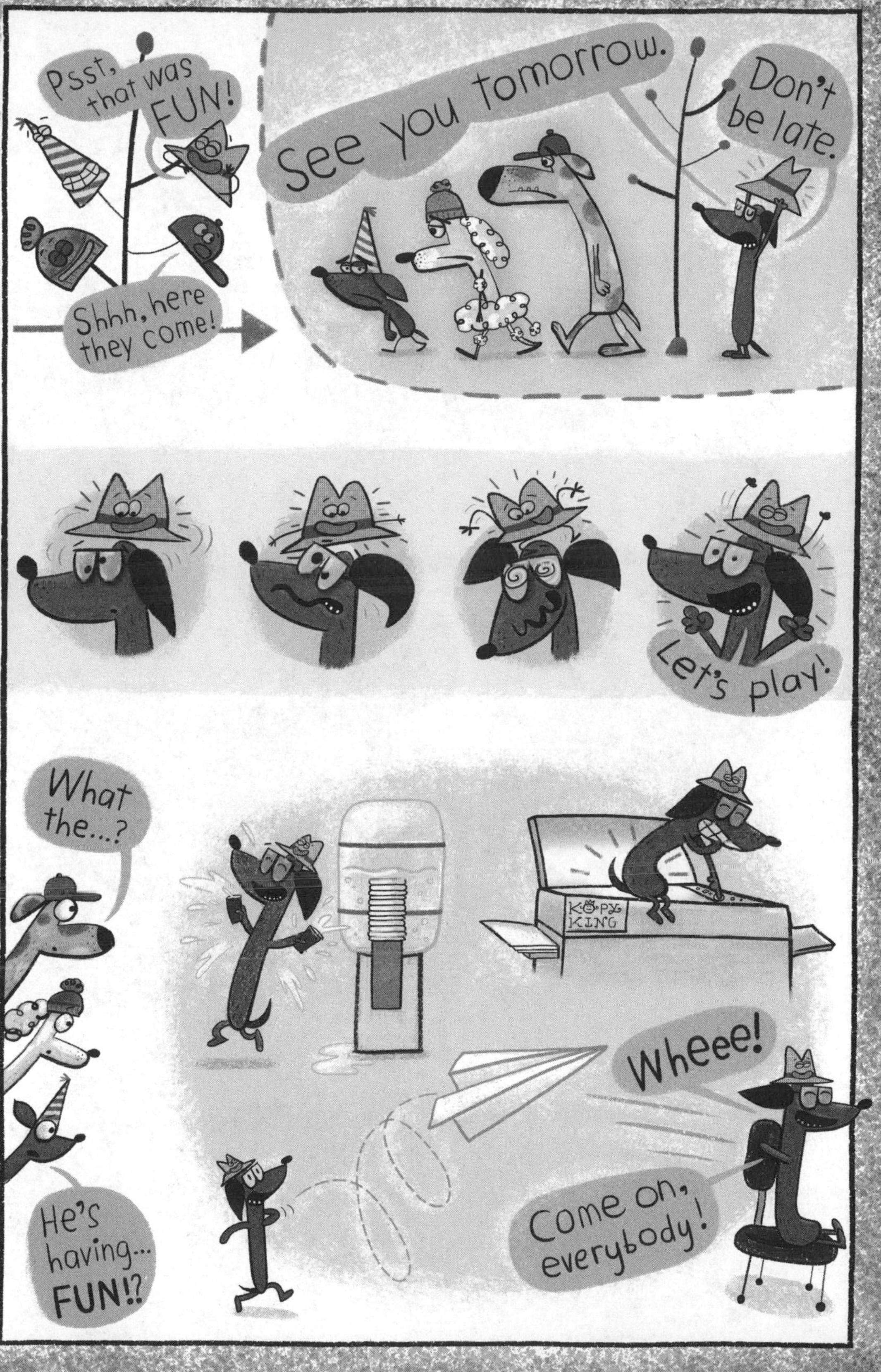
Psst, that was FUN!
Shhh, here they come!
See you tomorrow.
Don't be late.
Let's play!
What the...?
KOPY KING
Wheee!
He's having... FUN!?
Come on, everybody!

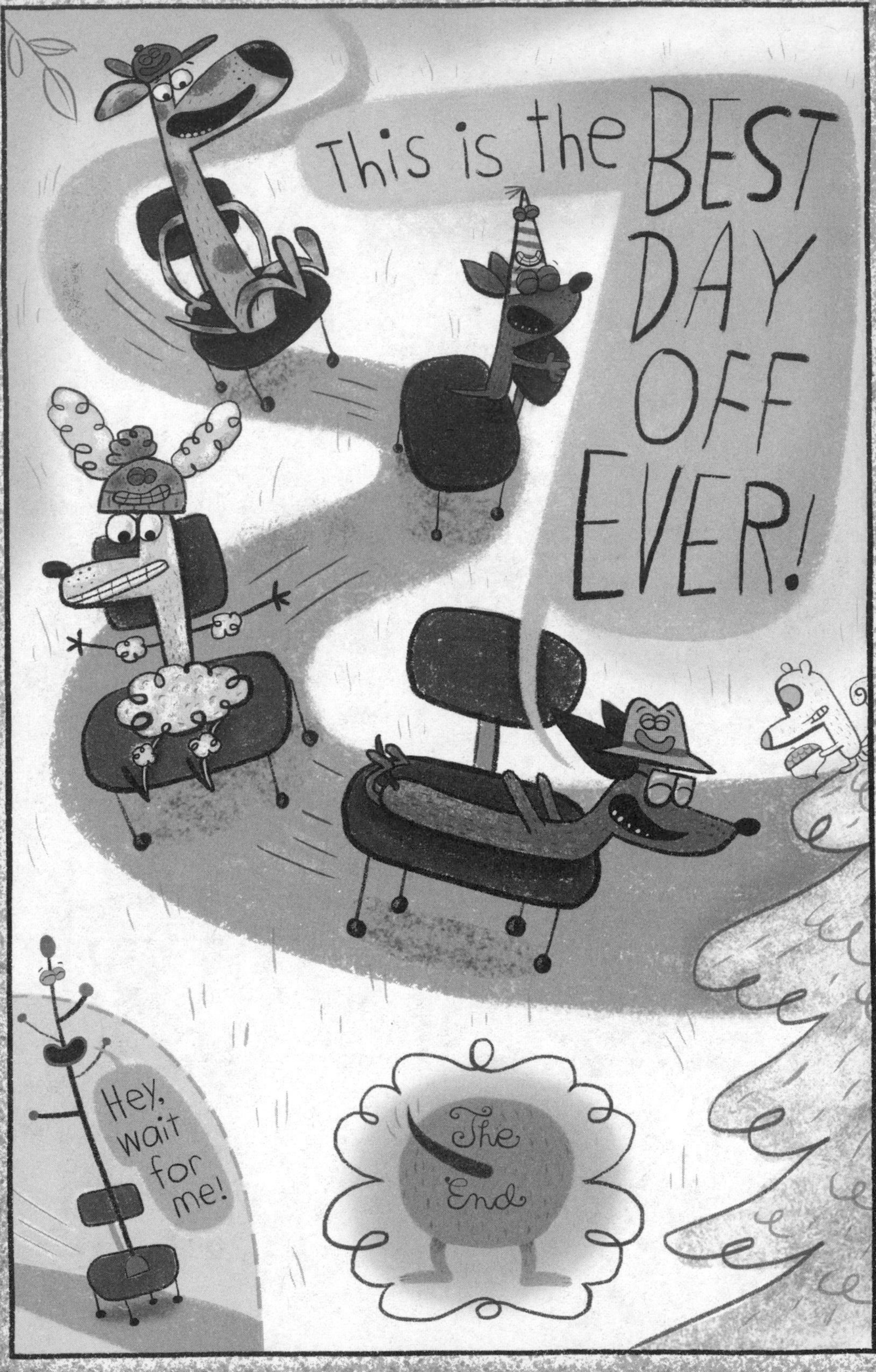
This is the BEST DAY OFF EVER!
Hey, wait for me!
The End

BY SHERMAN ALEXIE

The American three-line poem that uses haiku-ish elements, but is not a haiku: Put a famous or non-famous American in your first line (Beyoncé or your grandfather), then put an American, human-made landscape or place or object in the second line (Disneyland, Diet Pepsi, Hoover Dam), and then make those two American things collide in the third line.

Example:

> *My father wants to be buried*
> *In the same cemetery as Bruce Lee.*
> *Two dragons at rest.*

RESPONSE

BY KATE MESSNER

Waverly Woodson earned a Medal
of Honor on Omaha Beach,
His shiny-gold-star-blue-ribbon-
White-House invitation
Never came. Only the white boys
got those.

Author's note: I was researching my seventh *Ranger in Time* book, set during the 1944 D-Day invasion at Omaha Beach in Normandy, France, when I learned about Waverly Woodson, a member of the 320th Barrage Balloon Battalion, the only African American combat unit to come ashore on D-Day. Woodson was a medic with the unit, and even after he was wounded, he went on to rescue other soldiers from the water. Because of his heroism, he was recommended for America's highest military honor, the Medal of Honor. The recommendation reads: "This is a big enough award so that the President can give it personally, as he has in the case of some white boys."

But World War II happened before America's civil rights movement, and black soldiers weren't given the same rights as white soldiers. They were allowed to die for their country but had to eat in separate mess halls and live in separate housing. When the war ended, even though Waverly Woodson was recommended for a Medal of Honor, he was given a Purple Heart, for soldiers injured or killed in service, and a Bronze Star, the nation's fourth-highest honor, instead.

In fact, none of the 433 Medals of Honor the United States gave out after World War II were awarded to black men. Decades later, an independent army investigation determined that racism was to blame. In 1997, President Clinton awarded Medals of Honor to seven World War II veterans, only one of whom was still alive to receive it himself. Waverly Woodson wasn't one of those seven soldiers and has died now, but his family has launched a petition asking that he finally be given the medal he deserved for his courage on Omaha Beach.

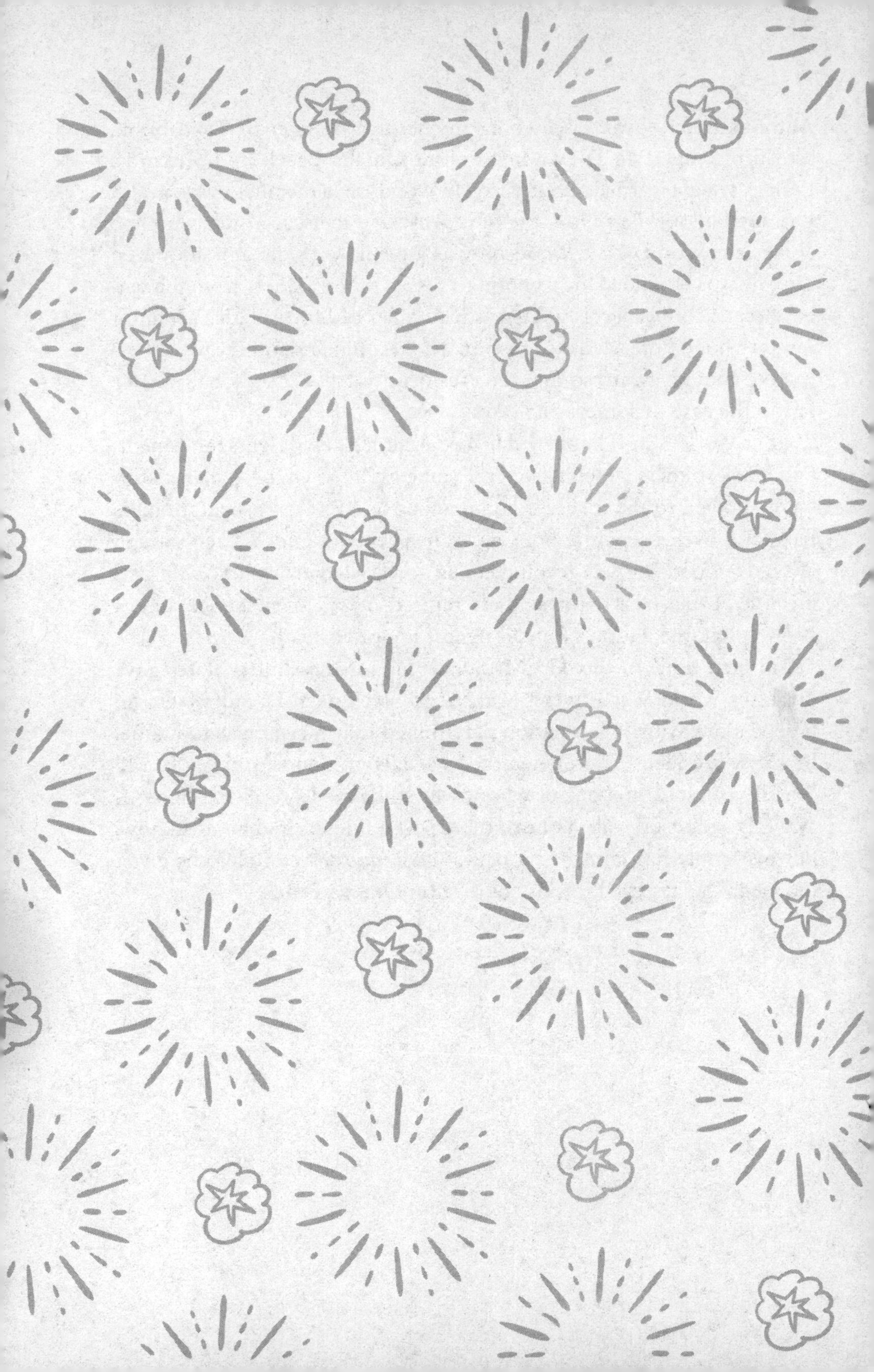

PROMPT

BY PETER BROWN

Create something that includes a tree looking out of place.

RESPONSE

BY LAUREN CASTILLO

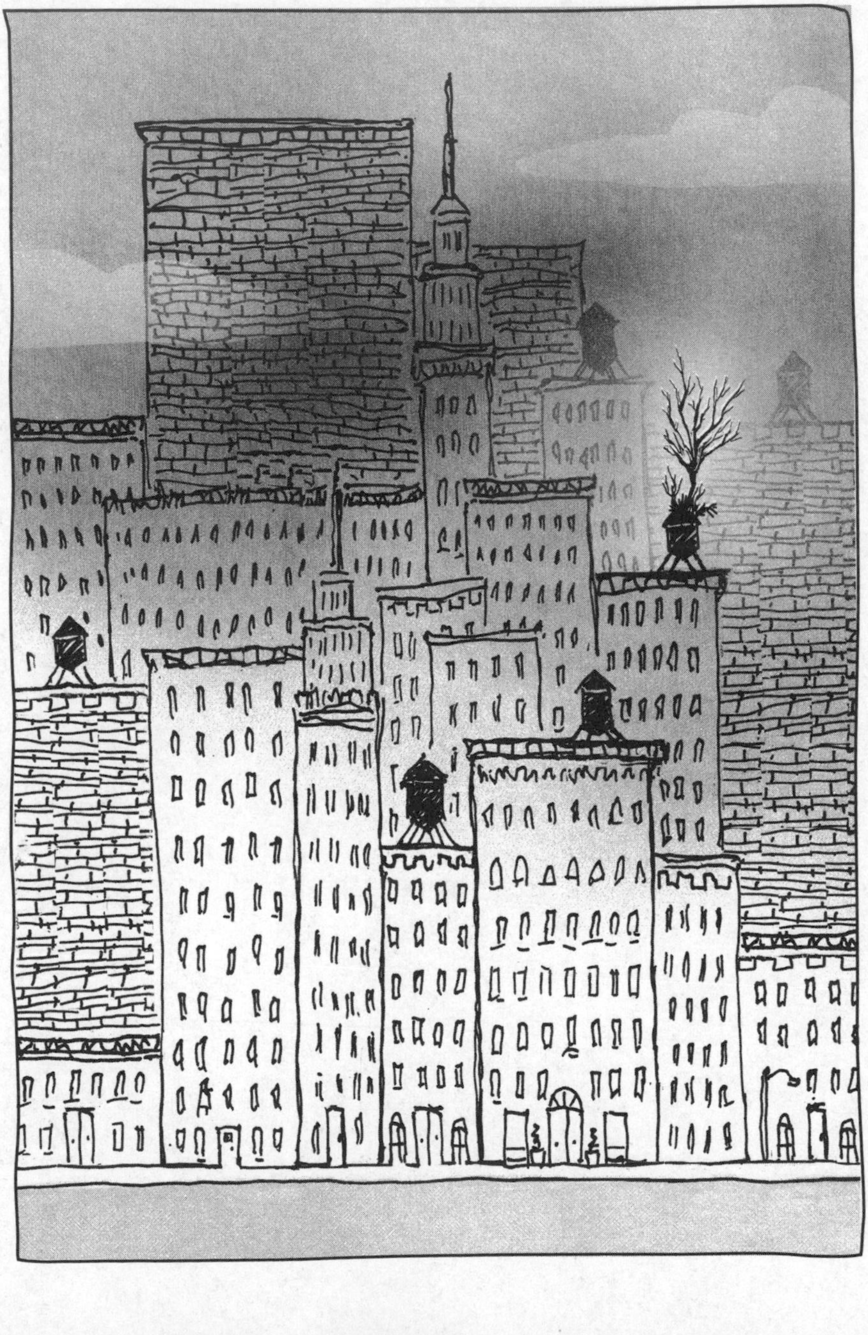

BY R. J. PALACIO

None of us knew where the lamp had come from, or how it had gotten here, or—most importantly—why it was lit. How could it be? It wasn't plugged in to anything. There wasn't even a plug! But somehow, the lightbulb was on, shining a yellow light from underneath the lampshade in the dark room. As we looked around, we realized that the light coming from the lamp wasn't like any light we had ever seen before. It seemed to light us from inside. It's hard to explain, but as I looked around at my friends in the room, I could somehow see inside of them, like they were made of glass. All their thoughts and feelings were illuminated. And as I looked at them looking at me, the thought quickly hit me: If I could see what they were thinking, they could see what I was thinking!

"Turn it off!" I said, grabbing the lamp to look for a switch, a knob—anything that would dim the light.

"Try taking the lightbulb out of the socket," Lee suggested.

I put my hand near the bulb, expecting it to be hot to the touch, but it was cool as marble. I tried twisting the lightbulb off, but it wouldn't move.

"Let's just break it," said Manolo, taking the lamp from my hands and slamming it, with all his might, against the wall.

The lamp just bounced off the wall like it was made of rubber.

This is crazy, I thought, shaking my head.

"No, what's crazy is that I just heard what you were thinking," said Manolo.

RESPONSE

BY DAV PILKEY

1.

None of us knew where the lamp had come from, or how it had gotten here, or—most importantly—why it was lit. How could it be? It wasn't plugged in to anything. There wasn't even a plug! But somehow, the lightbulb was on, shining a yellow light from underneath the lampshade in the dark room. As we looked around, we realized that the light coming from the lamp wasn't like any light we had ever seen before. It seemed to light us from the inside. It's hard to explain, but as I looked around at my friends in the room, I could somehow see inside of them, like they were made of glass. All their thoughts and feelings were illuminated. And as I looked at them looking at me, the thought quickly hit me: If I could see what they were thinking, they could see what I was thinking!

"Turn it off!" I said, grabbing the lamp to look for a switch, a knob—anything that would dim the light.

"Try taking the lightbulb out of the socket," Lee suggested.

I put my hand near the bulb, expecting it to be hot to the touch, but it was cool as marble. I tried twisting the lightbulb off, but it wouldn't move.

"Let's just break it," said Manolo, taking the lamp from my hands and slamming it, with all his might, against the wall.

The lamp just bounced off the wall like it was made of rubber.

This is crazy, I thought, shaking my head.

"No, what's crazy is that I just heard what you were thinking," said Manolo.

2.

Oh yeah? I thought. *What am I thinking now?*

"*Oh yeah?*" said Raj, in that stupid mocking tone he always uses. "*What am I thinking now?*"

The three boys chuckled to themselves for a moment. If there's such a thing as a mental high five, that happened, too. Then they stopped. Abruptly. They were all thinking the same *if I can see their thoughts, they can probably see mine* thing that I'd thought a couple of minutes ago.

What can I say? Boys are slow.

Lee, Manolo, and Raj each took a few steps back from the lamp. The looks on their faces echoed what they were thinking. They were terrified.

"Dudes, let's go," said Lee.

Just then, I realized that Charisse wasn't with us. She had come into the building with us. She'd led the way. She was the one who'd first noticed the tapping sounds. I looked around, but there was no sign of her. Oddly, there was no sign of anything that resembled the inside of a normal library. The ceiling was low. There didn't seem to be any doors. Or stairs. Or windows. Just bookshelves, and a few pieces of old furniture—messy and mismatched, but there wasn't—

Yeah, where is Charisse? Manolo said to me. Or rather, he thought it to me.

Stay out of my head, Manolo, I thought back at him.

But it was impossible to stay out of each other's heads. We could see each other's thoughts just as clearly as if they were being spoken out loud. And behind those thoughts, there were other things. Thought fragments. Dark whisperings.

Each of us was thinking several things at the same time. This is normal, I guess, although I've never really noticed it before. There were thoughts that were in the forefront—focused, declarative thoughts—but there were also quieter voices behind those thoughts. We all had them.

These quieter voices didn't seem to come from rational places. They were pure, reckless emotion. Once you noticed them, however, they had a way of taking over. These voices came from our darkest selves. I could tell, for instance, that Raj was ashamed about the way he looked. It was weird, because he'd never SEEMED like he was self-conscious. Apparently, his nose troubled him the most—he thought it made him look like a bulldog. But he was also embarrassed about his weight, about his "man boobs," as he referred to them. (But never publicly. At least not until now.)

Lee's quiet voices, the ones behind his own voice, were even darker than Raj's. They were bullying him. *They're all finding out what a phony you are, Lee*, his voice whispered to him. *They know about your dad. They know about the motorcycle. They know you're a liiiiaaaar.*

For the record, I didn't know any of that stuff. I didn't even know what the voice was talking about. *What motorcycle?*

"NO! STOP IT!" Lee screamed, slapping his hands over his ears to try and block the voices. It didn't work. *Ooooh*, Lee's dark, mocking voice whispered, *and Rachel's just finding out now that you like her. Why don't you look up at her, Lee? Look up at your one true love and see the disappointment in her eyes.*

"Aaaaand—he likes me," I groaned to myself. A half hour ago, that news would have thrilled me. But now—after hearing his *inside voices*—after seeing him cower from them like a little kid—I don't know. How could you like ANYONE if you knew what they were *really* thinking?

Suddenly, Lee dove for the lamp. He grabbed it and tore across the room toward the stairs. Then, taking two steps at a time, he bounded up to the next floor.

Wait a minute. Where did those stairs come from? They weren't there a minute ago...or were they? I guess they must have been.

Lee disappeared down an upstairs hallway, but we could still hear his footsteps. He was running at first. Then the sounds of his footsteps stopped. Silence.

Tap. Tap tap tappa tap tap, tap tappatappatappatap tap.

It sounded like someone was tap-dancing again, with a rhythm that got faster and louder until we could feel it shaking all around us. Underneath us, too. It made my bones hurt.

There was a scream. A woman's scream, I think. And then the footsteps above our heads came back again, faster and faster. Lee had left the lamp behind and was bounding down the stairs four at a time. The tap-dancing sound was getting closer. Louder. More painful.

"WEGOTTAGETOUTTAHERE!" Lee screamed. His voice was high and frantic, and it occurred to me that the scream I'd heard upstairs hadn't been a woman's voice. That had been Lee.

"What's wrong?" we all yelled, although it was difficult to hear our own voices above the deafening tap-dancing sound that was getting closer and closer.

"SERIOUSLY!" Lee cried, yanking at Manolo's hoodie. "WE G-GOTTA G-GET OUT OF HERE!!!" I could now see that he was crying. Like, blubbering. Like a baby.

"WHAT?" I yelled. "WHAT'S WRONG???"

"I—I think"—Lee stammered, gasping for breath—"I think I just found Charisse."

PROMPT

BY MINH LÊ

Author Anagram Challenge:

    1. Take the name of one of your favorite children's authors.

    2. Create an anagram from their name that sounds like it could be a title of one of their books. (Note: Feel free to use an online anagram generator if that helps.)

    3. Either (1) design a book cover for this hypothetical book; or (2) create a scene or compose a verse from the hypothetical book.

Anagram example: *Nursemaid Cake* by Maurice Sendak

(*Nursemaid Cake* totally sounds like it could be a Maurice Sendak book, right?)

Feel free to come up with your own, but here are some more anagram options in case you wanted to jump straight to step 3.

- *Label Every Cry* by Beverly Cleary
- *Sadder Clown* by Donald Crews
- *A Bitter Export* by Beatrix Potter

RESPONSE

BY VICTORIA JAMIESON

Anagram Challenge

1. Take the name of one of your favorite children's authors.

2. Create an anagram from their name that sounds like it could be a title of one of their books.

3. Either (1) create a book cover for this hypothetical book; or (2) write a scene or verse from this book.

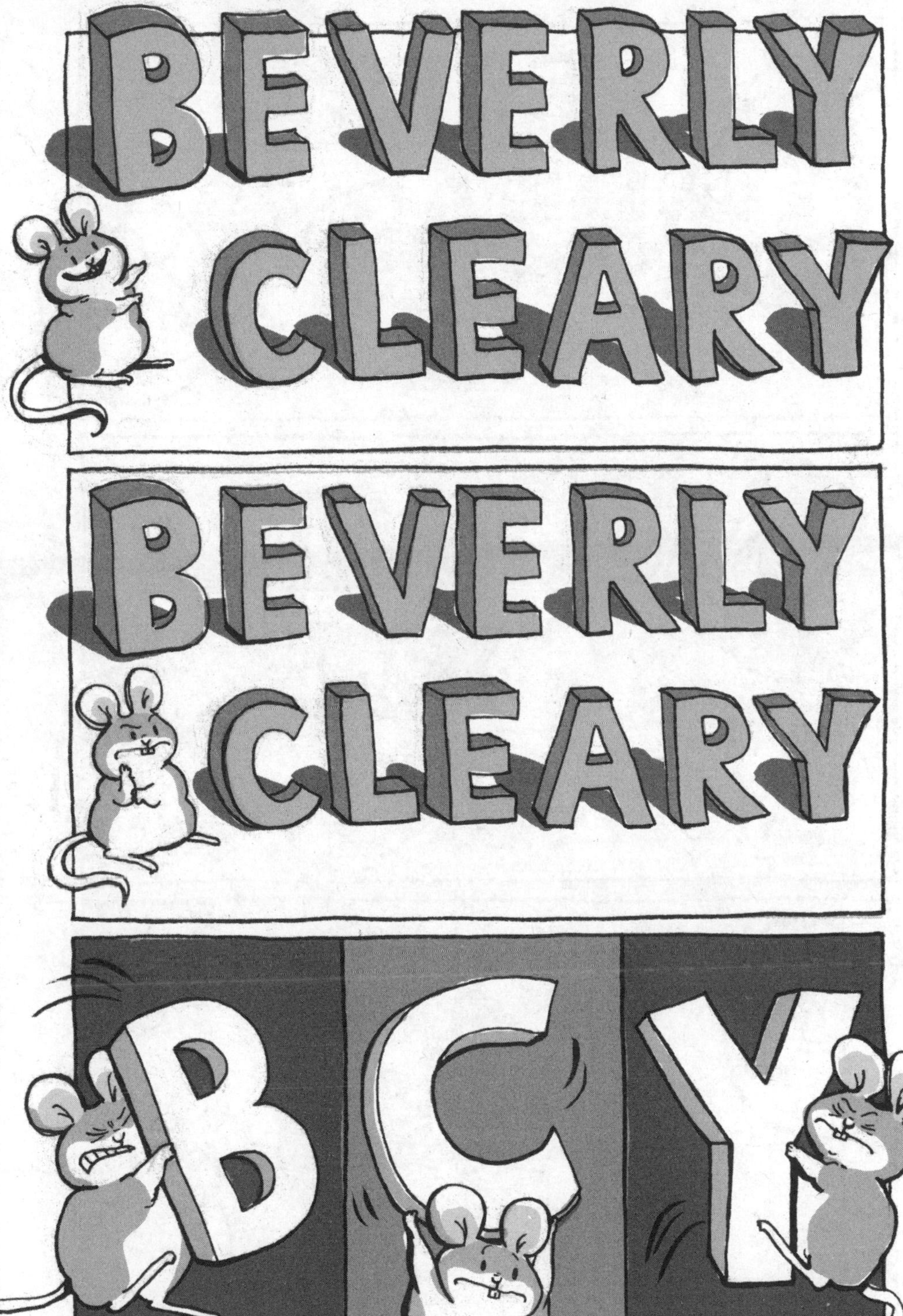
BEVERLY
CLEARY
BEVERLY
CLEARY
B
C
Y

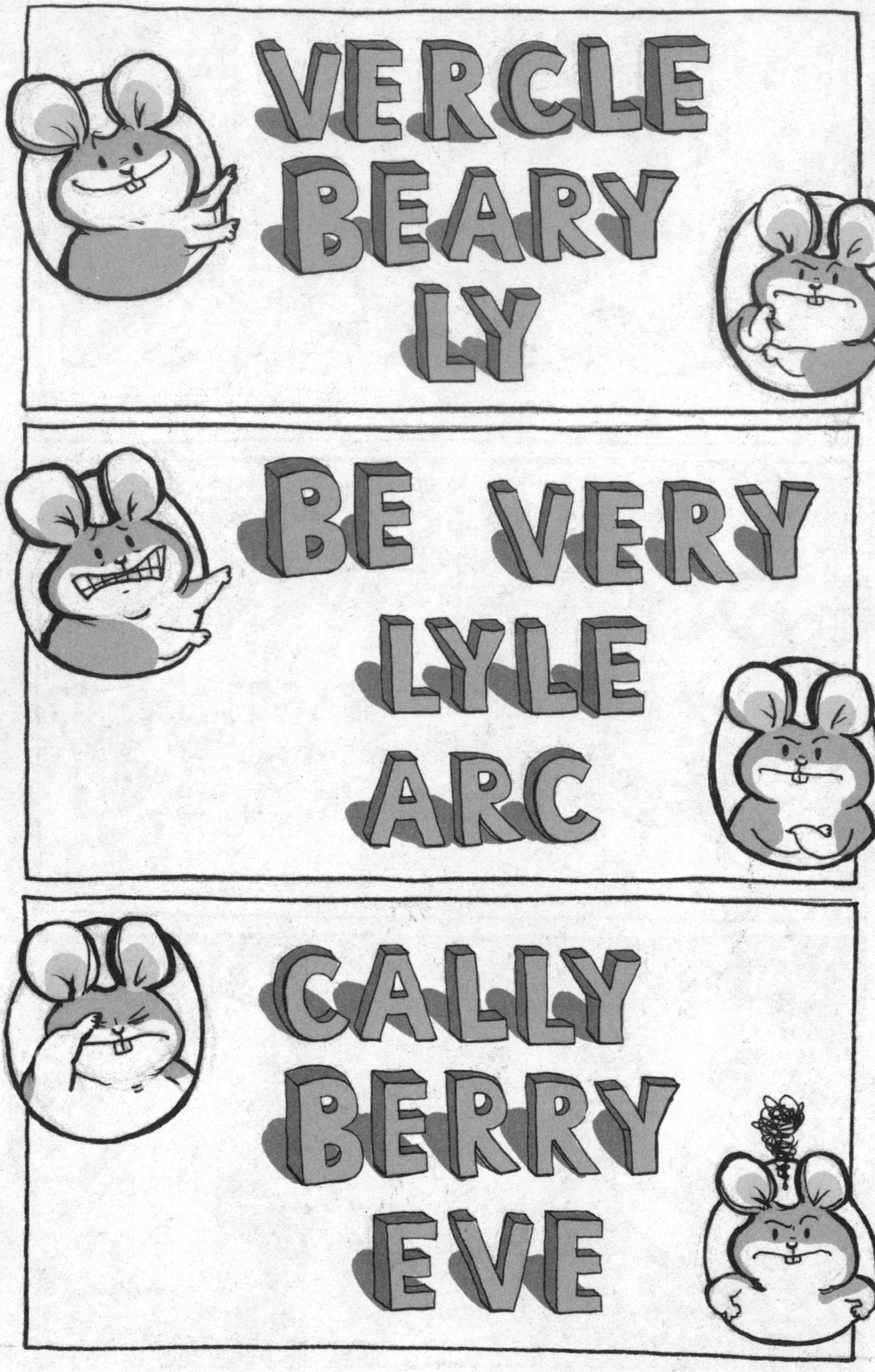
VERCLE
BEARY
LY
BE VERY
LYLE
ARC
CALLY
BERRY
EVE

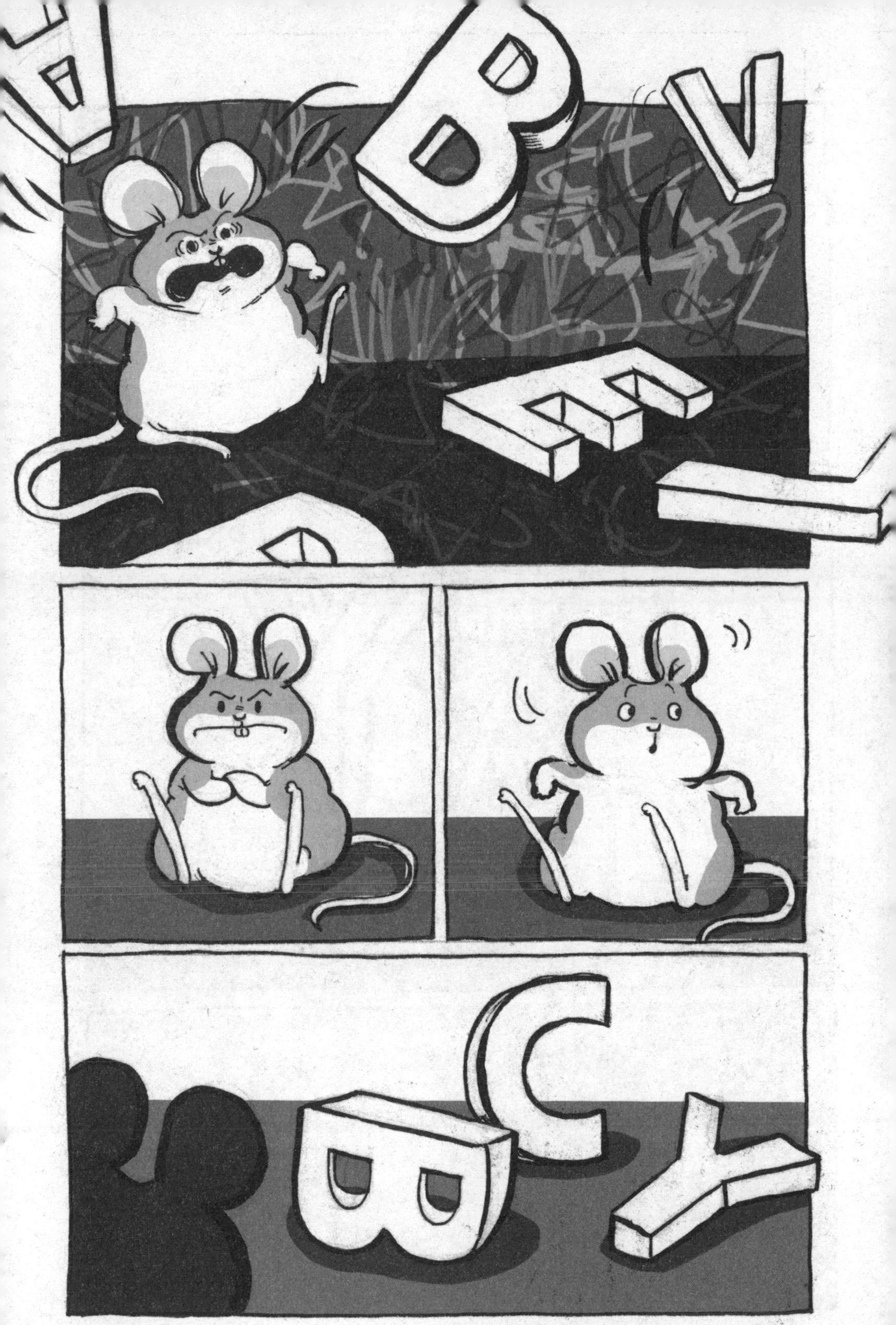

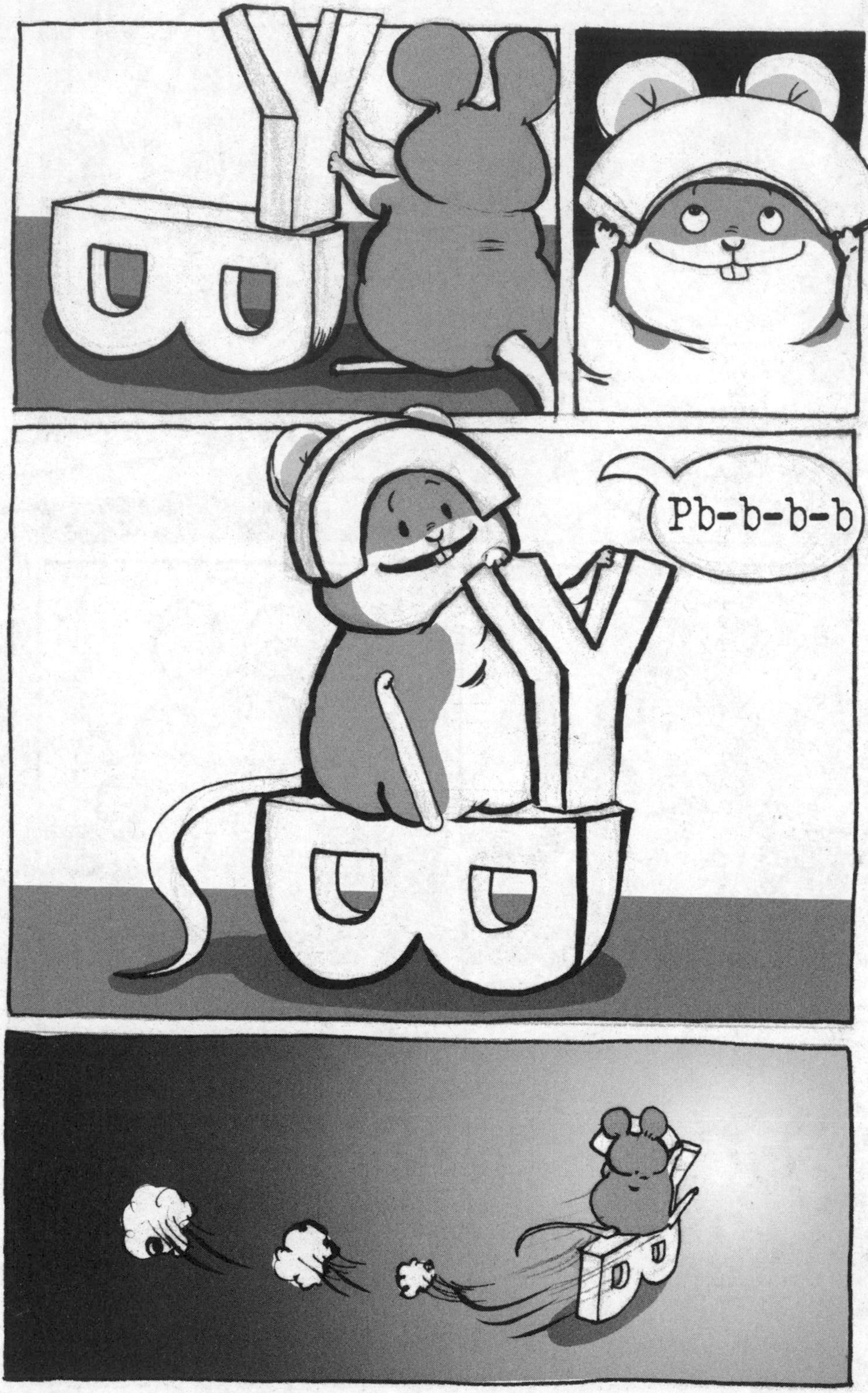
Pb-b-b-b

BY LAUREL SNYDER

Try to think of an abstract idea. For instance, you might choose "joy" or "hunger" or "stupidity." Now imagine that abstraction as a character. It can look like a person, an animal, or a creature of your own invention. Once you've got the character in your head, set it in motion. Make it DO something. "Joy" might ride a bicycle. "Hunger" might go to the movies. "Stupidity" might dig a hole. Tell me the story of what happens.

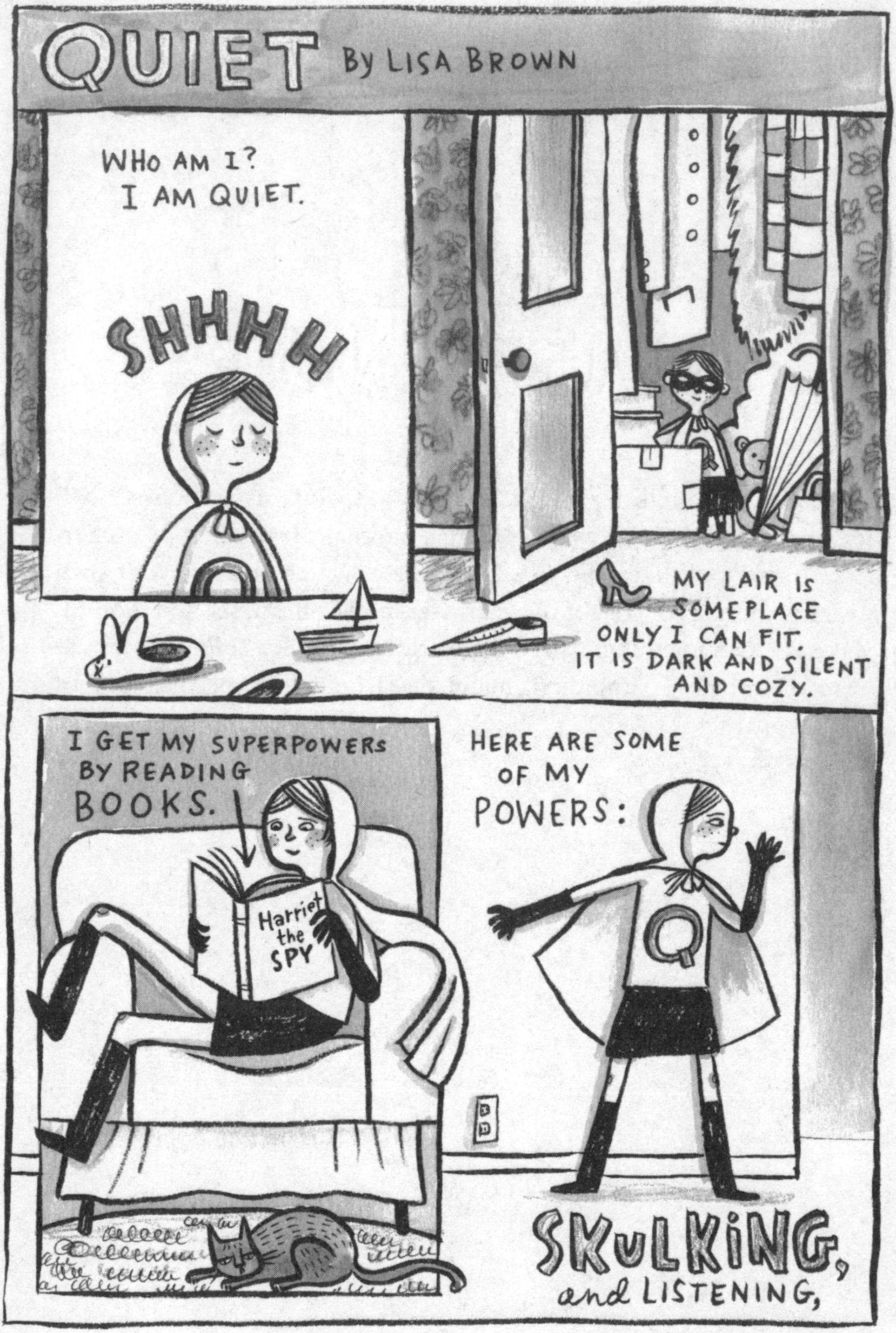
QUIET BY LISA BROWN
WHO AM I? I AM QUIET.
SHHHH
MY LAIR IS SOMEPLACE ONLY I CAN FIT. IT IS DARK AND SILENT AND COZY.
I GET MY SUPERPOWERS BY READING BOOKS.
Harriet the SPY
HERE ARE SOME OF MY POWERS:
SKULKING,
and LISTENING,

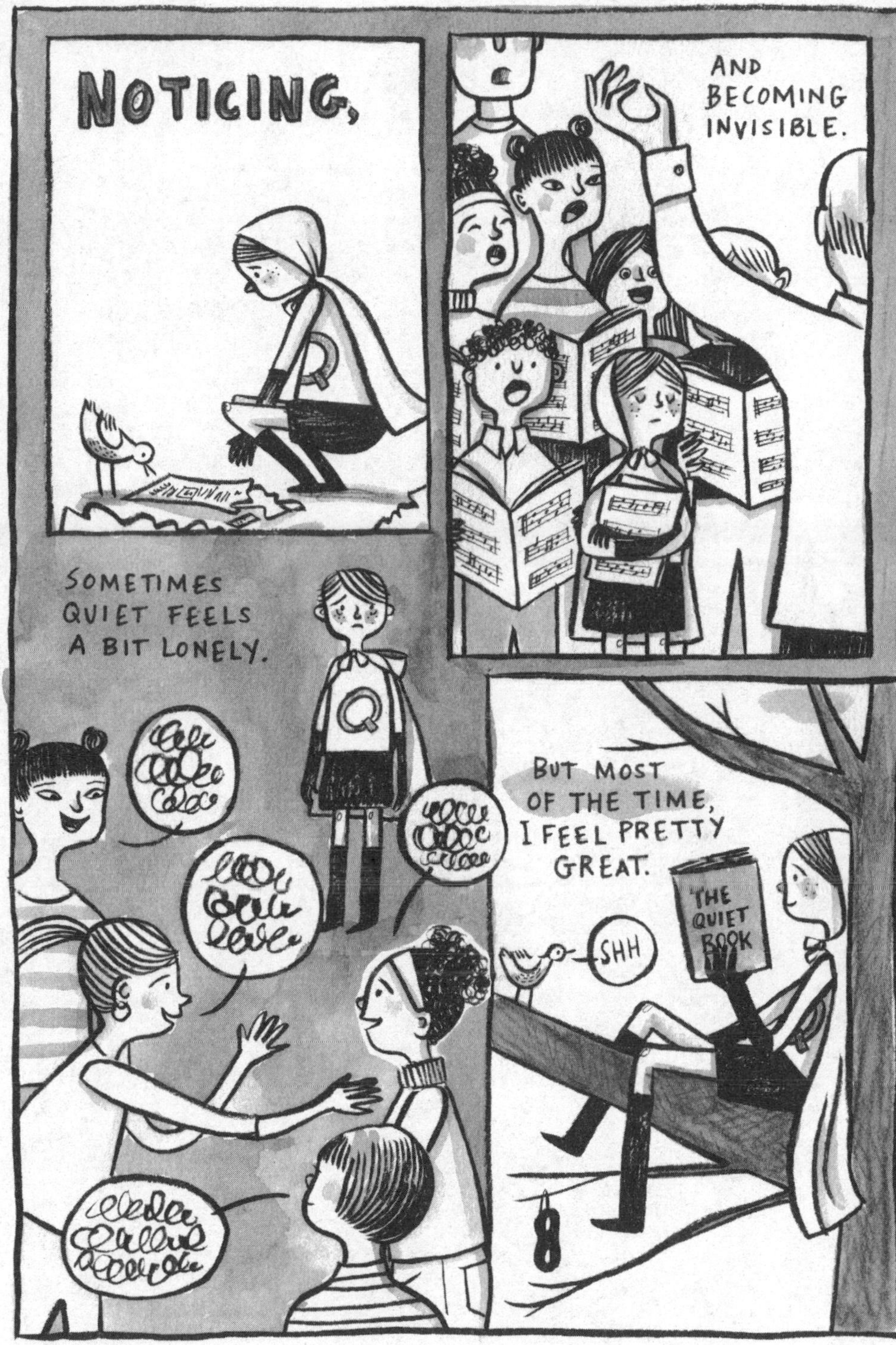
NOTICING,
AND BECOMING INVISIBLE.
SOMETIMES QUIET FEELS A BIT LONELY.
BUT MOST OF THE TIME, I FEEL PRETTY GREAT.
THE QUIET BOOK
SHH

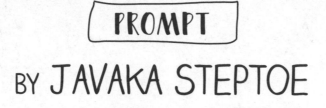

PROMPT

BY JAVAKA STEPTOE

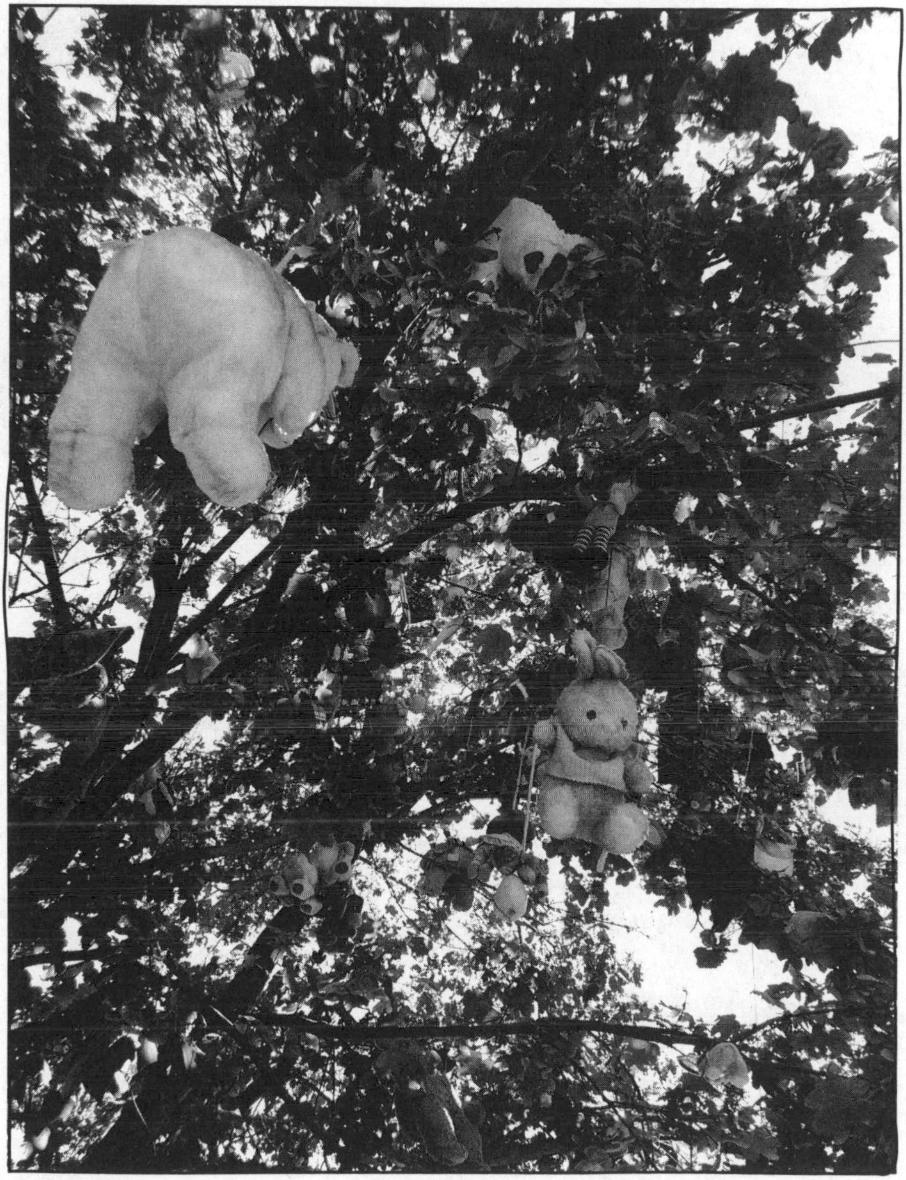

FLUFFLE-PICKING TIME
BY CHRIS GRABENSTEIN

With one whiff of the early morning breeze, Charlotte Applebee knew it was fluffle-picking time in Plush Grove.

The outdoors smelled like cotton candy mixed with the fresh scent of pillowcases dried on a clothesline. That meant the fluffles had already ripened on the branches of the trees in the five-hundred-acre orchard that had been in the Applebee family for six generations.

"The carnival men will be here soon," Charlotte said to Mr. Wiggles, her stuffed bunny rabbit, as she climbed out of bed and pulled on her flannel shirt and fluffle-picking overalls. "But don't worry. I won't let them take you."

The bunny rabbit, frayed and gray, was flopped between a pair of pillows looking limp and sad—the way it had looked for six years because it only had one eye and no wire to perk up its ears.

Charlotte went to her bedroom window to savor the sweet scent. "The fluffles smell plump and cuddly this year. I bet it'll be a good harvest. The best in years."

Although she was only eleven, Charlotte knew all the signs of fluffle-picking time. School would be closed for a week so the children could work in the orchards, helping their families pluck the ripe fruit out of the fluffle trees.

"The trees are heavy," Charlotte's father said proudly when she came down to the kitchen to eat a big breakfast of eggs, bacon, sausage, biscuits, gravy, waffles, fried chicken, and cornbread. It was what her dad called "a proper fluffle-picker's breakfast." They had to eat a hearty morning meal because fluffle picking was hard work and they only had a week to pluck every stuffed animal out of their trees or else they would "turn." They'd lose their cuteness. Their fleecy fur would become matted and tangled. Their button eyes might even pop out.

"School called," said Charlotte's mother. "It'll be closed for the week. All the fluffle farmers need every available hand they can find out in the orchards."

"Doc Hargrove's sending over his boy, Bobby," said her father. "He's your age, right, Charlotte?"

"Yes, sir," said Charlotte, stuffing her mouth with scrambled eggs and biscuit so she wouldn't have to say any more. Bobby Hargrove, who always sat behind her at school, was like a spoiled fluffle. Filled with bad stuffing. Rotten to the core. Bobby also thought that, since he was the doctor's son, he was better than all the "fluffle-picking hicks" in Plush Grove.

But Charlotte knew that nobody would even be able to pay to see Dr. Hargrove if the carnival men didn't buy up all the crates of stuffed animals that grew in the county's fluffle orchards each year.

"Trees are bursting with good variety this year," said Charlotte's father, putting down his coffee mug. "We've got heart-hugging white bears, monkeys wearing striped leggings, some blue whales, and a whole bunch of fuzzy brown bears."

"Blue whales are rare," said Charlotte's mother.

"Aya," said her father. "They're nice and plump, too. I figure it's that blanket of polyester I mulched around the roots back in June."

"But what makes them turn blue?" asked Charlotte.

"Sadness, I suppose," said her father. "We try to keep it away from the orchard but, every now and then, some seeps in."

"It's the price we pay for rainstorms," said her mother.

Breakfast finished, Charlotte headed out to the barn to grab her picking ladder and a stack of wood-slatted bushel baskets.

"You and Bobby can work the eastern orchards," said her father. "Your mother and I will head north and west."

"And try not to fall in love with any of the fruit," warned her mother.

"I won't, Mother."

"You sure did when you were little."

"She was only five," said her father, remembering when Charlotte had brought home Mr. Wiggles.

"Well, she's not five anymore," said her mother.

"Remember to toss any rotten fruit you find to the ground," said her dad, as if Charlotte didn't already know the basics of fluffle picking. "It makes good fertilizer."

"Yes, Dad."

Charlotte headed off to the eastern orchards, where the fluffle trees were lined up in tidy rows as far as the eye could see.

"Hey, wait for me!" shouted an annoying voice behind her.

It was Bobby Hargrove.

"Do I need a ladder?" he asked. "Last year, when I worked the Jenkins orchard, I had a ladder."

"You're a bushel boy this year," said Charlotte. "I'll pluck the fruit and toss it down to you."

"I'd rather be a picker than a packer."

Charlotte ignored him, set up her ladder, and started plucking stuffed animals off the branches. Her dad had been right: It was a very good harvest this year. She tossed down plush white teddy bears cradling red Valentine's Day hearts, purple gorillas, pink bunny rabbits, and a rare blue whale.

"Hey," cried Bobby. "Slow down!"

That made Charlotte smile. She started singing a fluffle-picking song (to the tune of "Frère Jacques") so she could pluck fruit even faster:

Picking fluffles, picking fluffles
One by one, one by one
Picking all the fluffles,
Picking all the fluffles,
Till we're done, till we're done

She was having so much fun, bombarding bratty Bobby down below, she didn't pay much attention to the dusty pink bunny with the bent ears, yellow knit sweater, and yellow paws.

"This one is rotten," said Bobby when he caught the bunny.

"What?" said Charlotte.

"This thing has three eyeballs!"

Charlotte scampered down the ladder.

"Let me see...."

Bobby handed it to her. "There's a shiny eyeball on its cheek. And look at that smile. It's sewed in upside down. What kid in their right mind would want this stupid bunny?"

"If it's a prize at a carnival booth..."

"They'd have to give it to the loser," sneered Bobby. "This bunny should've been harvested a week ago, before it grew an extra eye. Now it looks like a potato that's been in the potato bin too long."

Bobby tossed the floppy bunny to the ground.

"One bad bunny can spoil the whole lot!"

Charlotte nodded grimly. "Haul your bushel over to the holding crate," she said.

Bobby did as he was told. But not before he gave the limp bunny a good swift kick.

"We should chop off its head," he said as he walked away with his load. "It'll decompose faster if all the stuffing spills out."

"Go dump that bushel," said Charlotte. "I'll deal with the bad fluffle."

"Fine. Have all the fun. See if I care."

Charlotte knelt next to the bunny as Bobby disappeared around the trees. Her mother was right. She was too old to be bringing home stuffed animals, especially damaged goods. She buried the sad-looking, three-eyed bunny under a pile of yellow leaves that matched its ugly sweater and plush toes.

Bobby and Charlotte worked the orchard until sundown, with only a short break for lunch.

"Did you rip off its head?" Bobby asked at least a dozen times.

And every time he did, Charlotte would ignore the question and sing her annoying "Picking Fluffles" song again.

That night, after Bobby had gone home with a day's wages, Charlotte ate a late dinner with her parents. Nobody said much around the table. They were too hungry to chat.

"Well," said Charlotte's father when he finally pushed back from the table. "We best turn in early. Tomorrow's going to be just as much work as today."

"Not that we're complaining," said Charlotte's mother. "Didn't spy one rotten piece of fruit all day."

"Good harvest," said her father. "Best in at least six years."

Everybody said good night and headed off to bed.

Charlotte went up to her room, where Mr. Wiggles had been waiting patiently between his pillows all day long.

"Can you a keep a secret?" asked Charlotte. The stuffed bunny, of course, said nothing. His one button eye remained blank. "You want to know the best thing about fluffle-picking overalls?"

Once again, Mr. Wiggles didn't answer.

"They're big and baggy. Perfect for hiding stuff you were supposed to leave to rot under a tree."

She took out the three-eyed bunny with the bright yellow sweater. She had to peel away a wet yellow leaf before squeezing the freshly picked bunny into the pillow nook beside Mr. Wiggles.

Charlotte looked at her two castaway bunnies, their heads side by side. All of a sudden, Mr. Wiggles seemed to have two eyes again because his cheek was smooshed right up against the cheek where the extra button had popped up on the new bunny.

And the new bunny's sadly sewn frown? Somehow, it had turned itself upside down.

Charlotte smiled. Her father had been right.

It was a good harvest.

The best in at least six years.

PROMPT

BY VICTORIA JAMIESON

I Remember...

This one is easy. Set a timer for five minutes. At the top of a sheet of paper, write the words "I Remember." For five minutes, list as many things as you can that you remember. They can be good memories, bad memories, funny memories—your favorite teacher, holiday, birthday party, etc. Anything goes.

Pick one and begin creating!

RESPONSE

MATILDA AND ME
BY JOHN SCHU

Dear Dr. Mary Margaret Reed,

You might not remember me, but I remember everything about the year you were my fifth-grade teacher. You inspired me. You motivated me. You were patient and loving and exactly the type of teacher this shy and unsure-of-himself boy needed. You were larger than life in your sparkly rings and purple dresses.

I wanted to be you. I would go home from school every day and re-create your lessons in my bedroom that looked like a classroom. If you taught us about similes and metaphors, my imaginary students and cat and dog received the same lesson. If you read aloud from Maurice Sendak's *Chicken Soup with Rice: A Book of Months* (like you did on the first day of every month), I wrote the poem on one of my two chalkboards and recited it over and over again until it was memorized. Some of the best moments of my life took place in that bedroom with a piece of chalk in one hand and a book in the other.

A day rarely goes by when I don't think about your enthusiasm for books. If I close my eyes, I can still see some of the books I checked out from your classroom library: *One-Eyed Cat*; *Sideways Stories from Wayside School*; *Sarah, Plain and Tall*; *Maniac Magee*; and *James and the Giant Peach*. Oh, how I loved spending time with Ned Wallis, Mrs. Jewls's class, Caleb, Amanda Beale, and James Henry Trotter. They brought me much comfort and joy. Books have always helped me feel less alone and more connected to something bigger than myself—especially Roald Dahl's books. I read *Matilda* three or four times during the fifth grade. I wanted to rescue Matilda from Mr. and Mrs. Wormwood, discuss the books she was reading, and tell her about my favorite books.

I'll never forget the day I spotted a shiny new copy of *Matilda* in your classroom library. It stared at me, beckoning me to take it home forever. I could have borrowed it from you or asked my grandma to buy me a copy, but for some reason I needed to own **that** copy. I came up with a plan. Later that day during recess, I snuck back inside the school. Your classroom lights were off. The door was closed. With a racing heart and sweaty palms, I opened the door, bolted across the room, pulled *Matilda* down from the top shelf, and shoved it inside my backpack.

I should not have stolen your copy of *Matilda*, but I am glad I did. It lived in the back of my closet for three years. Whenever I felt frustrated or alone, I would take it out, open it up, and read a few pages. It always calmed me. I think it is the reason I give away hundreds of books every year. I hope someone will feel as connected to the book I give them as I feel connected to your copy of *Matilda*.

I spent a great deal of my childhood feeling different

and confused. Books saved me. *Matilda* saved me. You saved me. Thank you from the bottom of my heart.

Love,
John Schu, your former fifth-grade student

P.S. Twenty-seven years later, it is still one of my most valuable possessions.

PROMPT

BY SOPHIE BLACKALL

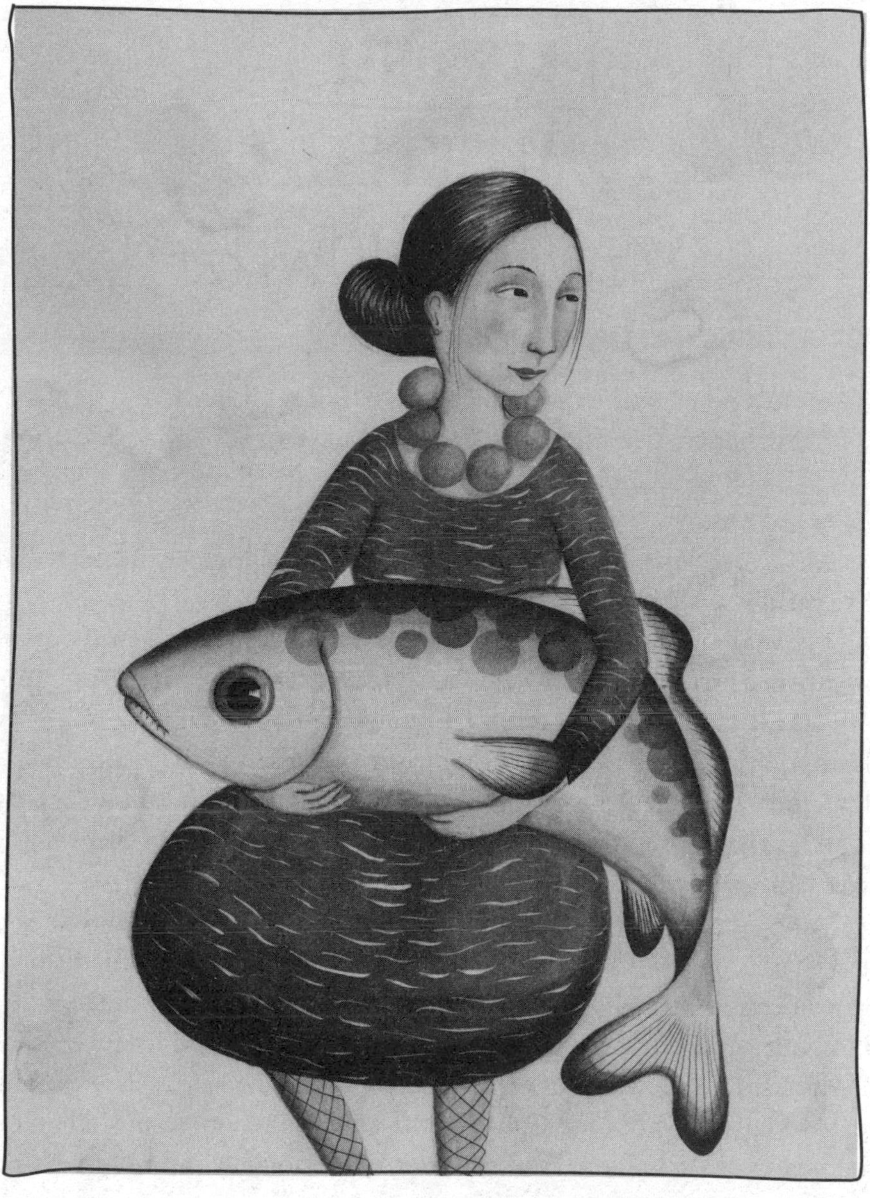

RESPONSE
MR. KEREL
BY ADAM GIDWITZ

My mom's new boyfriend wants me to call him "Mac."

"No thanks, Mr. Kerel," I say. "I think that's a little *premature*, don't you?" My biology teacher uses that word all the time. It sounds really grown-up.

Mr. Kerel's eyes look wet and glassy, as if I've hurt his feelings. But his eyes always look wet and glassy. Because he's a fish.

I have no idea what my mom sees in him. They met when she went on a fishing trip with her friend Georgia and Timothy Capetti's mom. She said it was a moms thing, and I couldn't come. Which was pretty disappointing, because I have often felt the "call of the open sea" (I don't know where I heard that phrase, but I think it sounds pretty cool). Living in the middle of the suburbs, I don't get to answer the sea's call very often. Or ever.

Anyway, she said it would be boring for me anyway, because they'd just be talking about "girl stuff" and letting the captain do the fishing. So you can imagine how surprised I was when she came home talking all about Mac, and how great he was, and what a good listener. "Was he the captain or something?" I asked. "No," she said. "The captain reeled Mac in just beyond Calvert Cliffs. We were gonna smack him on the head with a hammer and put him in a cooler with the other fish, but then he started talking, and he was just so charming and intelligent and funny. Georgia said he was a real catch, and we just died laughing. Hold on. I left him in the car."

So my mom ran out to the car and brought in the largest fish I'd ever seen. She was holding him in her arms like he was a baby, and he had these huge black-and-gray eyes and spots all along his back. "Hello, Chinami," he said. "I've heard so much about you. I'm Mr. Kerel." It's super awkward meeting your mom's new boyfriend. Especially when he's a fish.

He moved into my old toddler pool, out under the carport. Which also seemed premature to me.

The next Monday, at school, Timothy Capetti walked right up to me at my locker and said, "Is your mom dating that fish?"

I turned bright red. I blush really easily, and there were like twenty kids all within earshot. Including Prince Williams, who always makes me blush anyway. "I don't know." I shrugged.

The grade immediately went crazy with the news. "Chinami's mom is dating a fish!" "Ew, that's so weird!" "I wonder if they *kiss*!" "Hahahahahahahaha!" "Ho-ho-ho-ho-ho!" "Dah-ha-ha-ha!"

I hate Mr. Kerel.

Then came Jane Smiley's birthday party. I was totally psyched that I got invited, because Jane is kinda friends with the cool kids. She also hangs out with me in the library sometimes, helping Ms. Bruce, the librarian, shelve the books. I guess that's why she invited me to her party.

My mom told me that some parents were going to hang out at Jane's house while we kids played. "Get your shoes," she said. "Mac and I will meet you in the car."

"You are *not* bringing Mr. Kerel! No, Mom! Please!" But she insisted.

Twenty minutes later, we were walking into Jane Smiley's house. My mom had Mr. Kerel in a big plastic jug. Jane stared at us like we're a family of freaks. Which I think we are. But Mr. Kerel was really nice and charming to all the other parents. He made a joke, and they all laughed. I was staring at the floor as hard as I could.

Jane invited me downstairs, to their basement, which is one of those nice finished basements, with a TV and a big couch and a mini-basketball hoop. Some other kids were already there, including Jane's cool friends. Tim Capetti. Tiffany Young-Chang. Prince Williams. At first, they were talking about other things—some TV show I don't watch—but when the conversation died down, Jane went, "So, Chinami, you brought your fish?" The other kids went crazy. First they were laughing. Then they started creeping upstairs to peer through the door to the kitchen, spying on the parents as they talked. Someone reported that the parents were playing something called "the fish game." Mr. Kerel was leading it, of course. All the adults were taking turns naming a type of fish. The first person who couldn't think of a fish was out. Every time they named one, Mr. Kerel told them all about that species' personality. "Tunas? Oh, don't get me started. Big, dumb, and rude. Swimming around in this enormous school, pushing everyone out of the way. No, just go ahead and order the tuna melt. None of the other fish mind at all!" The adults were laughing. Downstairs, the kids were laughing, too. But at me.

And then Timothy said, "Hey, Chinami, maybe you should just make your stepdad into sushi!" Immediately, the other kids joined in. "Yeah! Chinami's Sushi Restaurant, starring Mac Kerel!" It's not funny. In fact, it's totally offensive—they're making the joke because I'm Japanese, I figured. Even Prince was laughing. And then someone said, "Chinami, are you *crying*?"

I didn't think I was crying. But I guess I was. I rushed upstairs and burst into the kitchen, my face burning so hot I'm surprised the tears weren't evaporating off my face. The adults all turned and looked. "Oh no," my mom muttered.

On the drive home, I let them have it. "I can't *believe* you brought Mr. Kerel to the party. I'm so embarrassed. I'll never be able to show my face at school again. I *hate* those kids. I *hate* you. And I *hate* Mr. Kerel!"

My mom and Mr. Kerel sat silently in the front. Mr. Kerel's seat belt ran through the handle on his jug.

But while it's true that I hate Mr. Kerel, I may have started to hate Mrs. Banks, my biology teacher, more. I used to kind of admire her. She seems like she knows everything. And when someone says something stupid, she just gives them this look that is like an icicle falling down your shirt. But today in biology, she handed back our tests, and I got a fifty. Out of a hundred. That's an F. A fail. And I studied really hard, too. I started to flip through, to see how I got *half* the questions wrong. And I was more and more incredulous (another good word that Mrs. Banks uses a lot) when I discovered that I *didn't* get half the questions wrong. I got a *couple* of them wrong. But it looked like I got most of them right. I should have done really, really well.

And then I got to the essay at the end. The question was: "Some people claim that changes in the oceans, such as rising temperatures, are caused by humans. But many scientists believe that climate change is natural, and not caused by humans at all. Explain why changes in ocean temperatures might be naturally occurring. Don't forget to use evidence." When I'd read that question, I'd been pretty sure it was one of those trick questions, where it sounds like the teacher wants you to say one thing, but actually, she wants you to say another.

So I wrote an essay about how people were causing temperatures around the world to go up, and the ice caps were melting, and polar bears were dying, and how it was because we were pumping smoke and exhaust into the air, and cutting down all the forests. We had upset the balance between carbon and oxygen in our atmosphere, and it was messing everything up. It was, I thought, a really good essay.

But across the top of it, in red marker, Mrs. Banks had written, "WRONG. NO EVIDENCE. 0 POINTS."

I couldn't believe it. Looking around the room, I could see that a few other kids were staring at their papers *incredulously* (double use! double points!). I raised my hand.

Mrs. Banks gave me the icicle-down-your-shirt stare. "Chinami?"

"Mrs. Banks," I said, "I don't think I should have gotten a zero on my essay. I used evidence to—"

Mrs. Banks cut me off. "You know one thing I *hate*? Grade grubbers. Kids who complain because they lost one point here, or one point there. You got the grade you deserved, Chinami. An F."

Everyone was staring at me. I felt like my face must have been redder than it had ever been in my life. With embarrassment. But also with anger. "Mrs. Banks, I am *not* grade grubbing. You gave me a zero on my essay, but I did exactly what you asked!"

"You did *exactly* what I asked?" she said, and gave a big, fake laugh. "I asked you to show, with evidence, that climate change is naturally occurring. You tried to show the opposite. Frankly, I find that insulting." She looked around the class. "And Chinami wasn't the only one. A lot of you are believing this propaganda that's meant to hurt American businesses. A coal plant in America is not killing polar bears in Antarctica! Cutting down a tree in South America is not killing turtles in Australia! And what about jobs! Don't you want your parents to have jobs? Isn't your father's job more important than a turtle in Australia?" She gave another fake laugh, really loudly this time. "And I'm a *biology* teacher!"

Finally, she turned to me. "Chinami, if you'd like to rewrite your essay so that it uses *evidence* to support the *truth*, I am prepared to give you extra credit. You won't be able to get an A, but maybe you can pull out a C. Does that sound fair?"

At home that night, I sat in front of my composition notebook, my head on my arm, a sharpened no. 2 pencil between my fingers, and I stared at the faint blue lines running across the page, with the faint pink one crossing them along one border. I had written my name at the top. That was it.

My mom came into the kitchen, with Mr. Kerel in his jug. She put Mr. Kerel down on the table across from me. "How was your day, honey?" she said.

I mumbled something that sounded like a combination of "horrible" and "a catastrophe."

"What happened?"

"I don't want to talk about it."

Mr. Kerel poked his head above the water in his jug. "I can leave, if that would help."

"Can you?" I asked, sitting up. "Can you leave? How? You can't walk! My mom has to carry you everywhere!"

Mr. Kerel slid back down into the water. My mom's face turned red. I immediately felt awful. I bet my mom's face looked right now like mine did in biology today.

"Sorry," I said.

"It's okay," said Mr. Kerel.

"I just got an F on my biology test."

"But you studied so hard!" said my mom.

"And it wasn't even that I got a lot of answers wrong. It was all because of the stupid essay." I told them everything that had happened.

My mom's face went from red to gray. She looked at Mr. Kerel. Mr. Kerel looked at her, and then at me. He said, "Chinami, would you mind if I spoke to your school principal?"

"No!" I shouted. "Mrs. Banks hates grade grubbing! And you're not even my dad!"

"I promise I won't bring up your test at all," Mr. Kerel said. "Your principal won't have any idea that's why I'm there."

I stared at him. His huge, fishy eyes gazed at me over the edge of his jug.

"This is important, Chinami," he said. "Please." I shrugged. And then he added, "And don't write that stupid essay. Better to get an F telling the truth than a C by lying."

A tiny corner of my mouth smiled.

Three weeks later, there was a special assembly at the school. Our teachers didn't seem to know any more about it than the kids. We all just filed into the old auditorium, with its tattered red stage curtains and worn gray carpet, and plopped down in the squeaky chairs. Once everyone was settled, our principal came out, thanked the teachers for giving up some of their class time for this important speaker, and left the stage again. She came back in carrying a very large jug of water.

With Mr. Kerel inside.

She put Mr. Kerel on the podium, next to the microphone. I could feel the eyes of all the kids in my grade sliding to me, and then back to the stage, and then back to me. The kids in other grades had no *idea* what was going on.

Mr. Kerel started to speak. At first, there was a commotion in the auditorium. A lot of people were really surprised. Of course. But as he continued, people settled down. He was talking about growing up.

"It wasn't easy," Mr. Kerel said, "being the only talking fish in the sea. Other fish would tease me, with their blub-blubs and their bubbles. They would laugh in their fishy ways. None of them could speak a word of human language. But I could. It just came naturally to me. I would hang out around the fishing boats, hear the humans speaking, and pretty soon I could do it myself. You'd think that would make me special. I could hear what kind of bait the humans were using. What kind of flashing steel hooks they'd be dropping down into our homes, to trap and kidnap and kill us. I tried to tell the other fish, but I was a freak. They didn't want to listen to a freak. They refused to believe me.

"And I'm a freak up here on the land, too. So you might not believe me," he went on, "when I tell you what's going on in the ocean. Coral reefs—which are essentially cities for fish—are dying. Imagine the buildings of Houston or Dallas falling down on people every day, the farms in Indiana just going brown and barren. That's what our reefs are like. And it's not just the reefs. I had a friend named Dolly—a dolphin, incredibly smart gal, spoke in these squeaks and laughs, such a funny lady—who ate some human garbage and choked to death. And I used to be pals with a whole bunch of cod. Except there are pretty much no cod in the Atlantic anymore. They're all gone. A whole species, just wiped out."

The kids in the audience were now silent. I looked down and saw Mrs. Baker in the front row. Her face was like stone.

"What's killing all my pals? Destroying the cities we live in? Is it a war? Is it a plague?" asked Mr. Kerel. "No. It's oil rigs blowing up underwater. It's people throwing garbage in the ocean—or even littering on the streets, which goes into drains and gets washed into the ocean. It's everyone driving their cars everywhere they go, which raises the temperature of the planet, and kills the coral that makes up our reefs. Maybe you don't believe me, because I'm just a talking fish. But I'm up here talking to you because I don't want to live in the oceans anymore. Most of my friends down there are dead."

Mrs. Banks was looking at her lap.

After Mr. Kerel finished, there was some applause. Our principal picked up his jug and carried him offstage. As we filed out of the auditorium, I expected the kids to start teasing me again. But the only who said anything to me was Prince Williams, who appeared at my shoulder in the middle of the crowd of kids and said, "That was the best assembly we've had in a long time."

The sun is bright and the sea is shining today. My mom and I are in the prow of a small sailboat. The captain is in the back, handling the sheet and the rudder. The wind is strong, so the sail is full and taut. My black hair is blowing into my mother's face, and her hair is blowing straight out like a flag.

I call out, "Mr. Kerel!" But he dove out of sight a few minutes ago, and he doesn't respond. I call again. "Mr. Kerel!" Nothing. The sailboat plows over the waves, bouncing with the chop. I breathe in deeply. The sea smells wonderful. So salty and clean. "Mr. Kerel!" I call again. No response.

My mom looks overboard, slightly nervous. She and Mr. Kerel have plans to get married in the fall. I'm going to be the flower girl.

"Mac!" I shout. Suddenly, Mr. Kerel comes leaping out of a wave, spraying water in a cascade of droplets that are lit up in the sun like a rainbow.

"Show-off," my mom mutters. But she's smiling.

I smile up at her, and then look back out to the sea. Mr. Kerel leaps out of the water again and does a twist and a flip, and then goes plunging back into the waves. He's not so bad after all, I guess.

PROMPT

BY DAN SANTAT

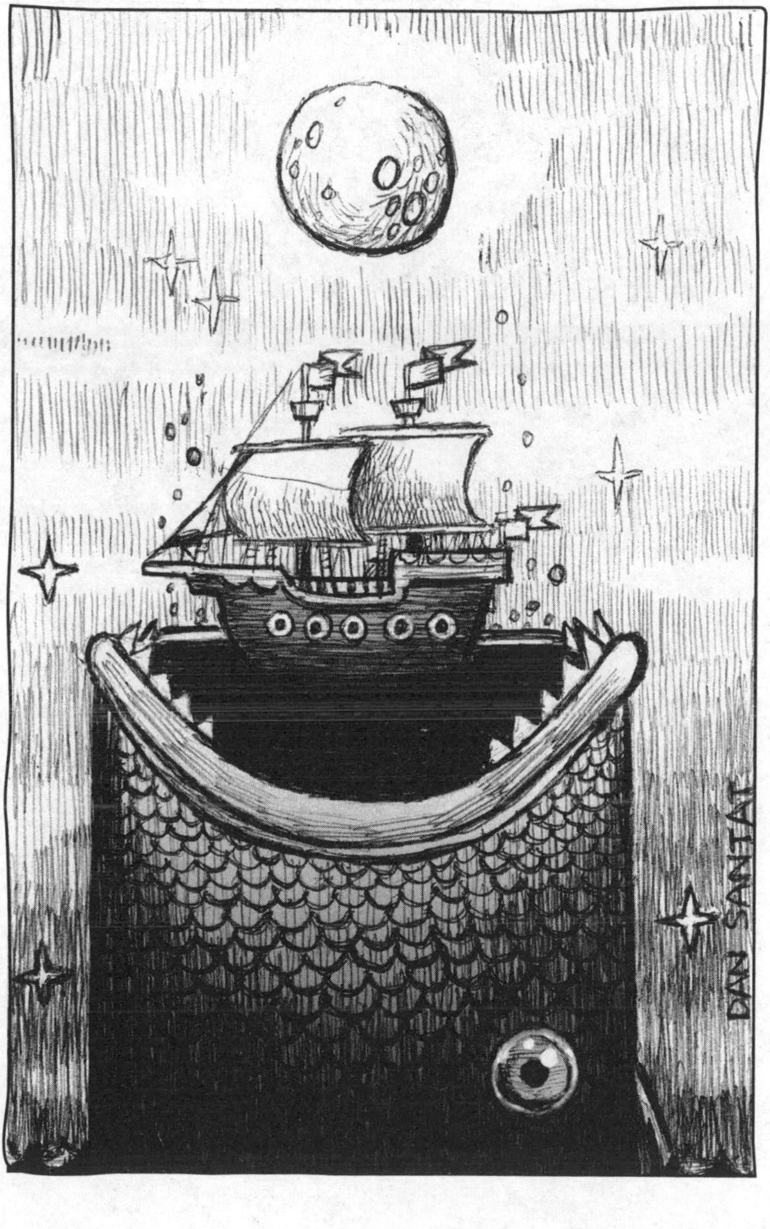
DAN SANTAT

RESPONSE

BY TOM ANGLEBERGER

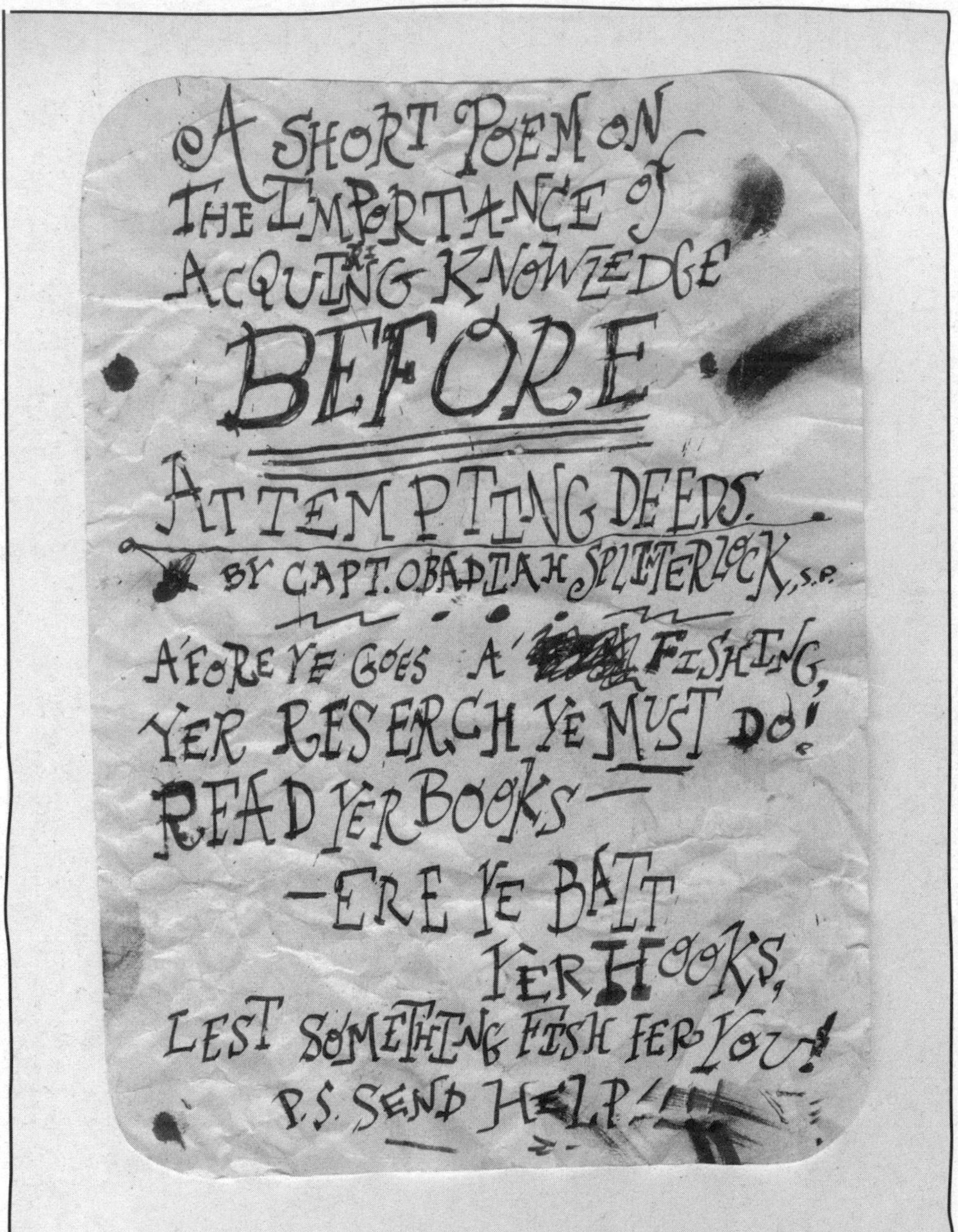
A SHORT POEM ON
THE IMPORTANCE OF
ACQUIRING KNOWLEDGE
BEFORE
ATTEMPTING DEEDS.
BY CAPT. OBADIAH SPLITTERLOCK, S.P.
AFORE YE GOES A FISHING,
YER RESERCH YE MUST DO!
READ YER BOOKS —
— ERE YE BAIT
YER HOOKS,
LEST SOMETHING FISH FER YOU!
P.S. SEND HELP!

PROMPT

BY NAOMI SHIHAB NYE

Write a dialogue poem—a back-and-forth between human and something or things not human.

> *Sea, are you watching me?*
>
> *I have no idea who you are. Speck*
> *on my shore, blot on my sand…*
>
> *Sea, are you weary of your motions?*
> *etc.*

REFLECTIONS ON A CONVERSATION

BY KAT YEH

Deep breath now | won htaerb peeD
I'm ready | ydaer m'I
Looking good | doog gnikooL
This is it | ti si sihT
Wait…is that a hive? | Um, I think that thing's a zit

Who said that?

          I did.

But you are…

          Me.

and you call this a zit?

          I just say what I see.

But you're my reflection
you do what *I* do
you see what *I* see—

          (coughs to self)
          Says you!

Look, stick to your job
It couldn't be clearer:
I do stuff—you follow
now act like a mirror!

                              You want a reflection?

—without being harassed
I've got a meeting—

                              —we both do
                              So, I'll make this fast:

                              I can offer reflections

          Like this | siht ekiL

There you go!

                              but Reflection can mean
                              more than one thing,
                              you know...

                              Hit it!

Wait, I don't have time for—

Reflection can mean thought—I mean think—I mean thinking—
    I mean taking information in and tell me that it's sinking in
        and tell me that you're letting go of rules inside your head
    and you're taking roads less traveled and you're forging paths ahead
    'cause that bendy twisty turning and that change in point of view
        means you're smashing through the old and coming up with
                              something new
                    Take a look again—
            it doesn't even matter what you see
                True reflection is the chance
            to live with pos—si—bil—ity

73

Wow...that was really—
        SO DON'T GO LOOKING
        FOR REFLECTIONS
        —SELF-REFLECT
        NEVER QUIT
        THAT IS ALL
        THAT'S THE TRUTH
        THAT'S MY RHYME
        And that's a zit.

        (mic drop)

...

                            I know...too far

Just that part at the end
But you gave me a lot
to reflect on, my friend

So, what's next?

                            We have a meeting!

We have a meeting!
Let's go!

                            Hey...Me?

Yes?

                            You got this

            We got this | We got this
                I know | I know

PROMPT
BY DEBORAH FREEDMAN

THE ASCENT

BY R. J. PALACIO

...and so we climbed. She on her ladder, me on mine. How far we climbed was impossible to tell in the nothingness around us. The ground was just a memory now, something sensed but not seen. Like the stars above us, glimmering invisibly in the daylight, the earth below us was there but not there. For a brief second I thought of my mom, the atoms and dust of her body in the ground now, her soul with the stars. "Energy can be neither created nor destroyed; rather, it transforms from one form to another." I heard this quote in my sixth-grade science class not too long after my mom died, and it made me love science.

I was tired of the climb, I have to admit. But watching Julia climb her ladder, always just a few yards higher than me, kept my legs from stiffening, kept my hands from cramping up. I would look around, lose my will, second-guess our decision, but then I'd look over at her. She never looked down. Her eyes were fixed upward on the object of our ascent. We had gotten much closer. We could see the vague clouds that shrouded the towers. White tendrils were looping in and out of the cosmic ladders. Before, from the ground, the white mist had appeared unmoving, as slow as ordinary clouds. But now we saw how they roiled like rapids, how they sparkled with something like tiny lightning bolts. It's like the clouds were illuminated from within by millions of tiny Christmas tree lights. Again, I pushed away thoughts of Mom, making me hot chocolate on Christmas morning. *Focus, Clare!*

I can't deny that I was afraid. I can't deny my teeth were chattering though I wasn't cold. Would the cloud be cold when we passed through it? Would the tiny electrical charges burn us? Would we fall?

"Clare! How are you doing?" It was like she could read my mind.

I looked over. Julia had paused in her ascent and was looking at me. She waited for me to catch up to her so that we were finally at the same level on our respective ladders.

"I'm kind of nervous," I admitted quietly.

The ladders were about twenty feet apart, but we didn't have to raise our voices to talk to each other across the chasm. There were no other sounds besides the sounds of our voices.

"We'll be fine," she said.

"How can you be so sure?"

She looked up. She shrugged. "I just know it." Then she smiled at me. "But look, you can go back down if you want to. I'll tell you what I find."

This is the way it had always been for us, for as long as I've known her. She was the brave one, the explorer, the leader. Me, I was the follower, the encourager, the helper.

When we first discovered the ladders in the forest, she was the one who instantly named them "cosmic ladders." She was the one who immediately said, "Let's climb them." I was the one who said, "No, let's go tell someone about them."

"We're the ones who were brought here," she pointed out. "We followed the signs. We followed the crow. We found these ladders for a reason. We were meant to climb them. One for you, one for me. It's destiny."

"I think we should go back and tell your parents about them, Julia," I persisted, the voice of reason.

"If we leave, they might not be here when we come back. Maybe they're magical."

"That's totally ridiculous."

"All right, but maybe they're like cosmic ladders or something. Maybe they're like...what are they called, in outer space, like black holes? Where you travel through time?"

"Wormholes."

"Yeah. Maybe they're kind of like wormholes. Maybe those towers are rockets or something. Maybe they'll connect you, Clare."

She stopped short of saying it, but I knew what she was thinking. I was thinking it, too.

"Okay," I said.

Now she nodded happily, spit into her palms, rubbed them quickly, and started climbing again.

I sighed deeply, made the mistake of looking down, and felt a shiver run up my spine.

"Don't look down, Clare!" she shouted.

"Fine fine fine," I grumbled, but then I looked up and resumed climbing.

I can't say how much longer we climbed. I lost track of time. An hour? Two hours? I don't know. What I do know is that, at some point, I could feel the white mist around me. It was like we were climbing through the lightest form of water, a soft silky puddle of breathable milk.

When my mom died, it was the strangest thing walking around afterward, being alive when she wasn't. Everything was the same, life went on for everyone around me, but it was like the earth had shifted for me. I had been learning about the cardinal points in school, and I remember thinking: *There's no North for me anymore. There's South and East and West, but North is gone. My compass won't work anymore.*

I also remember people telling me, over and over again, that she would always stay with me, in my heart, in my memory. But that just made me wonder, *Am I still with her? Wherever she is now, wherever she's going, will she remember me? Is she thinking of me?*

Ugh, I wish I could rein in my thinking. *Focus, Clare!*

I was so lost in my thoughts that I didn't realize we'd arrived until Julia whooped and hollered. I looked up. Directly above me was a little island balanced on the top of the ladder. It looked like the upended bottom of a giant tree, though there were no roots or anything. Just very round rocks, like bubbles of stone, covering the bottom of the island. I touched one. It was smooth and warm. It wasn't attached to the bottom of the island by anything I could see, but it didn't move when I grabbed it. With my other hand I grabbed another rock, and pulled myself up enough to be able to latch my leg around one of the lower rocks on the end. Then I pushed up and scrambled over the side.

I stayed crouched in front of the tower for a few minutes, not daring to look down, or even to look across at Julia. I could feel my heart beating furiously in my forehead. I could feel myself starting to panic. I closed my eyes and willed myself to stop trembling.

"Clare, are you okay?"

"No! I'm not!"

"Everything will be fine!"

I looked over at Julia. She was smiling, her eyes shining.

"They're much smaller than I thought they'd be!" she said.

I finally got the courage to look up at the tower in front of me, and I knew she was right. For some reason, from below, it had appeared much larger, but now it was no bigger than a small shed. It was like one of those water towers you see on top of buildings when you walk over the Brooklyn Bridge. Except that these towers had doors with doorknobs that glowed like lightbulbs.

"Are you ready?" said Julia, taking hold of the doorknob on her tower door. "Let's go in at the same time."

She didn't even hesitate to feel if the doorknob was hot to the touch first. She just grabbed it.

I'm telling you, the girl is fearless.

I stood up and took hold of my doorknob. It was cool to the touch, though I would have thought, from the way it was shining, it would have burned my fingers badly.

"Okay," I said. "I'm ready."

"I'll see you on the other side!" she answered giddily. She kind of laughed as she said it. I think, for the first time, she was a little nervous.

She opened the door and walked inside. The door closed behind her.

I turned the doorknob to my door, head down, fingers trembling. But, even as I willed myself to walk inside, just as my thoughts caught up to my heart, I knew I couldn't do it.

I knew I wouldn't even look inside....

PROMPT

BY DAV PILKEY

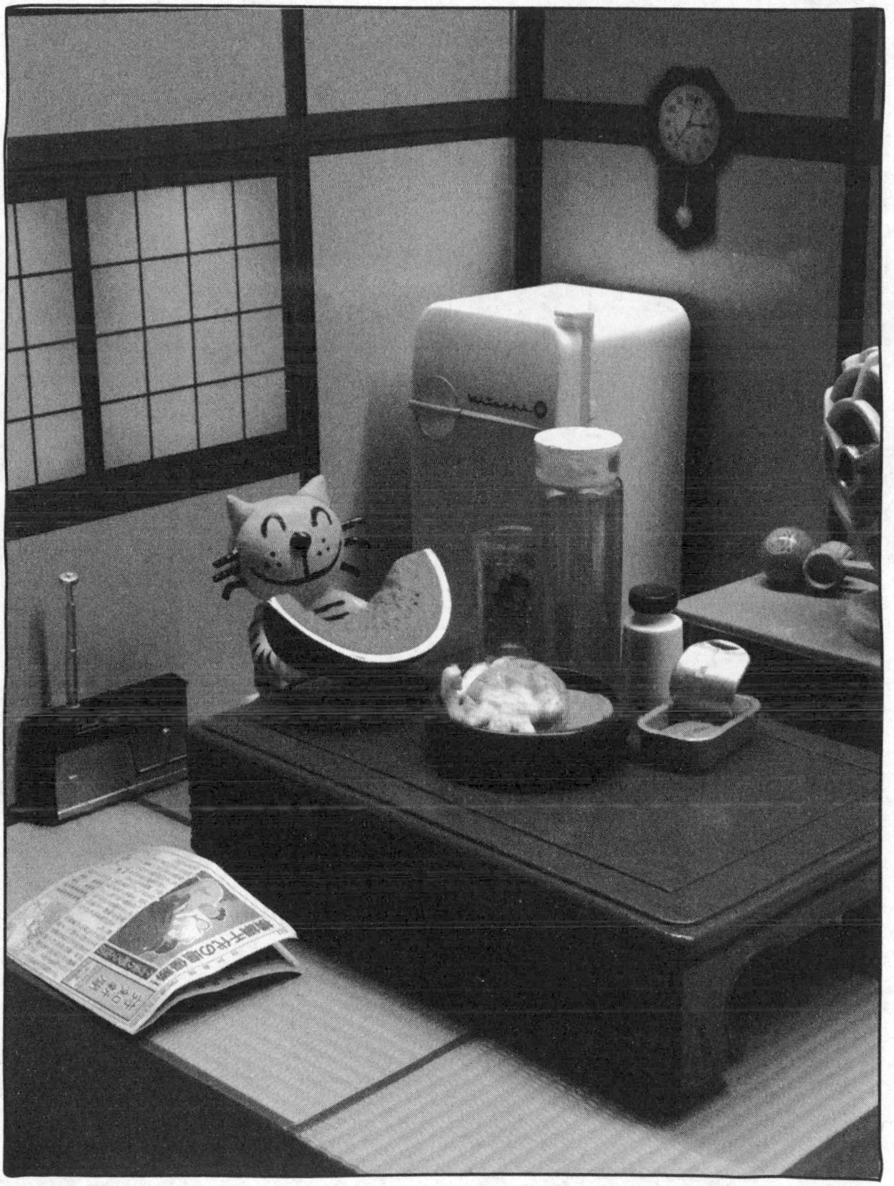

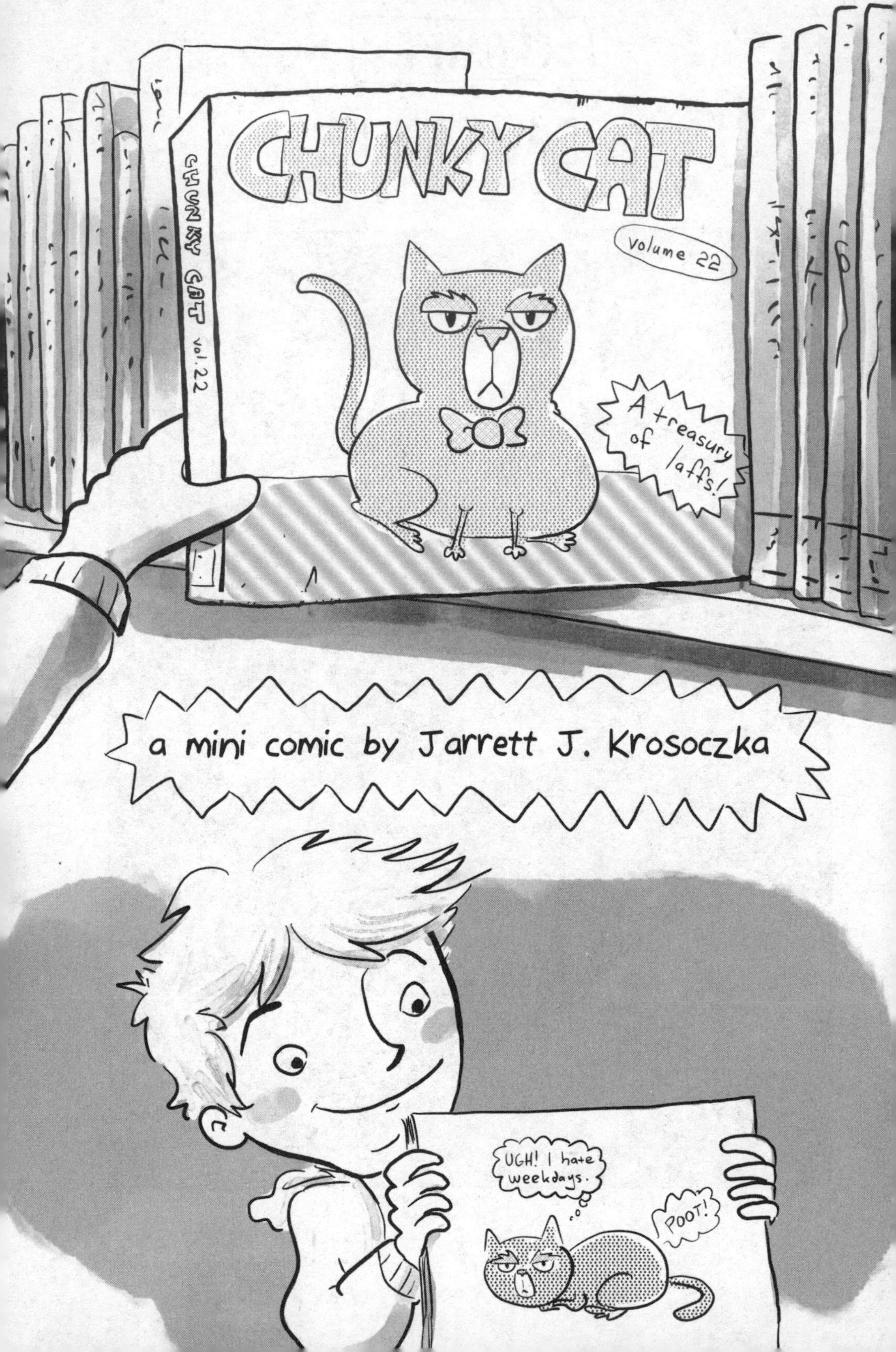
CHUNKY CAT
volume 22
CHUNKY CAT vol.22
A treasury of laffs!
a mini comic by Jarrett J. Krosoczka
UGH! I hate weekdays.
POOT!

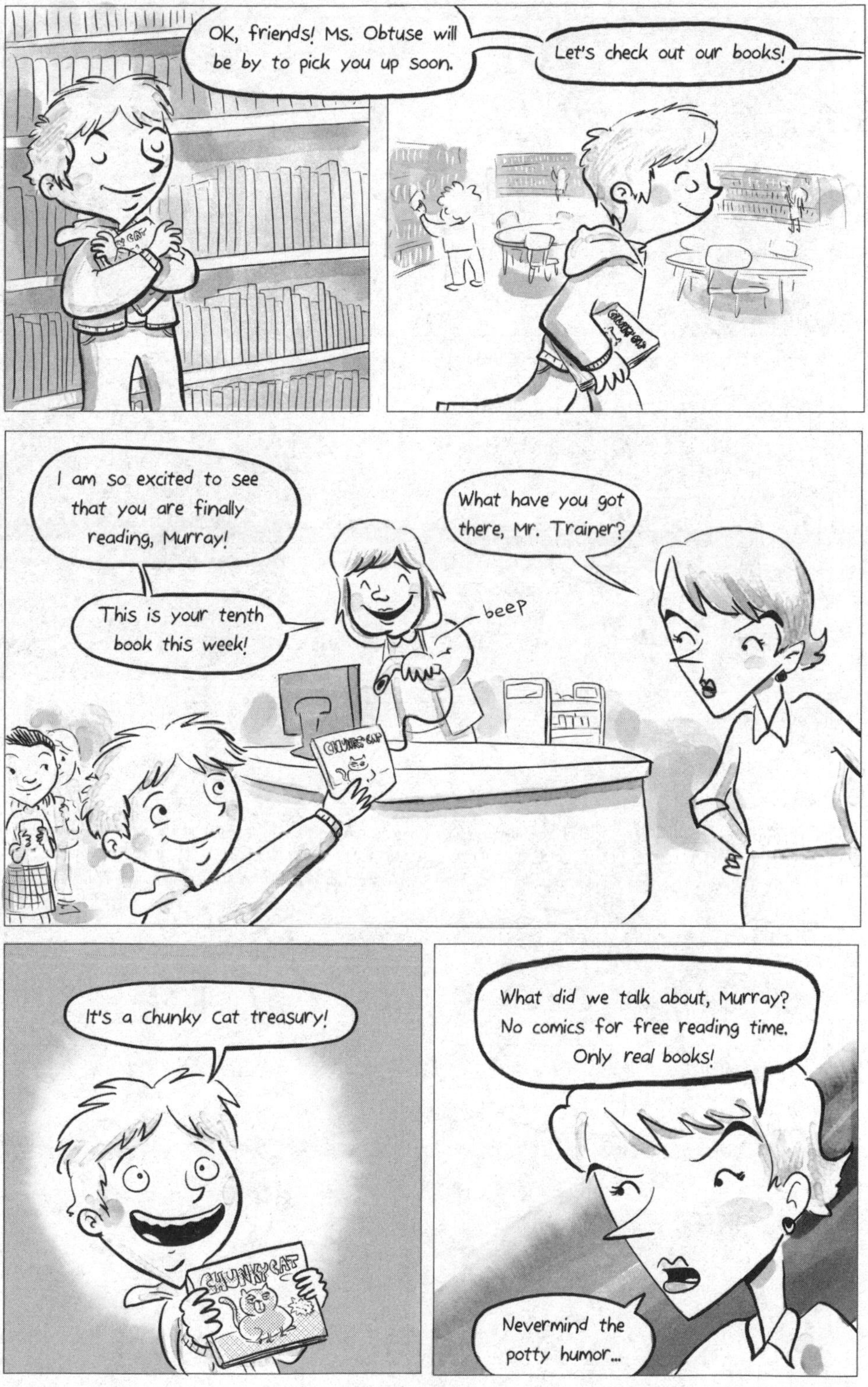

OK, friends! Ms. Obtuse will be by to pick you up soon.
Let's check out our books!
CHUNKY CAT
I am so excited to see that you are finally reading, Murray!
This is your tenth book this week!
beep
What have you got there, Mr. Trainer?
It's a Chunky Cat treasury!
CHUNKY CAT
What did we talk about, Murray? No comics for free reading time. Only real books!
Nevermind the potty humor...

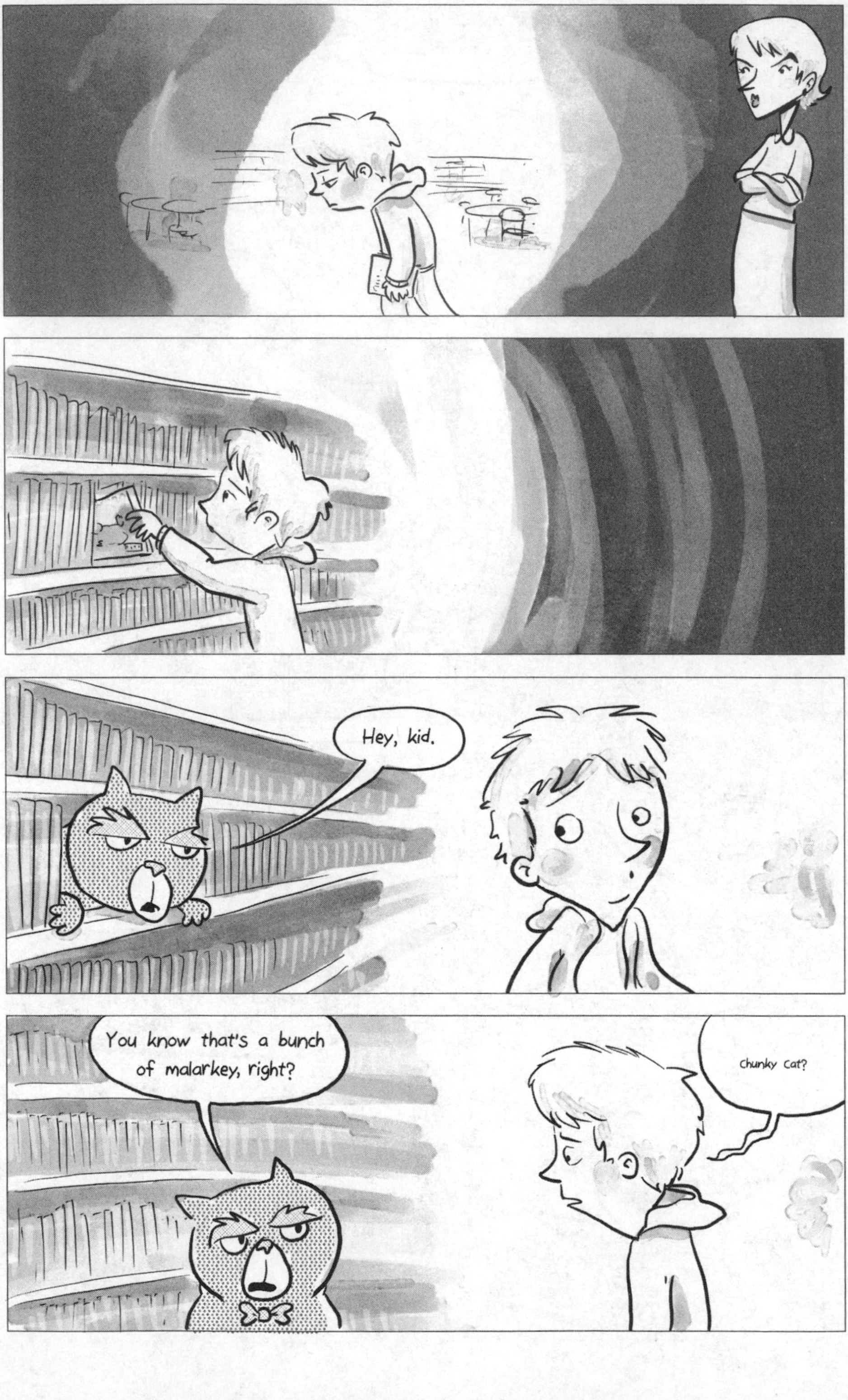
Hey, kid.
You know that's a bunch of malarkey, right?
Chunky Cat?

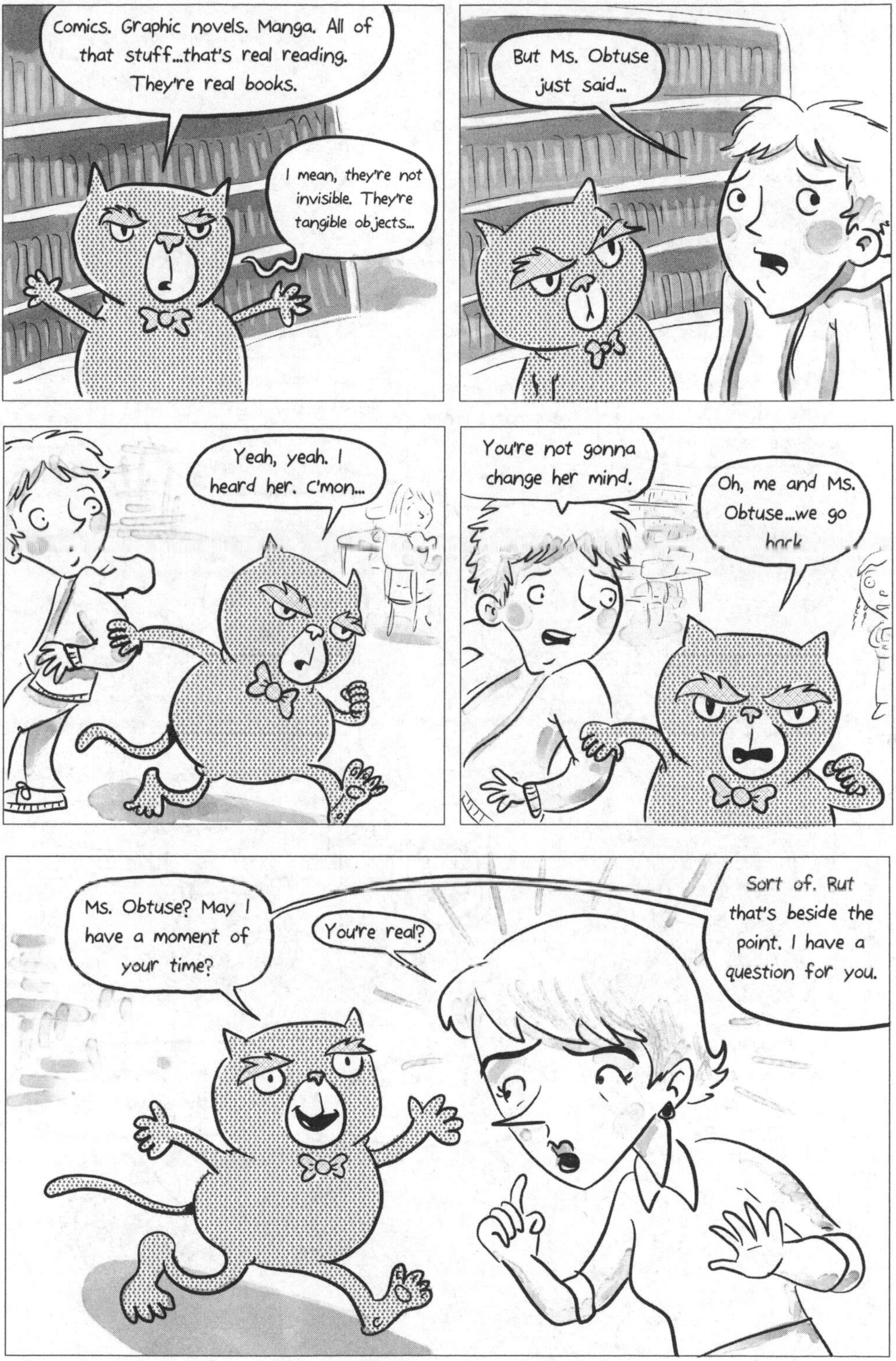
Comics. Graphic novels. Manga. All of that stuff...that's real reading. They're real books.
I mean, they're not invisible. They're tangible objects...
But Ms. Obtuse just said...
Yeah, yeah. I heard her. C'mon...
You're not gonna change her mind.
Oh, me and Ms. Obtuse...we go back
Ms. Obtuse? May I have a moment of your time?
You're real?
Sort of. But that's beside the point. I have a question for you.

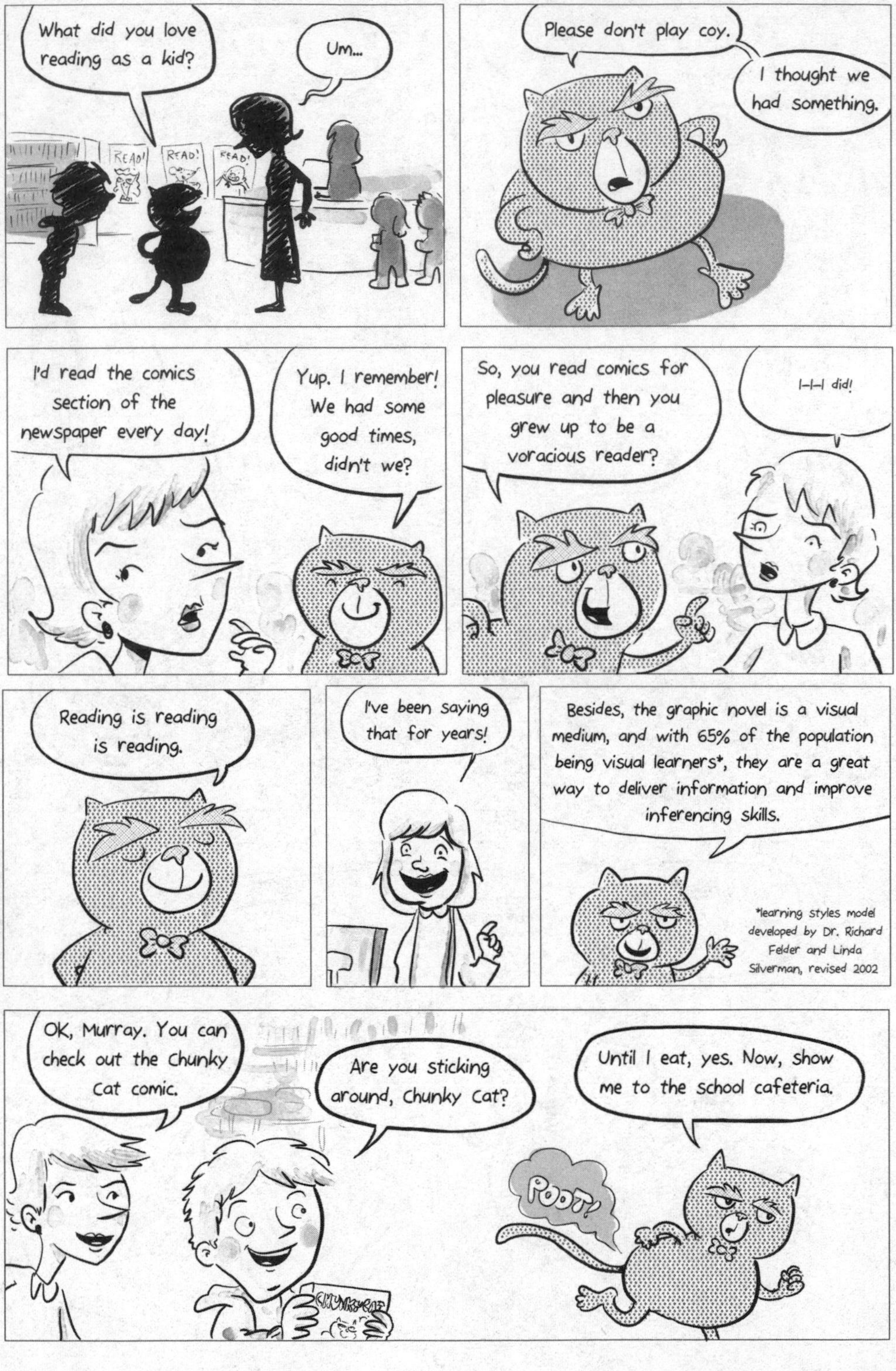
What did you love reading as a kid?
Um...
READ!
READ!
READ!
Please don't play coy.
I thought we had something.
I'd read the comics section of the newspaper every day!
Yup. I remember! We had some good times, didn't we?
So, you read comics for pleasure and then you grew up to be a voracious reader?
I-I-I did!
Reading is reading is reading.
I've been saying that for years!
Besides, the graphic novel is a visual medium, and with 65% of the population being visual learners*, they are a great way to deliver information and improve inferencing skills.
*learning styles model developed by Dr. Richard Felder and Linda Silverman, revised 2002
OK, Murray. You can check out the Chunky Cat comic.
Are you sticking around, Chunky Cat?
Until I eat, yes. Now, show me to the school cafeteria.
POOT!

PROMPT

BY DEBBIE RIDPATH OHI

Weird. How could I have not noticed that door before? This was crazy.
I reached for the knob.

RESPONSE

THE LEPER'S SPOTS
BY DANIEL NAYERI

...and they lived happily ever after. The lovers would set off to Peking, the genie back to the cosmopolis of his bottle, and the mouse...the wily mouse asked for the three phoenix tail feathers to make a little nest. The lovers could hardly refuse after all she had done to help them, and there were no practical uses for the feathers anyway. So the mouse... the wily mouse had her nest, which became a throne, which became a gallows, which became a tomb.

But for now, they lived happily ever after.

For now they thought the story was ended.

Alas, no story ever ends.

Little did they know.

We are born naked with no teeth, and we will die naked with no teeth, but the story is infinite in all directions. A thousand and one tales of a thousand and one nights in a thousand and one mouths.

Each is a door in a labyrinth of time. And you, little one, are there. You might crouch beside the doors you know, and sleep in their threshold.

Or you might wander.

Or you might come across a door in a hall you have known all your life and say, "Weird. How could I have not noticed that door before? This is crazy." You might reach for the doorknob and open it (the door).

Just like that, a new story begins.

But also, in another part of the labyrinth, another you would never dare open a strange door.

And that story goes on as well.

There are a thousand and one *yous* and a thousand and one doors.

For the mouse and the lovers and the phoenix and the genie, this was a cold stone door in the deepest part of the maze.

The orphan boy had rousted the evil king with the help of the animals. The princess was imprisoned in her aviary with her dearest birds. The wily mouse led the boy through the walls of the palace to the throne room.

In some forms of the story the boy dies here at the hands of the genie, who has become a sand behemoth.

But in this one, the pieces fell into place just so.

The phoenix saved the princess, but drowned.

All that remained were the three feathers the genie ripped away in his monstrous fist.

As the genie turned his attention to the boy, the wily mouse stole his bottle from beside the king and gave it to the boy, who wished the king into oblivion, and for the princess to have her arms turned back into flesh (they were glass), and—perhaps unwisely—for the genie to return to his bottle, never to grant another wish until the end of days.

The princess would have preferred to be consulted on that last one.

She would have wished the phoenix back to life.

That made no sense to the boy. Certainly if they had had four wishes, that would have been it, but as it stood, the genie was too dangerous.

They *would* have had four wishes if the boy had given her the bottle, said the princess.

This was undeniable.

The boy lost the thread of conversation.

Well, anyway, he said, her hands had been glass just seconds ago.

The princess had been tutored by the astronomers in elocution, argumentation, and logic.

So? she said.

So the genie was banished to his bottle, back to the family that missed him, and the lovers had their first true quarrel, which the mouse helped resolve. She had had four husbands and knew that underneath every fight is a different fight about a different thing altogether.

By the time the lovers finally kissed, the mouse had performed three great boons—sneaking the boy into the palace, grabbing the bottle, and resolving the quarrel—for which she received the three tail feathers.

In one version of the story she simply eats the phoenix feathers and becomes a molten mouse, a demon to cats.

But in this one, she bowed and scraped her whiskers on the floor in thanks. When no one was looking, she snatched up all three feathers in her paws and squeezed them to her chest. They smelled like sulfur and singed her hair a little, but to the mouse they were the touch of a god… or an angel near enough in status.

From that day onward, the lovers had very little to do with their mornings and so they made up new laws (lawful: sandwiches; unlawful: sand witches). The princess, now queen, rebuilt her aviary. The boy, now king (but always in his heart of hearts a mongrel) made a law to protect the animals that had helped him in his adventures—the sparrow that carried news to him in the dungeon, the ants that brought him food, his army of stray dogs, and of course, the mouse…the wily mouse.

The law was simple, whispered into his ear by the mouse: The sultanate of animals would be ruled by kindness. Killing another creature, however small, was thenceforth illegal.

Was this wise? asked the princess that evening as they walked in the gardens. Or never mind that, was it possible? It seemed to her the laws of nature abound. And that law is not the kindness of hearts, but the kindness of parts. *The kind of tooth or claw you've got, in life, is more or less your lot.*

To the boy—who had recently gone from guttersnipe to king, who had made three impossible wishes, and who had somehow come to enjoy the affection of the only girl he had ever loved—nothing seemed impossible.

Sometimes the beasts go to war over the decree.

This time, they simply didn't listen.

As they say, the leper cannot change his spots, and the leopard doesn't want to.

In three days, the mice, and the moles, and the lizards, and especially the ant queen stood before the boy and the princess demanding justice for their newly dead.

The young queen remained steadfast in her belief that the law was to blame.

When the king demands something the people cannot give, even the most loyal servants become outlaws, she said to her husband over dinner.

He quite obviously agreed, but had few alternatives. What if we said no killing every *other* day? he offered.

The mouse—who was in the habit of eating from their table—swished her whiskers in the negatory direction.

The second decree was more modest. There would be no killing *within* the palace walls.

That should be easy enough to obey, said the boy to his bride, hoping to have won back her approval, as they fed the birds.

The aviary is off the palace ground, technically, he noted aloud.

She made a confirming noise.

He wondered if they would have secrets between them now.

In the new world, the palace cats were least happy.

The mouse moved her nest from a hole behind the pantry to a roof beam above the throne room. The three tail feathers splayed out of it like a high-back chair. From her seat above the crown, the mouse became a judge for the animals that measured below a hand's width—a ruler of the small rule. If a house spider gave in to the urge and devoured a moth, he would be dragged before the mouse—it was agreed that she had the boy's ear, and he was too busy scolding the cooks. From the roof beam, she hung the spider by his own rope.

Inside the palace was a revolting peace, but outside it there began the stirrings of revolt.

A safe city for mice? they would say (the other mice). Why shouldn't *our* litter be so lucky?

They had not heard of the hanging judge, only that a mouse could swagger before the nose of a cat in an open hall and fear for nothing but the sneeze.

When the princess looked out of her window one evening as she brushed her hair, she saw a congress of prey animals gathered outside the walls to express the injustice.

Husband, she said, *have you noticed the hens pecking at the western gate?*

The boy made no response. He sat before the mirror. In all his life scraping for survival in the streets, he had never seen himself so clearly. He parted his hair on the left, then on the right, then tousled it, then combed it back.

In one story the riches of the palace cripple the boy into indolence.

In this one he returned to the world and said yes, and the squirrels were on the other side.

He admitted that if the squirrels had managed a consensus, there was something wrong. The palace guards were used to uprisings during the evil king's reign, and so began preparations. They shut the inner gates and mustered the reserve archers.

They won't do much against an army that can skitter over walls, said the princess. *Or burrow under*, said the boy. They would have to go out and speak to them from the ramparts. It could all be resolved, surely, if everyone wanted nothing more than fairness.

The boy passed the comb through his hair a last time. When he inspected it, he saw a louse. He hid the comb immediately under the table and looked over his shoulder to make sure the princess hadn't seen the shameful reminder of a time—just a few days ago—when the boy slept in the flea-ridden garbage heap behind the grand bazaar.

He squeezed the louse between his thumb and fingernail.

Should we go? asked the princess. She was interrupted by the door of the royal bedroom slamming open. A horde from the palace zoo—

the lion, the dogs, the jackals, and the badger rushed into the room and seized upon the boy.

None dared touch the princess when she gathered herself and rose from her chair.

She walked behind them as they pushed the boy before the mouse... the wily mouse, who sat on her nest of phoenix feathers and tamed all the cats and beasts, who ruled, judged, and executed all her enemies by hanging them from the rafters. They dangled below her throne like the tassels of a carpet.

The trial was short.

The boy shouted that he loved her—the princess—as the animals put the noose around his neck.

The mouse laughed, because she had seen how far apart their lives began, and never believed they would last in love.

She gave the command.

The rhino pulled the rope.

The gorilla held his legs (the boy's).

They roared when it was over.

The princess—whose turn it was to exclaim something—was missing.

In one version of the story, she abandons the boy and becomes a lonely wanderer.

In this one she appeared on the rafter, towering above the mouse, as if by magic.

Magic? said the mouse in disbelief.

It was indeed magic.

The princess had made three wishes: for mouse and her nest to fly into the very center of the ocean, for the boy's neck to be made whole (it was broken), and for her dearest phoenix to return.

All three came true.

The tail feathers sparked into new flame.

The boy coughed and awoke.

And the mouse...the wily mouse disappeared from the story forever.

How? asked the boy as she helped him down from the gallows.

I snuck the genie's bottle into my pocket when they rushed into our room, said the princess.

But he doesn't grant wishes anymore.

I know, said the princess. *That's why I asked to speak with his wife.*

In one version of the story they kiss. Actually, in many versions of it. There is much kissing.

In some, they fall apart.

The labyrinth is full of doors, remember, and the story is infinite in all directions.

In some the wily mouse becomes a lord of the sea and returns for their heads. In one the chickens outside overrun the palace before anyone can tell them the good news. In several versions the boy and the princess are just too different and quarrel constantly. But in this one they practice love, and difficult compromise, and have lots of fat babies.

And this time they live happily—not always, but most times, and if not *ever after*, then at least until…

…the end.

BY LEMONY SNICKET

Write a paragraph about one specific thing that makes it clear you are thinking about another specific thing entirely.

LOST & FOUND
BY JENNIFER L. HOLM

I was sitting in the nurse's office because of a spider.

I had been looking for my jacket in the Lost and Found box. I'd left it on the playground at recess the day before. The Lost and Found box was stuffed to the brim with random stuff: dirty zip-up fleeces, stray socks, knit caps, empty lunch boxes. And it had smelled weird—like mold and stale peanut butter crackers and maybe rotten milk.

As I'd rooted around looking for my jacket, I'd felt a sting. When I'd looked down, a little spider ran across my hand. A moment later, my hand had started throbbing and the underside of my wrist had swollen up to the size of a golf ball. My teacher had taken one look at it and sent me to the nurse's office.

I'd never imagined myself sitting in the nurse's office because of a spider bite. Then again, I'd never imagined myself doing a lot of things. Like living in Atlanta.

Everything was different here. The houses. The streets. Even the school. Instead of an outdoor lunch court, there was a stuffy cafeteria. But the biggest difference was the cold. It was November and freezing. I would still be wearing shorts if I was back in California.

I missed my old home. I missed the sun. Most of all, I missed having a friend.

We had moved here at the end of October, and for some reason the friend groups had already cemented by then. Kids were nice enough, but I didn't have a person of my own. A kid I could count on: who sat with me at lunch or talked to me on the playground or just shared jokes with me. Moving to Atlanta was a big opportunity for my dad, but all it had been for me was lonely.

"How are you feeling now?" the nurse asked the girl sitting next to me. The girl was breathing into one of those asthma inhalers.

The girl shrugged.

"Why don't you sit there and we'll see how you're breathing in a few minutes," she told the girl and then turned to me. The nurse was wearing a shirt with kittens on it.

"What can I do for you?" she asked.

I held out my hand.

"Oh dear," she said. "Did you fall?"

"A spider bit me."

"Hmm," she said. "Let me go get some ice for it. That will help."

She disappeared out the door and the room was silent.

"That's so cool," the girl said.

"What?"

"That you got bit by a spider!" Her nose wrinkled. "Was it a tarantula?"

I shook my head. "Tarantulas don't live around her. They like the desert."

"How do you know?"

"I used to live in California. We had a tarantula in our garage."

Her eyes bugged open. "Really? Did it ever bite you?"

"Tarantulas are big and furry and don't like people. They're scaredy-cats."

"I like spiders," she admitted.

"Me, too," I said. "The ones that don't bite, I mean."

"Yeah," she said with a laugh.

"My dad took pictures of Old Spidey. He was the tarantula who lived in our garage."

"Really? Can I see them sometime?"

"Sure," I said.

She smiled at me. "I'm Meera."

"I'm Nevy," I said.

As Meera asked me more questions about tarantulas, I felt warm for the first time since moving here. Because while I had lost my jacket, I had found something more important.

A friend.

BY LINDA SUE PARK

She threw it off the bridge into the river, and watched it disappear downstream.

RESPONSE

BY SOPHIE BLACKALL

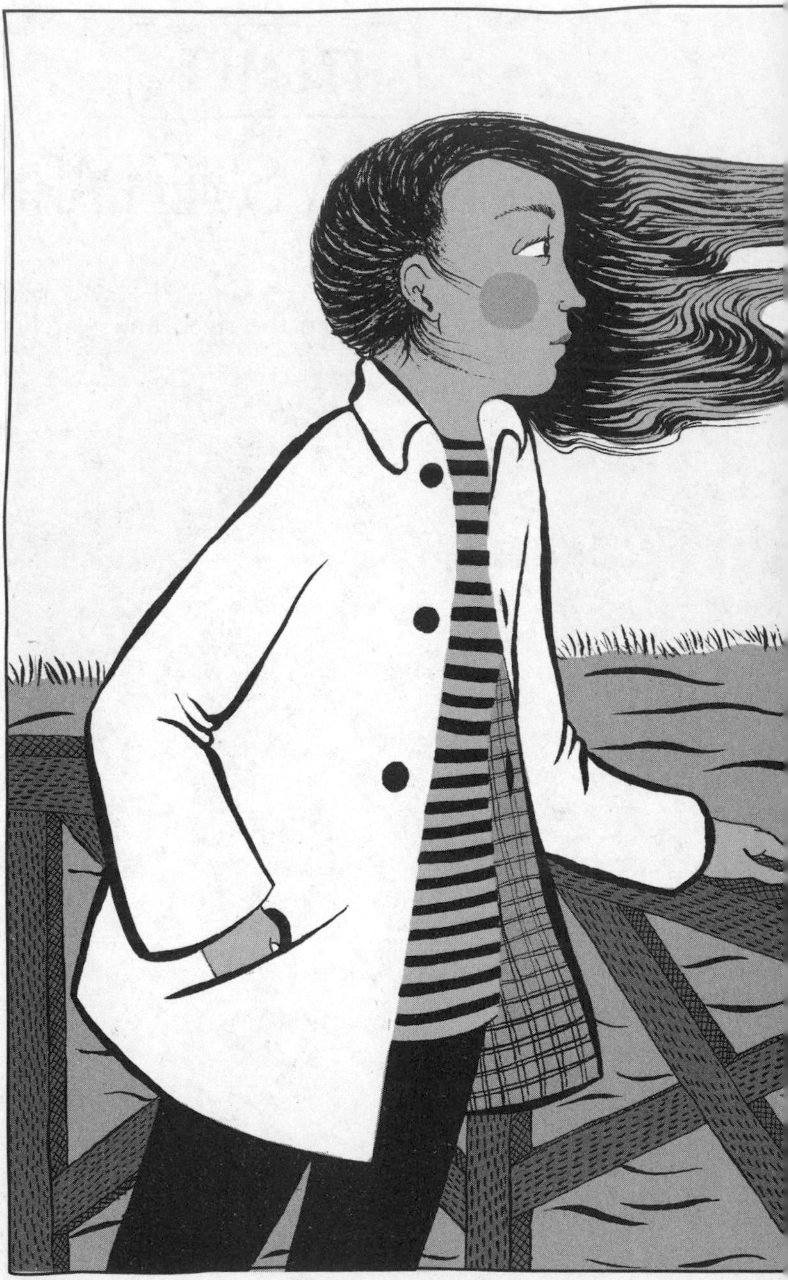

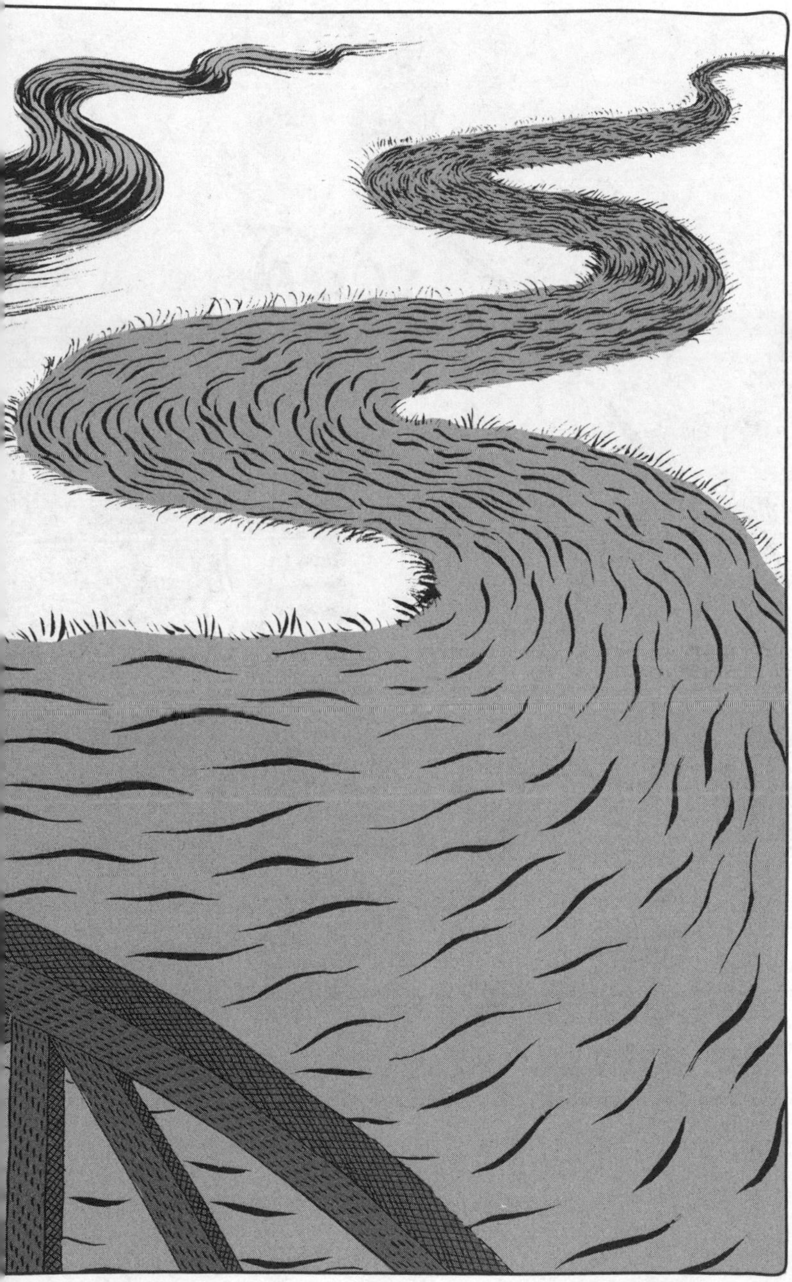

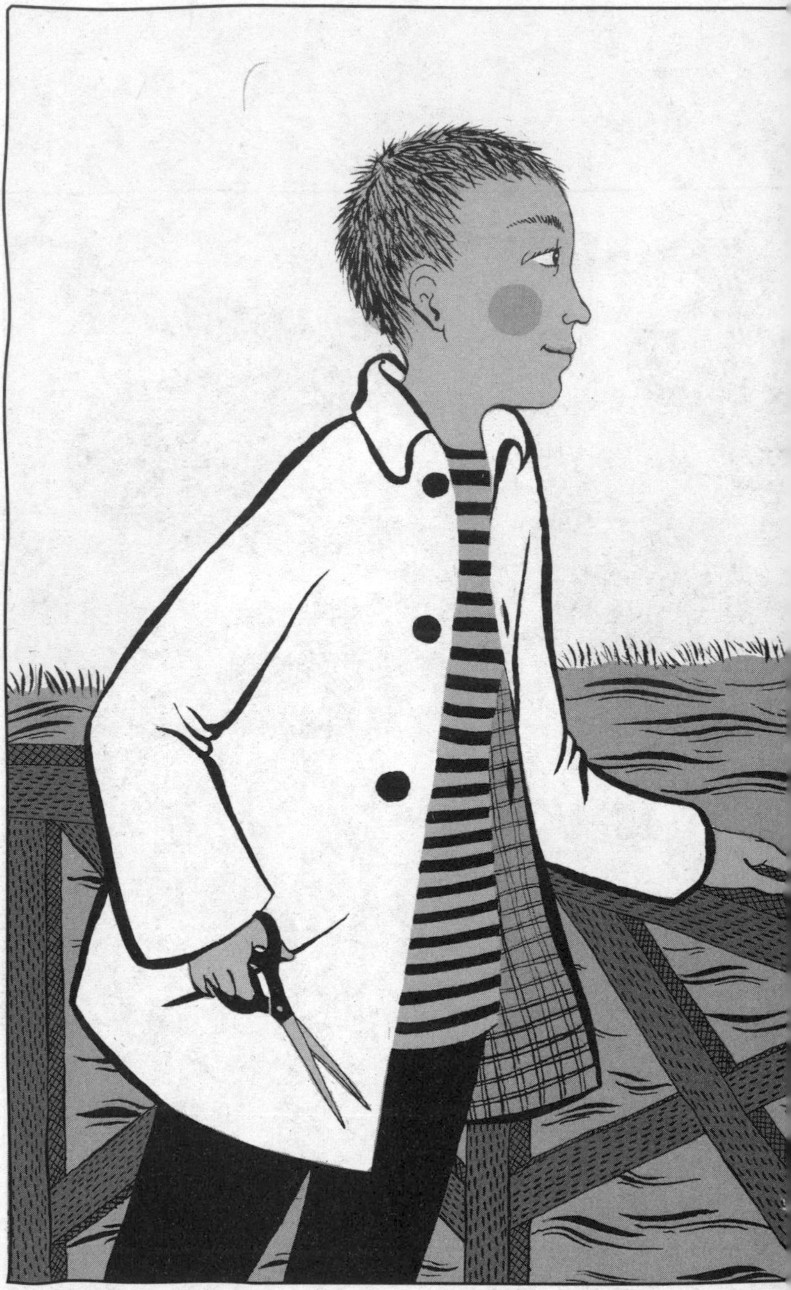

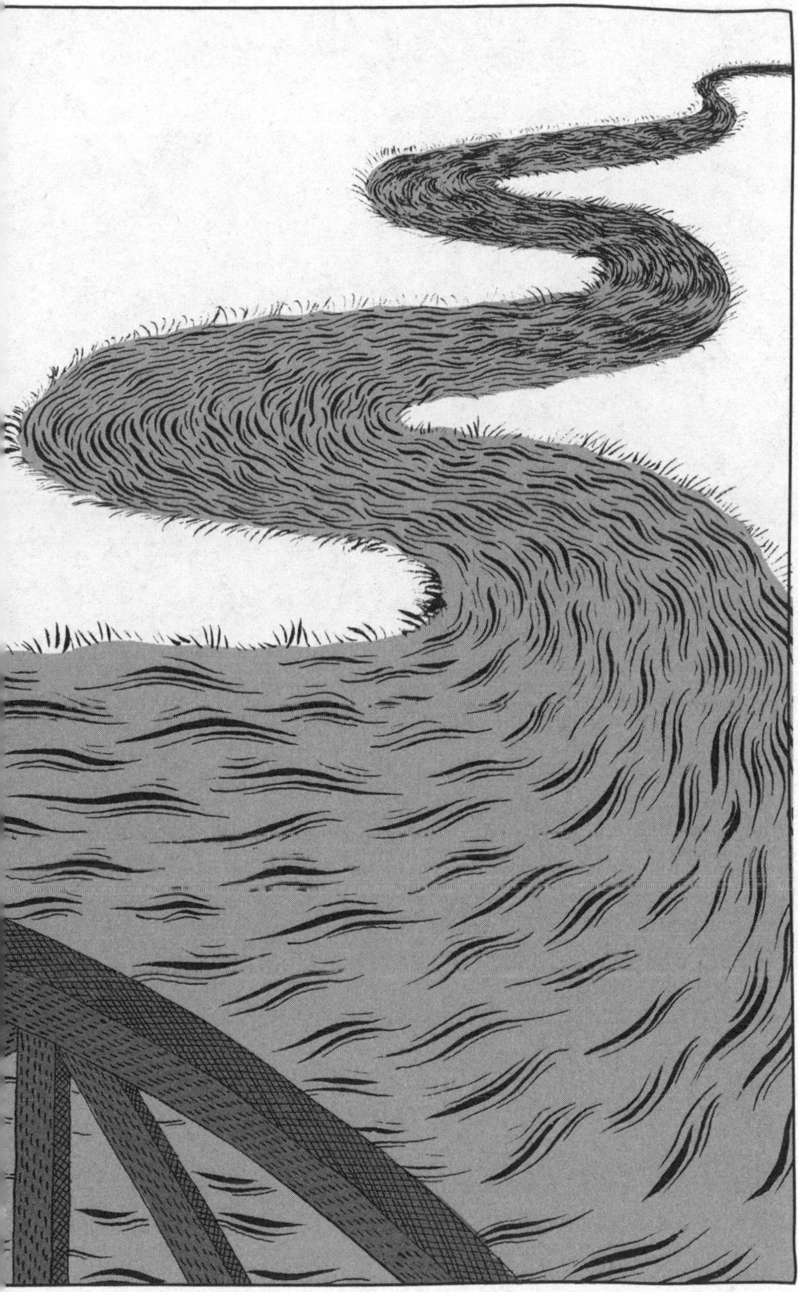

PROMPT

BY LINDA URBAN

The fairy-tale/folktale character of your choosing calls home to explain why they might miss curfew.

BY DEBORAH FREEDMAN

HICKORY
DICKORY
DOCK...

the
mouse
ran
up
the
clock

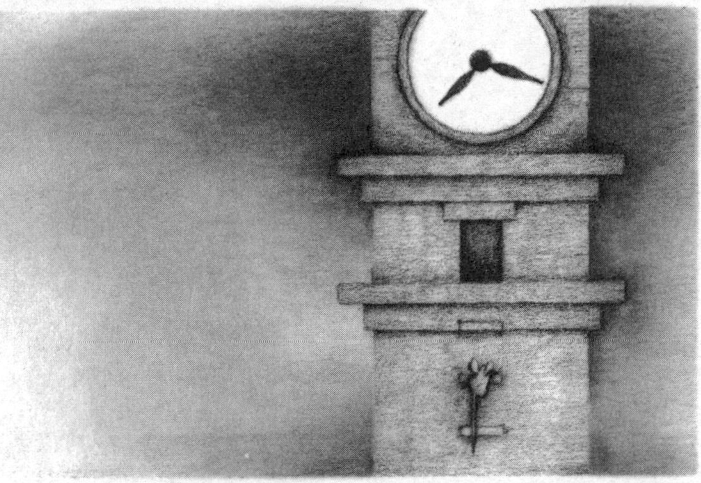

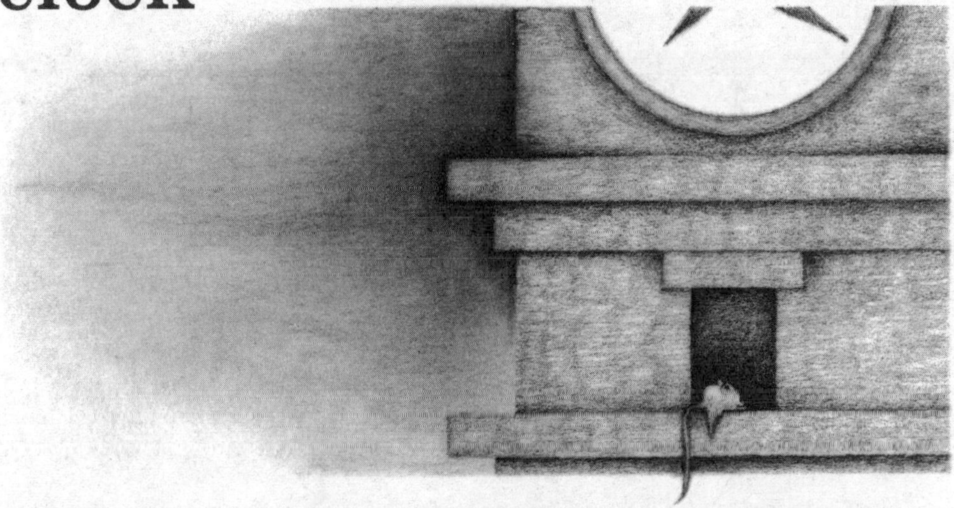

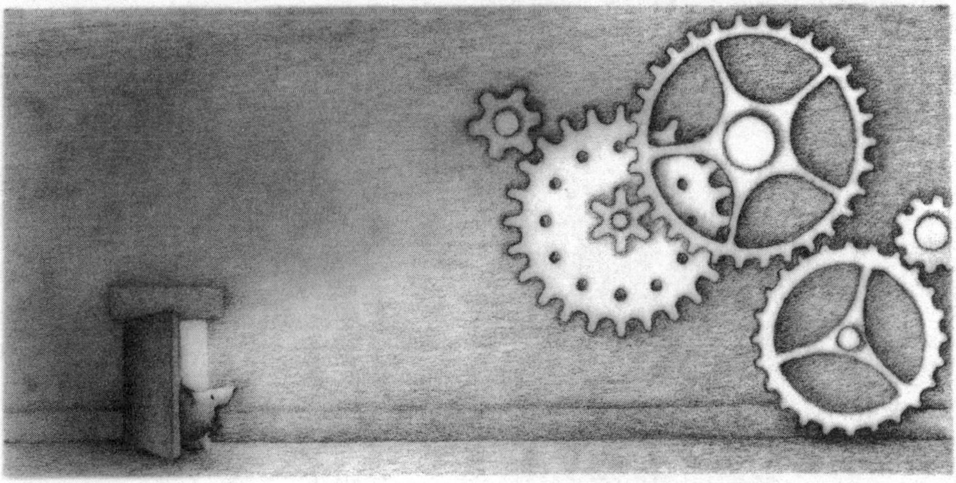

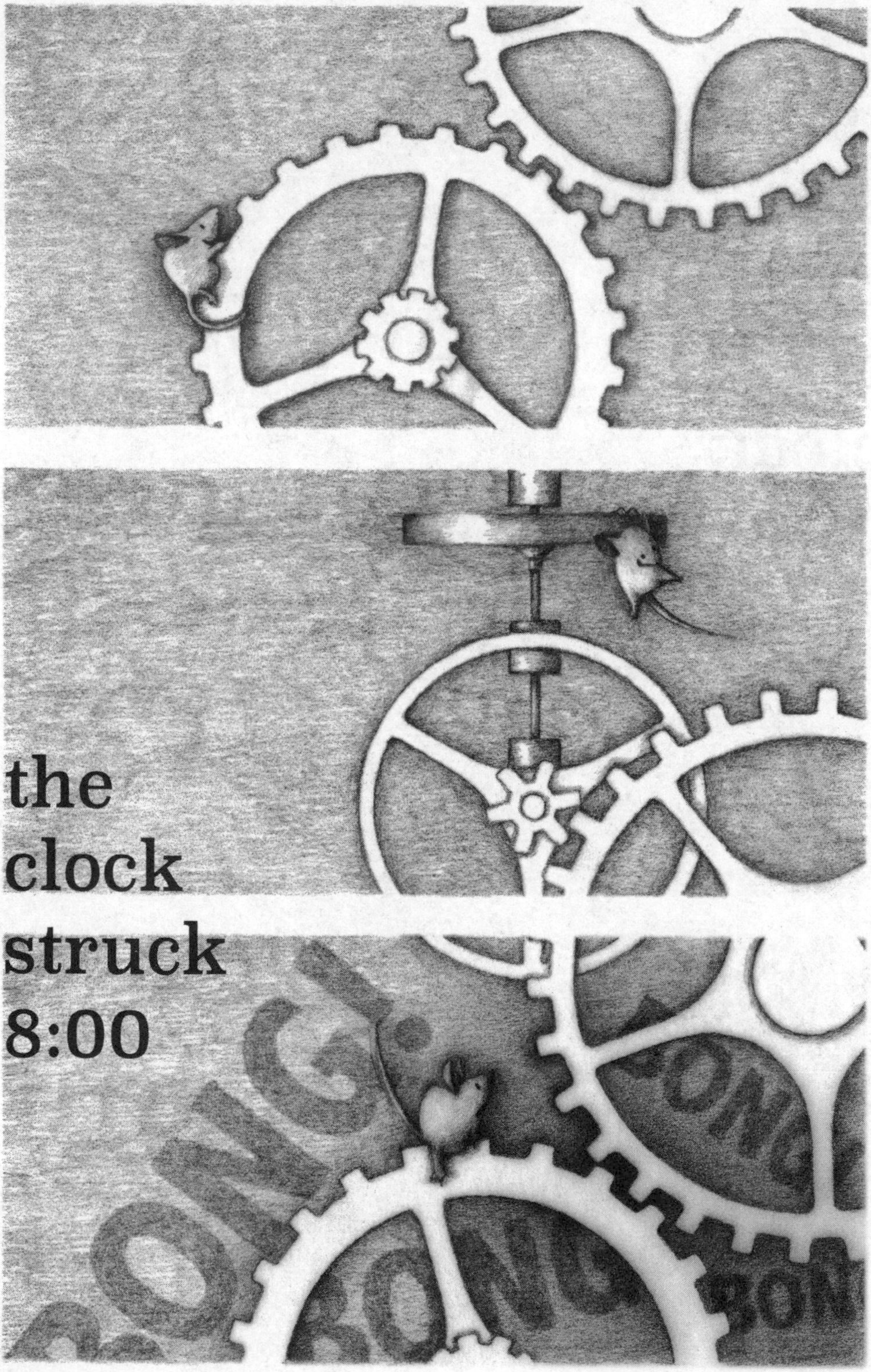
BONG!
BONG
BONG
BONG

the
clock
struck
8:00

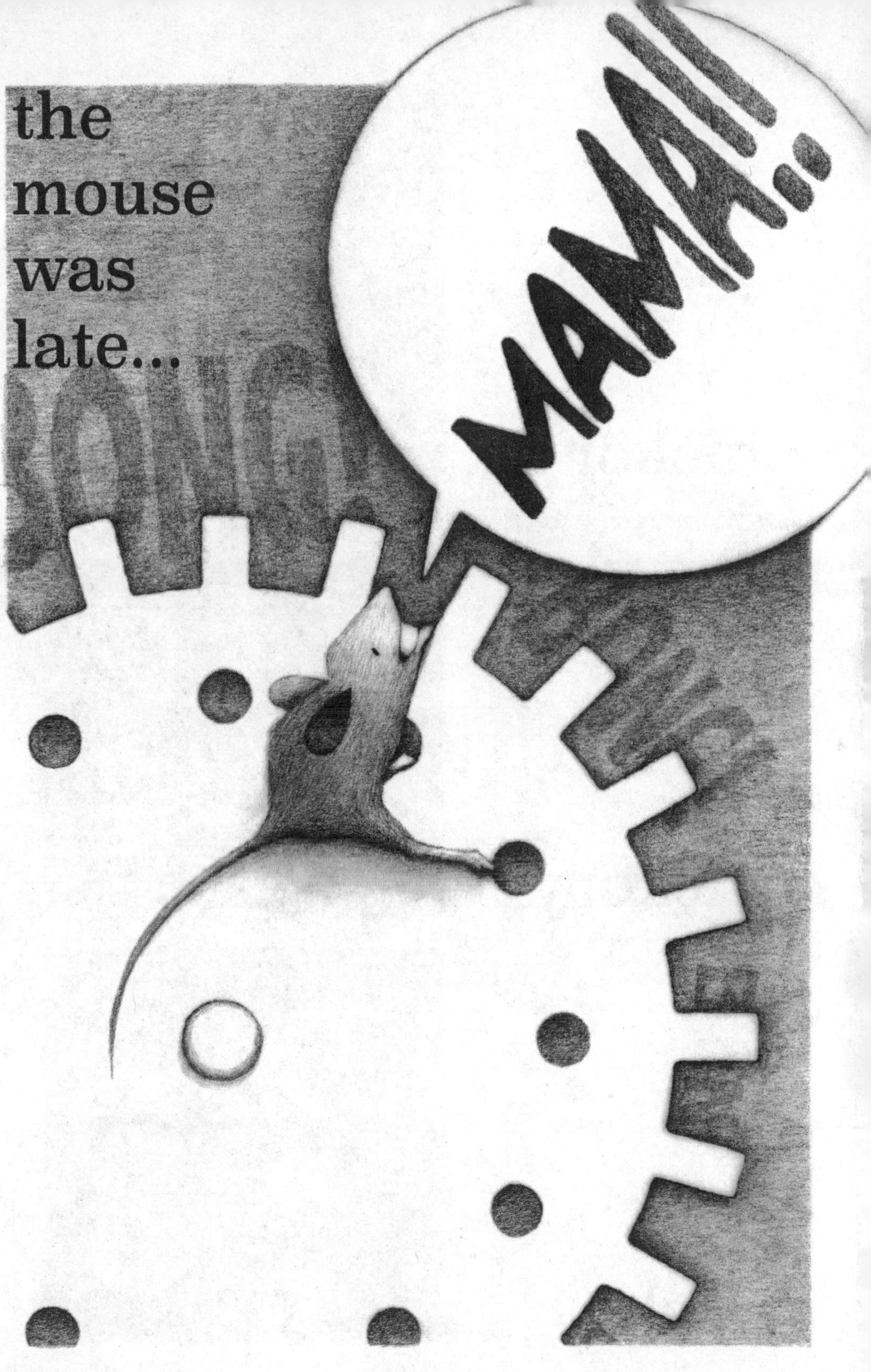
the mouse was late...
MAMA!!

hickory

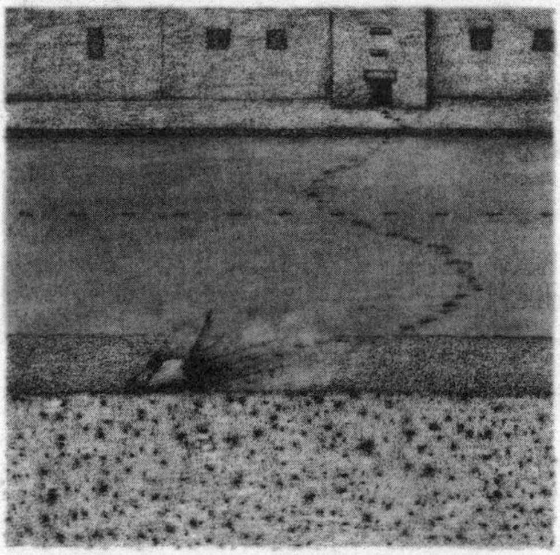

dickory

dock.

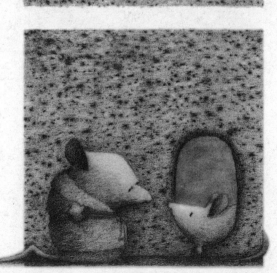

PROMPT

BY JOHN SCHU

My school librarian turned into a fly on the fifth day of fourth grade.

CHANGES
BY SHERMAN ALEXIE

My librarian turns into a fly—
Into the last word of this lion.
But my librarian is too shy to roar,
So my librarian turns into a crow—

Or wait, maybe my librarian turns
Into a raven. What's the difference
Between a crow and raven? I'd ask
My librarian, but the library is now

One enormous book. Each word
Is the same size as the cow
Who jumped over the sun. Why
The sun and not the moon? Ask

Your librarian about the difference
Between nocturnal and diurnal.
And now the library has become
The moon. My librarian is

An astronaut. My librarian is
A comet passing between the sun
And moon. My librarian becomes
The universe. My librarian becomes

The mirror at the end of the universe.
Look in the mirror. Read the reflection
Like a book. I have become the librarian
And the librarian has become me.

You can become a librarian, too.
Just pretend you are this word
And that word and that word, as well.
Just pretend you are a bird,

And if you still don't know a raven
From a crow or sparrow or jay,
That's okay. Just fly your way
Along the ornithology shelf

Until you see a book with wings
Like yours. Or better yet, say
Hello to the birds and words
You don't recognize. Ask them

To tell you a tale filled with joy
And sadness and defeat and glory.
Oh, wait, I am the librarian
Who just turned into every story.

BY KATE MESSNER

The building was seven stories tall, and the elevator doors closed before I noticed that the buttons weren't labeled with floor numbers. Instead, each one was inscribed with a year: 1775, 1850, 1920, 1944, 1962, 1980. The seventh button only said "Surprise Me." There was nothing to push to make the doors open again, and no option to call for help. I'd have to choose one....

42, YOU'RE IN THIS ROOM
BY ANDREA DAVIS PINKNEY

The building was seven stories tall, and the elevator doors closed before I noticed that the buttons weren't labeled with floor numbers. Instead, each one was inscribed with a year: 1775, 1850, 1920, 1944, 1962, 1980. The seventh button only said "Surprise Me." There was nothing to push to make the doors open again, and no option to call for help. I'd have to choose one....

And so, I did—1962.
As soon as the doors opened,
I heard The Voice.
A spirit-guide, gently leading me
into this time and place.

The Voice—low, confident, friendly.
The Voice—filled with an elder's wisdom
and the soul of someone who knows.

But what was happening here?

I let The Voice tell.
I watched and listened.

The Voice spoke. It said:
42, you're in this room.
Proud.
Head high.

Today you don't need to turn
the other cheek.
Today you're ready to be inducted,
among so many greats.

How many home runs did you make?
Fact: 137, to be exact.

Home-runner.
That was you, 42.

Dirt flying off your cleats,
spraying glory-dust into the face
of anyone who tried to stomp
on your dignity.

Well, later for them. Way later.
Because while they attempted to rob your
inner equanimity,
you were stealing all the bases—
and guarding them, too.

42, second baseman, protected that plate
with pride.
Even when hatred rained onto so many
just-mowed diamonds,
it could not dull your shine.

That's why we're here today, 42.
To honor your bat-power.
To praise every game you ever played—

and changed.
To celebrate the color-line win that scored
big for integration on the field.

Yes, 42, you're in this room. At last.
Fifteen years after you stepped up
to the major leagues.

It's about time the stars aligned
to spell out your brilliance.
Whew, it took a long minute for them to
include you, didn't it, 42?

You're no doubt accustomed to slow
progress.
But, Lord, getting this acknowledgment
went way past the ninth inning.
Overtime is an understatement.

But it's not your way to complain.
That isn't like you, 42.
Today you're in this room,
and that's what matters.

Look, here are a few good numbers that
helped you make history.
They're lining up to greet us.
Marching proudly to sing your praises
in a victory parade.

42: The dignity digits that decorated your
Brooklyn Dodgers jersey
and had fans chanting:
  "Forty-two,
  forty-two,
  forty-two!"

'52: That's when your Topps card
came into view.
Did you know that single slice of card-
board
is now a collectible, worth more money
than a vintage mitt?

'62: An important year. Here. Now.
This moment.
This beautiful day on your legacy's
landscape, when the world rejoices
in your awesomeness.

When, 42, you enter this room.
The first black athlete to make it in.

You, 42.
The game-changer who always brought
your A-game.

We stand with you, 42.
Applauding your achievement.
Shouting your number, and your name.

Here comes the pitch!
Here comes *you*, eager to meet it.

Hey, mighty righty—swing!

Send that crimson-stitched white leather
flying straight to the sun's eye,
rising high on hope's horizon,
while you glide through this room
to stand alongside these amazing guys
who are honored to be here with...

You, 42.
Grace under segregation's fire.
You, 42
Sheer sportsmanship.

42, you.
Smooth, personified.

July 23, 1962.
Cooperstown, New York.
Jackie Robinson, welcome to
the National Baseball Hall of Fame.

PROMPT

BY KAT YEH

You have a brand-new audio translation app on your phone. Just as you click on it for the first time, your dog starts barking. And words begin to appear on the screen....

RESPONSE

BY JAVAKA STEPTOE

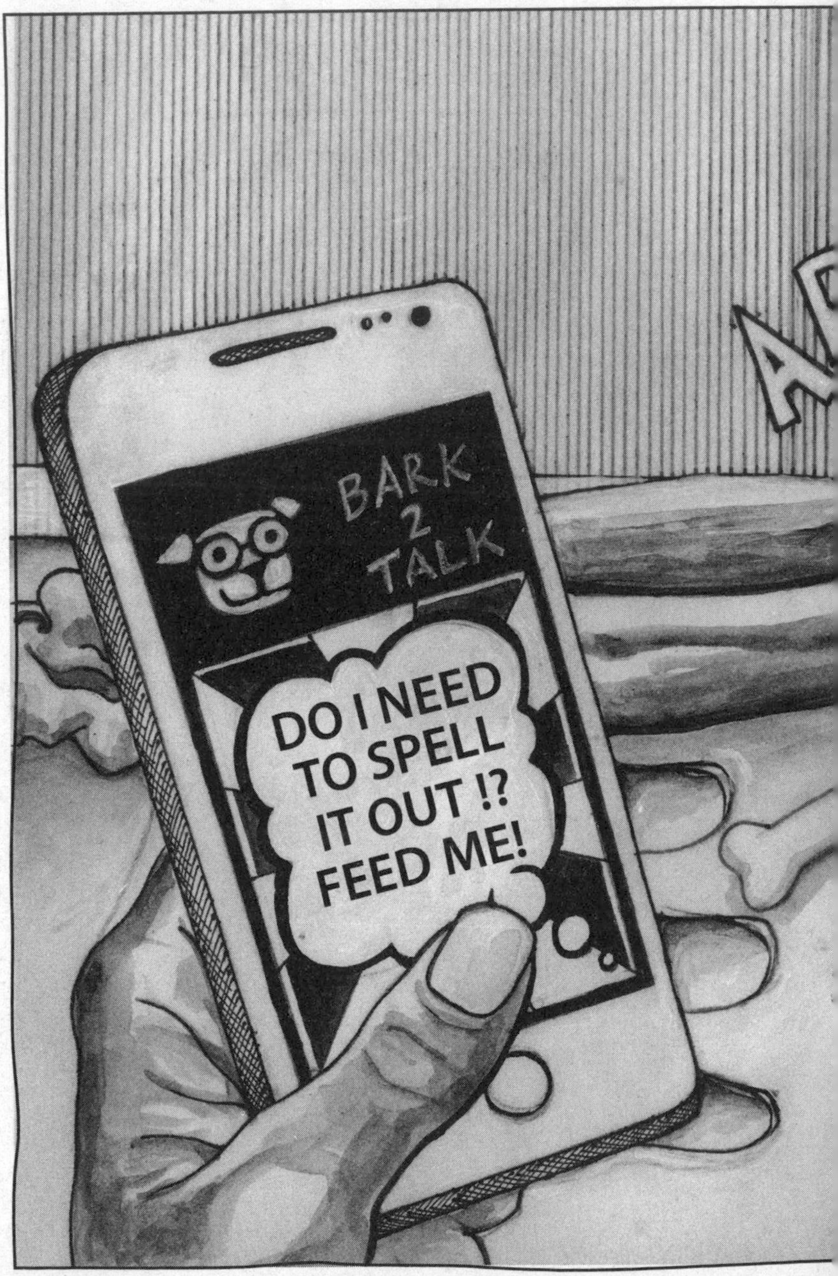
BARK 2 TALK
DO I NEED TO SPELL IT OUT !? FEED ME!

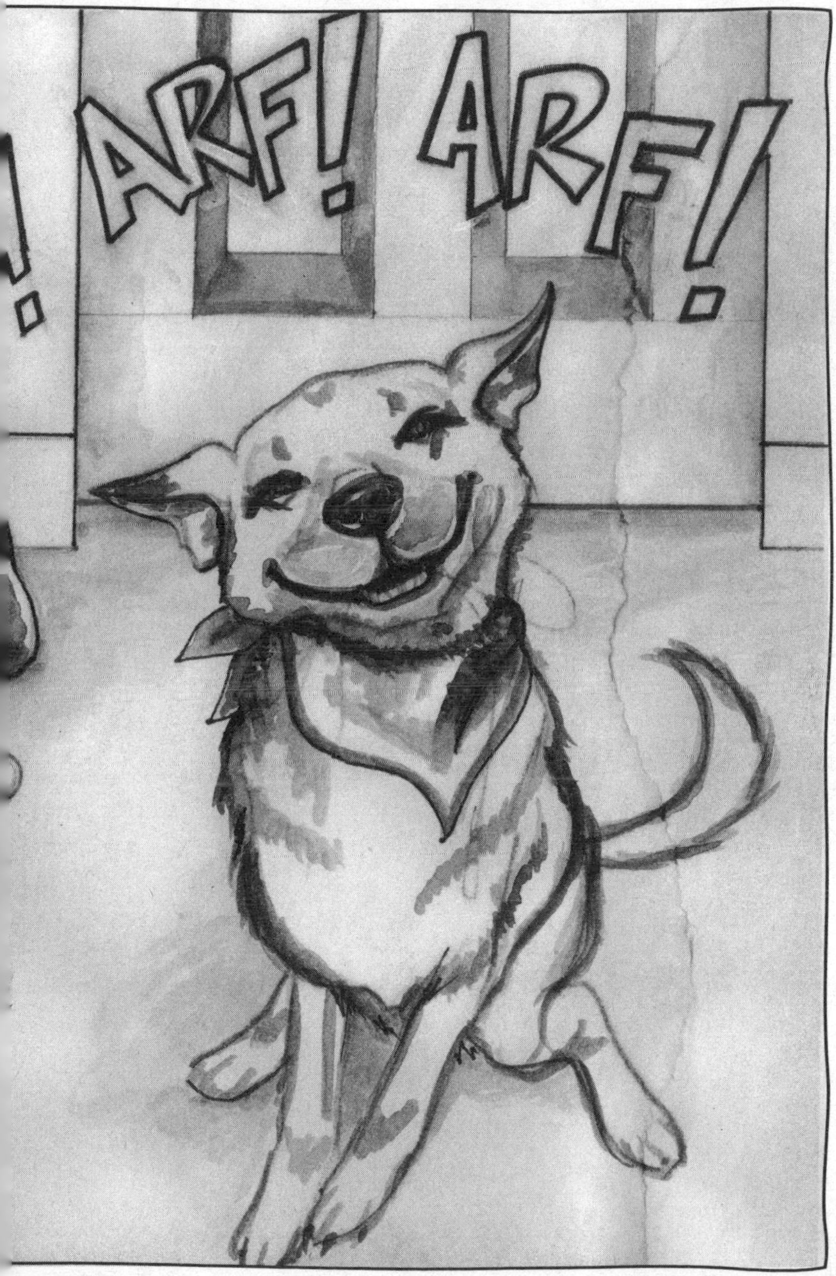
ARF! ARF!

PROMPT

BY FRANK VIVA

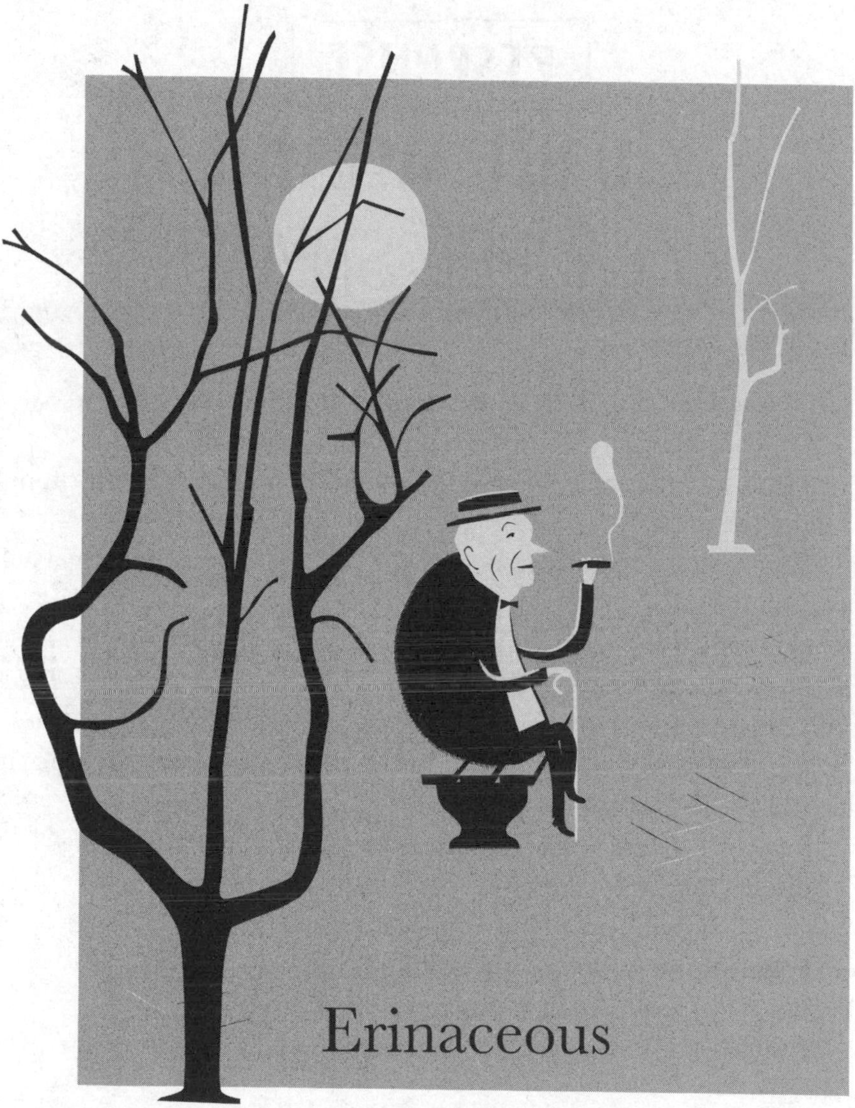
Erinaceous

CHANCE MEETING
BY LAUREL SNYDER

A girl found Edmund, deep in the wood. She wore a *very* red dress.

"Come to my party!" cried the girl. "Join our fun! Huzzah!"

"Thanks all the same," replied Edmund. "I am not much for fun. I am more for quiet."

"But we have balloons!" shouted the girl. "And lemonade! We will play games!"

"No thank you," said Edmund. "I am happy where I am."

The girl did not understand. "*Here?* How can you be happy *here*? You have nothing here!"

"On the contrary," said Edmund. "I have plenty—a sturdy place in which to sit, and a thing to think."

"Really?" asked the girl. "What is the thing you are thinking?"

"Just a thing," said Edmund. "It doesn't concern you."

"Oh…" said the girl. "But you look so lonely."

"Lonely is not a look," said Edmund. "Lonely is a feeling."

"Well, you look *alone*, at any rate," said the girl.

Edmund shook his head. "Alone and lonely are not the same. Not at all."

The girl began to feel itchy. "I was only trying to be kind," she said.

Edmund shrugged. "It's nice to try."

"Well, humph!" said the girl. "I've changed my mind. *You* are no longer welcome at my party. *You* are odd, and confusing, and far too prickly!"

"Dear girl," said Edmund, crossing his legs. "We *all* have prickles. I just wear mine on the outside."

For that, the girl had no reply. She ran away. Loudly. Home. Never to be seen again in that wood.

So Edmund returned. To himself. And the thing he had been thinking, before the red dress interrupted.

Though what that was, we will likely never know....

PROMPT

BY LIESL SHURTLIFF

Sticks and stones may break
Our bones might crumble to dust
But words will create....

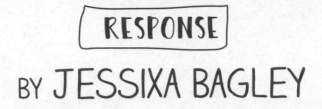

RESPONSE

BY JESSIXA BAGLEY

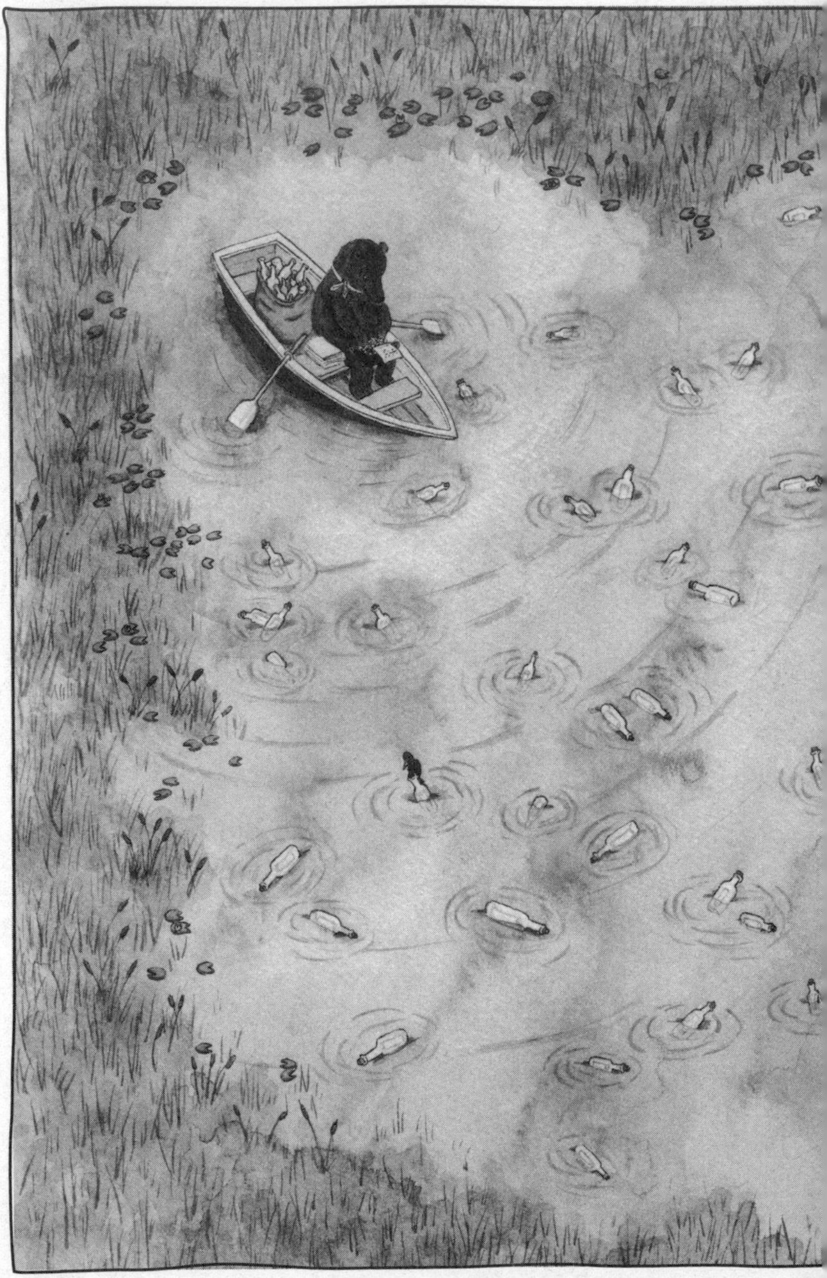

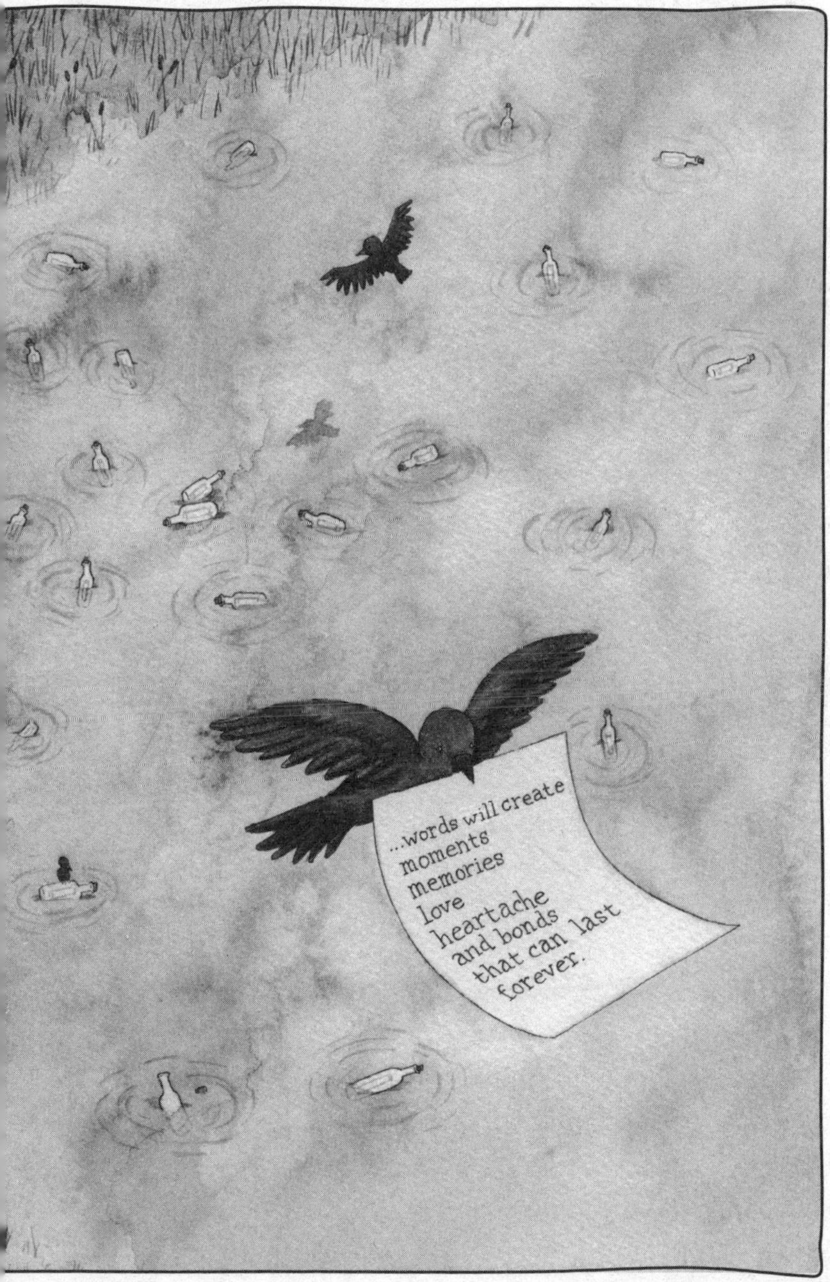
...words will create
moments
memories
love
heartache
and bonds
that can last
forever.

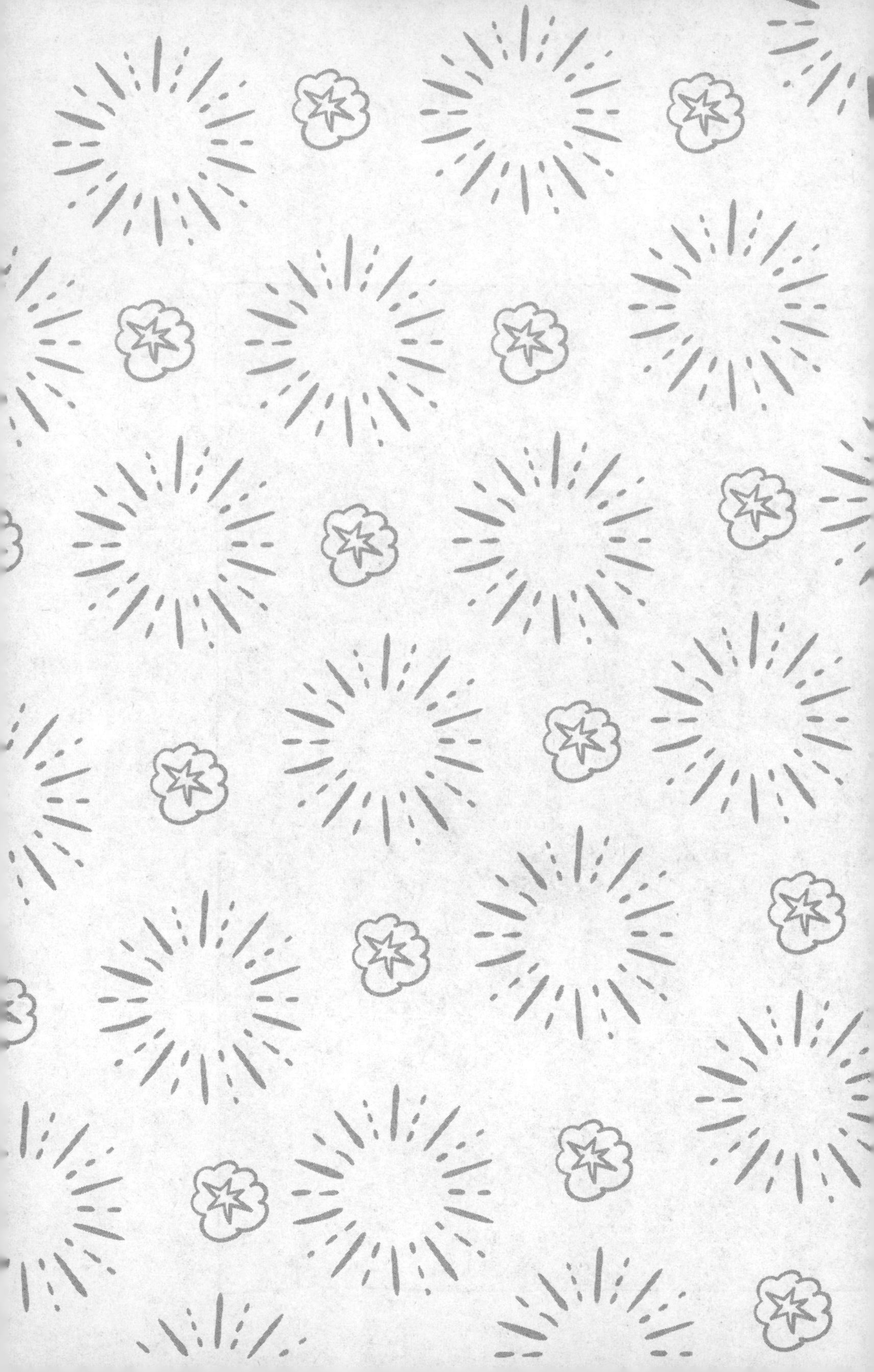

PROMPT

BY LAUREN CASTILLO

THE PORTAL TO ANYWHERE
BY TRACEY BAPTISTE

I wasn't wearing the right shoes
For a walk in the forest
But I wanted to go someplace
Away from there
Anywhere
And I knew these woods
Since I was three
When we lived in the green house
With the backyard that opened to the trees
My shiny shoes squeaked over the broken twigs
And scuffed on stones
Until I found our spot
Mine and Carly's
The one where we had built the portal to anywhere
A thing no one had done before
That only she and I could make again
It had taken us to the edge of the universe

And under the ocean for a ride on the
back of a kraken
And to a robot's house in the middle of
a cloud
And didn't that mean something special?
Something secret?
Something you should never ever ever tell
anyone else?
Didn't it?
Well, I walked all the way here
In my new black shoes
That were not for walking in the woods
at all
And I piled the stones
Large ones to small ones going in a spiral
I made a pattern of the light and dark
ones
And the rough and smooth ones
Then I piled the twigs on top
Like we used to
Weaving them into each other
Like a nest
And I sat in the middle and squeezed my
eyes shut
So hard that tears ran down my cheeks
And I wished
And when I opened my eyes
Nothing had happened
So I tried again
And again
Until the day grew cold
But the portal never opened
It wasn't possible without Carly
It needed both of us
So I climbed out

It was a long way home
And I had forgotten my jacket
But the air crackled
The hair on my arms stood on end
And when I looked back
The portal had opened
Anyway

PROMPT

BY ANDREA DAVIS PINKNEY

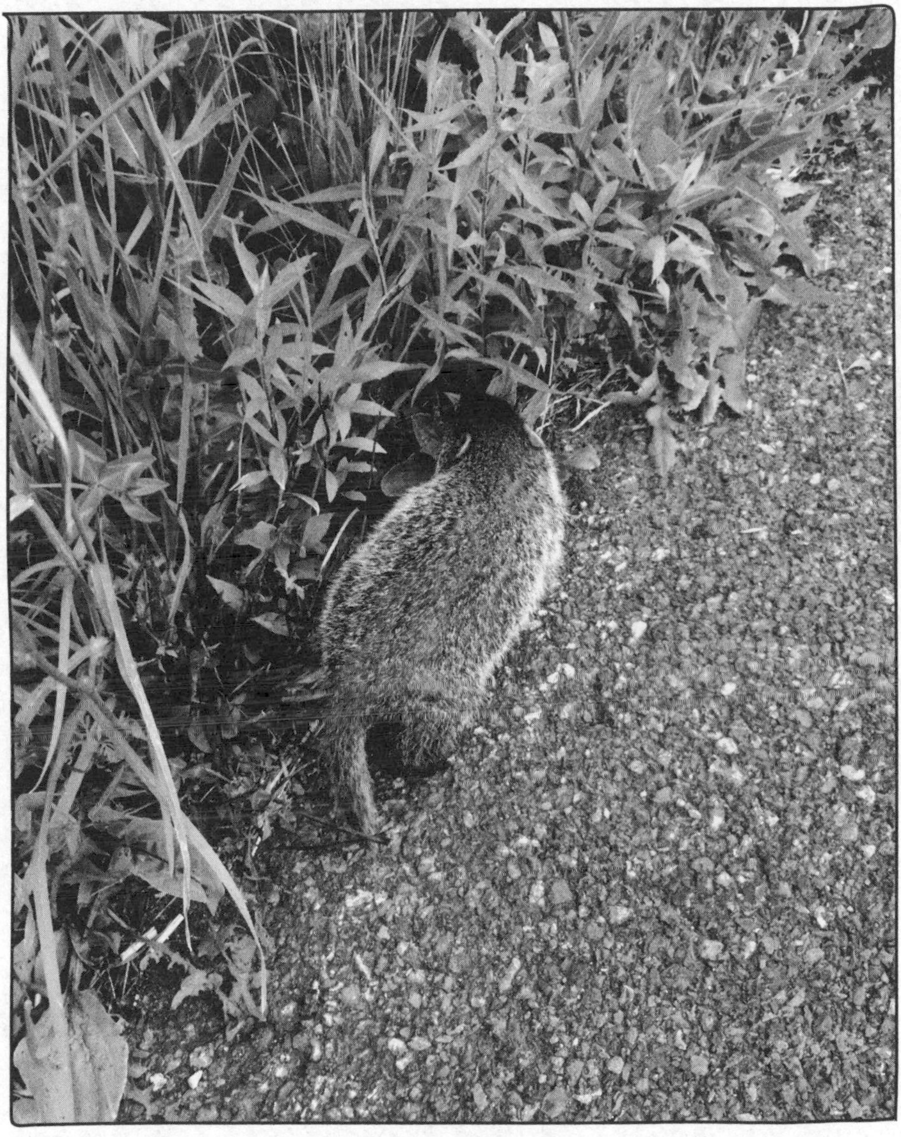

THE TRAP
BY LINDA SUE PARK

In fall, the leaves are reddish brown.
They drift and linger on the ground.
And iron jaws are buried deep
in rusted and forgotten sleep.

A fox runs wild, with grace and ease,
through days of youth and groves of trees.
A sudden snap: The jaws awake
and fox-flesh tears, and fox-bones break.

With questions he can never ask,
he must begin the ghastly task.
And soon the earth is reddish brown.
The stains spread slowly on the ground.

His teeth and will, to forge the key:
Escape, at last, on only three.

Author's note: When I received my prompt, I couldn't tell what the animal in the photo was. However, my immediate response was a flashback: to a poem I had started writing way back in college. It was a poem about a fox, which I had never finished to my satisfaction.

The animal in the photo is NOT a fox. But my mind got fixed on "fox," and there it stayed. I typed out what I could remember of the original; it was only a line or two. I worked with those lines until I finally ended up with the attached sonnet.

Creativity often happens in strange and convoluted ways...and sometimes an idea has to go on the back burner until the right time— even if it's forty years later!

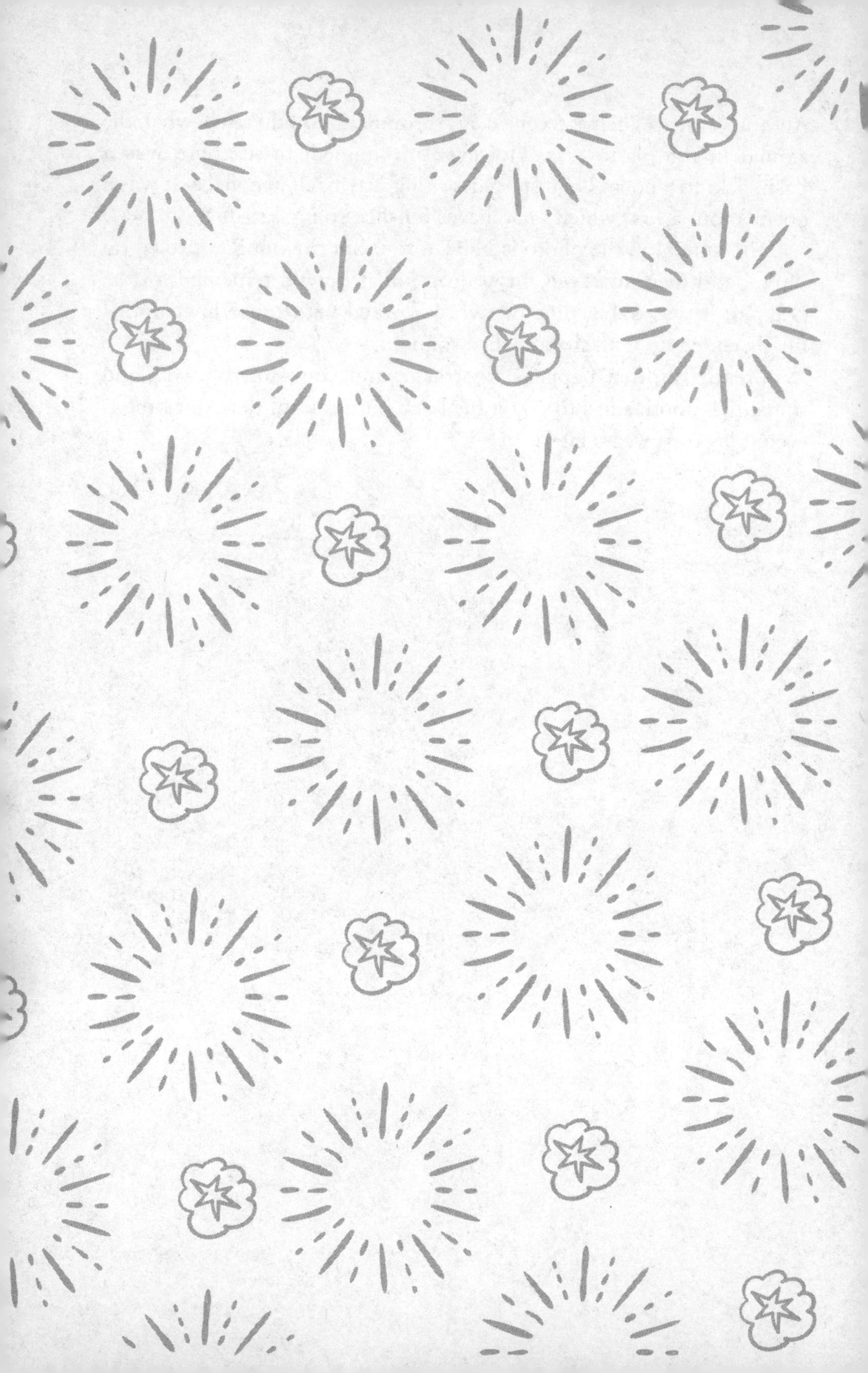

PROMPT

BY MARIKO TAMAKI

The guy next door.

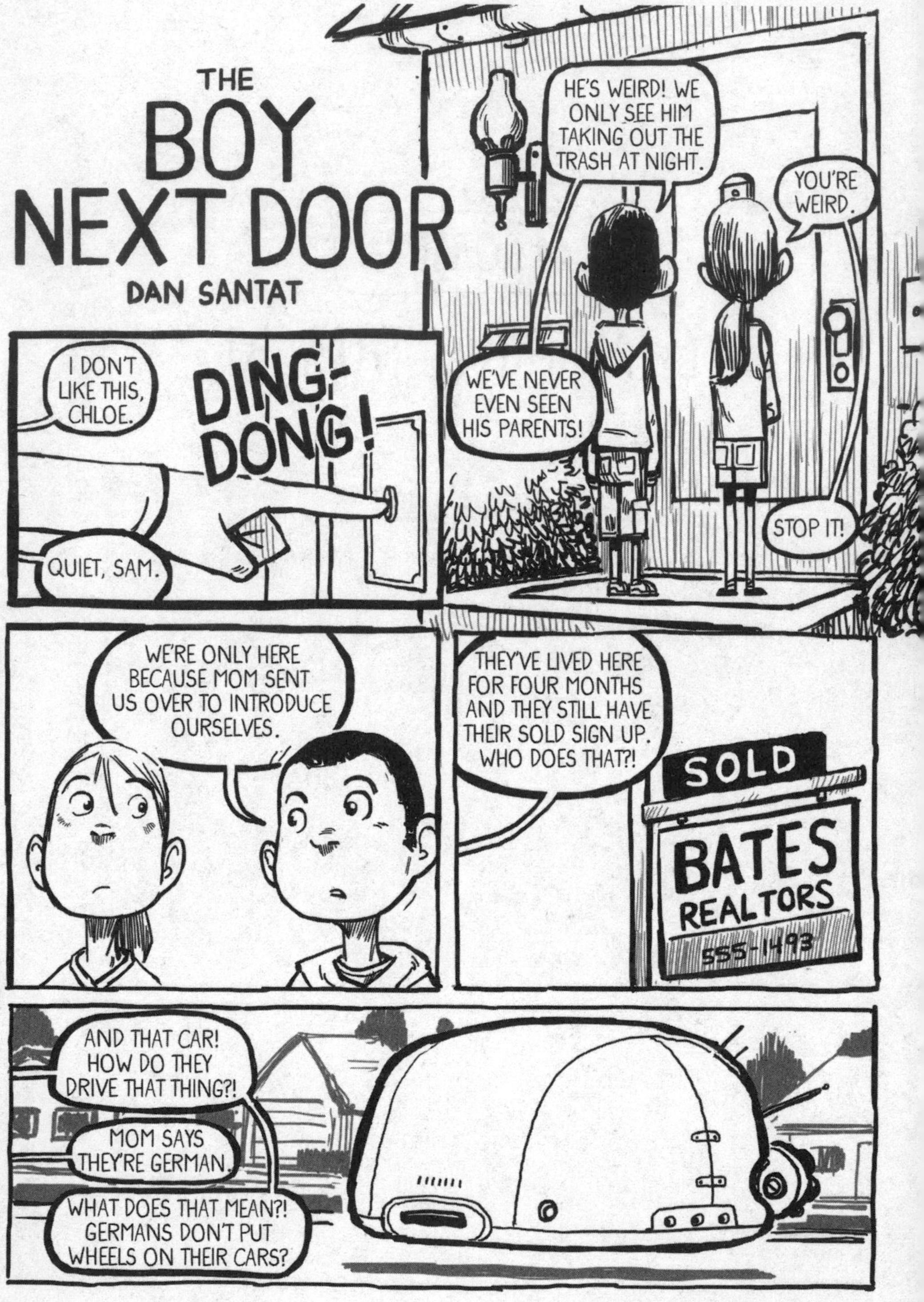
THE BOY NEXT DOOR
DAN SANTAT
HE'S WEIRD! WE ONLY SEE HIM TAKING OUT THE TRASH AT NIGHT.
YOU'RE WEIRD.
WE'VE NEVER EVEN SEEN HIS PARENTS!
STOP IT!
I DON'T LIKE THIS, CHLOE.
DING-DONG!
QUIET, SAM.
WE'RE ONLY HERE BECAUSE MOM SENT US OVER TO INTRODUCE OURSELVES.
THEY'VE LIVED HERE FOR FOUR MONTHS AND THEY STILL HAVE THEIR SOLD SIGN UP. WHO DOES THAT?!
SOLD
BATES REALTORS
555-1493
AND THAT CAR! HOW DO THEY DRIVE THAT THING?!
MOM SAYS THEY'RE GERMAN.
WHAT DOES THAT MEAN?! GERMANS DON'T PUT WHEELS ON THEIR CARS?

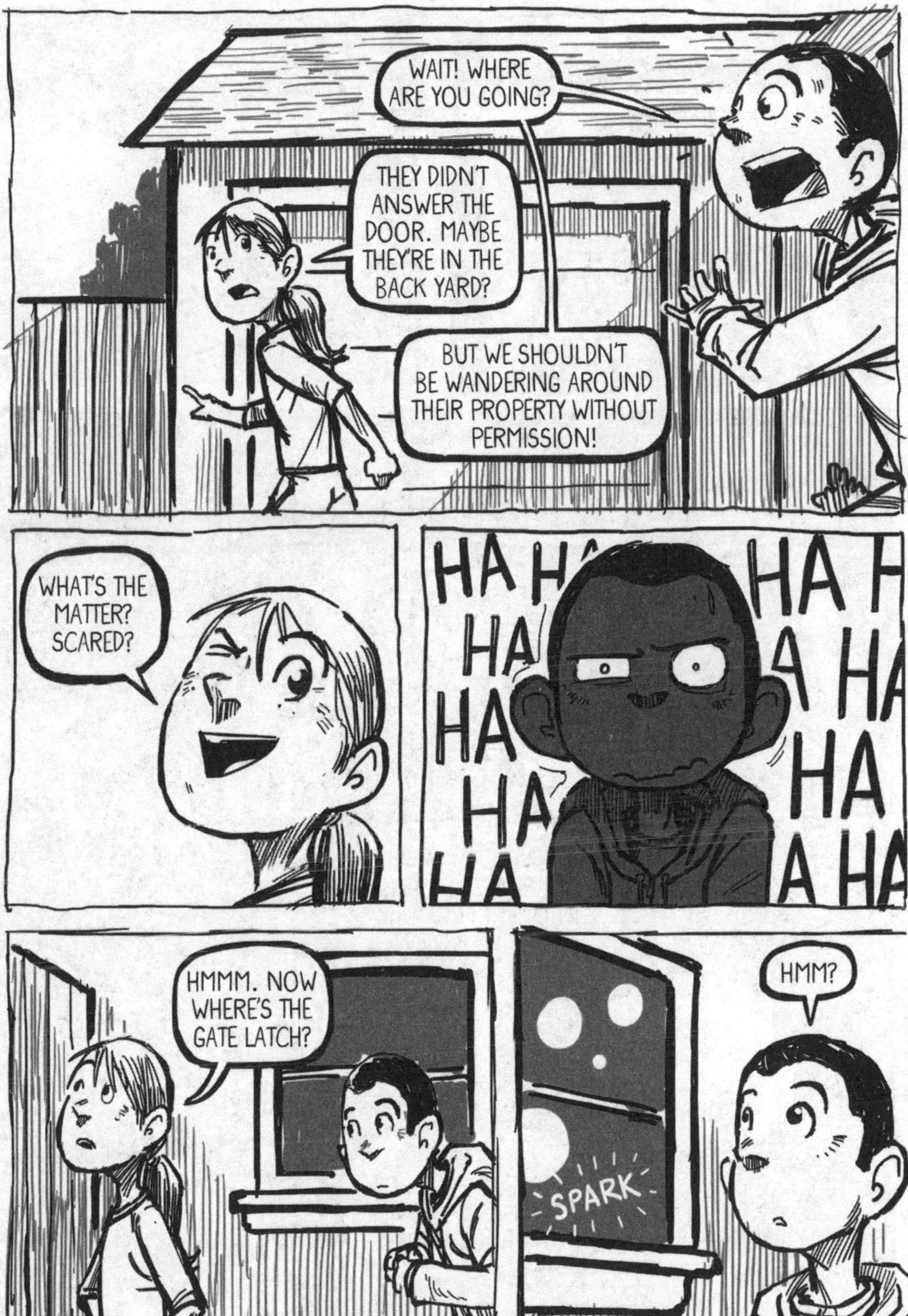

WAIT! WHERE ARE YOU GOING?
THEY DIDN'T ANSWER THE DOOR. MAYBE THEY'RE IN THE BACK YARD?
BUT WE SHOULDN'T BE WANDERING AROUND THEIR PROPERTY WITHOUT PERMISSION!
WHAT'S THE MATTER? SCARED?
HA HA HA HA HA HA HA HA HA HA HA HA HA
HMMM. NOW WHERE'S THE GATE LATCH?
SPARK
HMM?

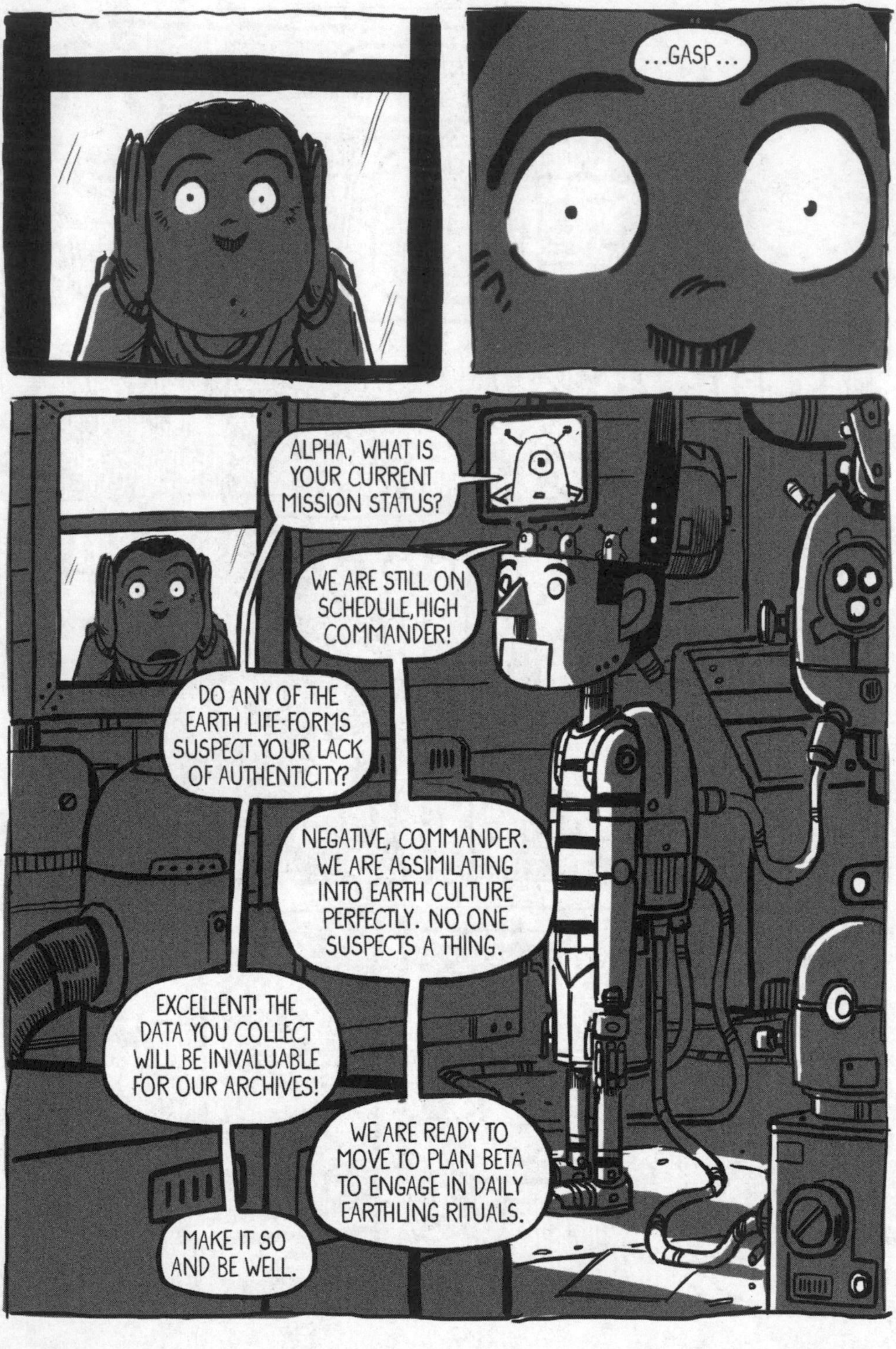
...GASP...
ALPHA, WHAT IS YOUR CURRENT MISSION STATUS?
WE ARE STILL ON SCHEDULE, HIGH COMMANDER!
DO ANY OF THE EARTH LIFE-FORMS SUSPECT YOUR LACK OF AUTHENTICITY?
NEGATIVE, COMMANDER. WE ARE ASSIMILATING INTO EARTH CULTURE PERFECTLY. NO ONE SUSPECTS A THING.
EXCELLENT! THE DATA YOU COLLECT WILL BE INVALUABLE FOR OUR ARCHIVES!
WE ARE READY TO MOVE TO PLAN BETA TO ENGAGE IN DAILY EARTHLING RITUALS.
MAKE IT SO AND BE WELL.

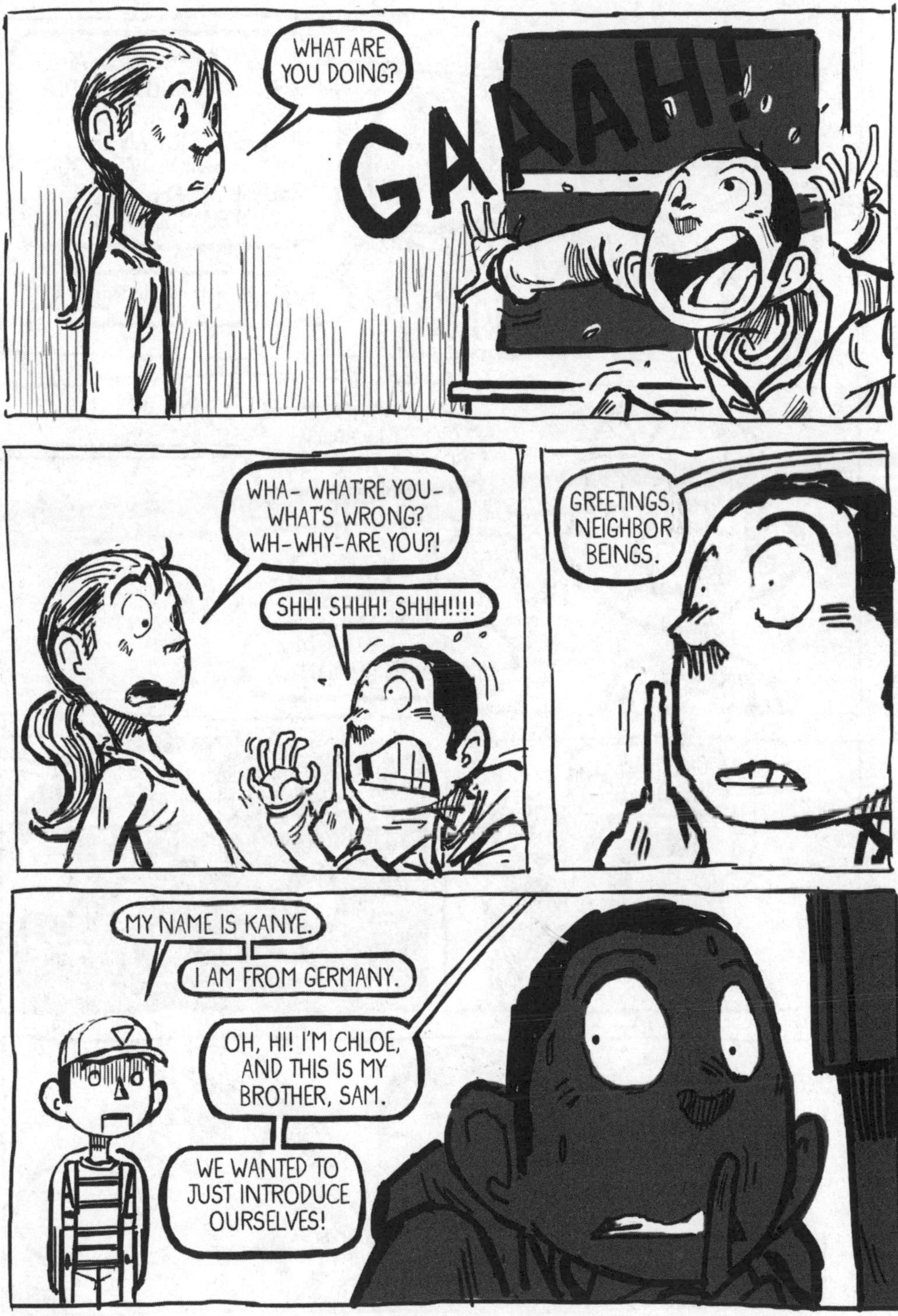
WHAT ARE YOU DOING?
GAAAH!
WHA- WHAT'RE YOU- WHAT'S WRONG? WH-WHY-ARE YOU?!
SHH! SHHH! SHHH!!!!
GREETINGS, NEIGHBOR BEINGS.
MY NAME IS KANYE.
I AM FROM GERMANY.
OH, HI! I'M CHLOE, AND THIS IS MY BROTHER, SAM.
WE WANTED TO JUST INTRODUCE OURSELVES!

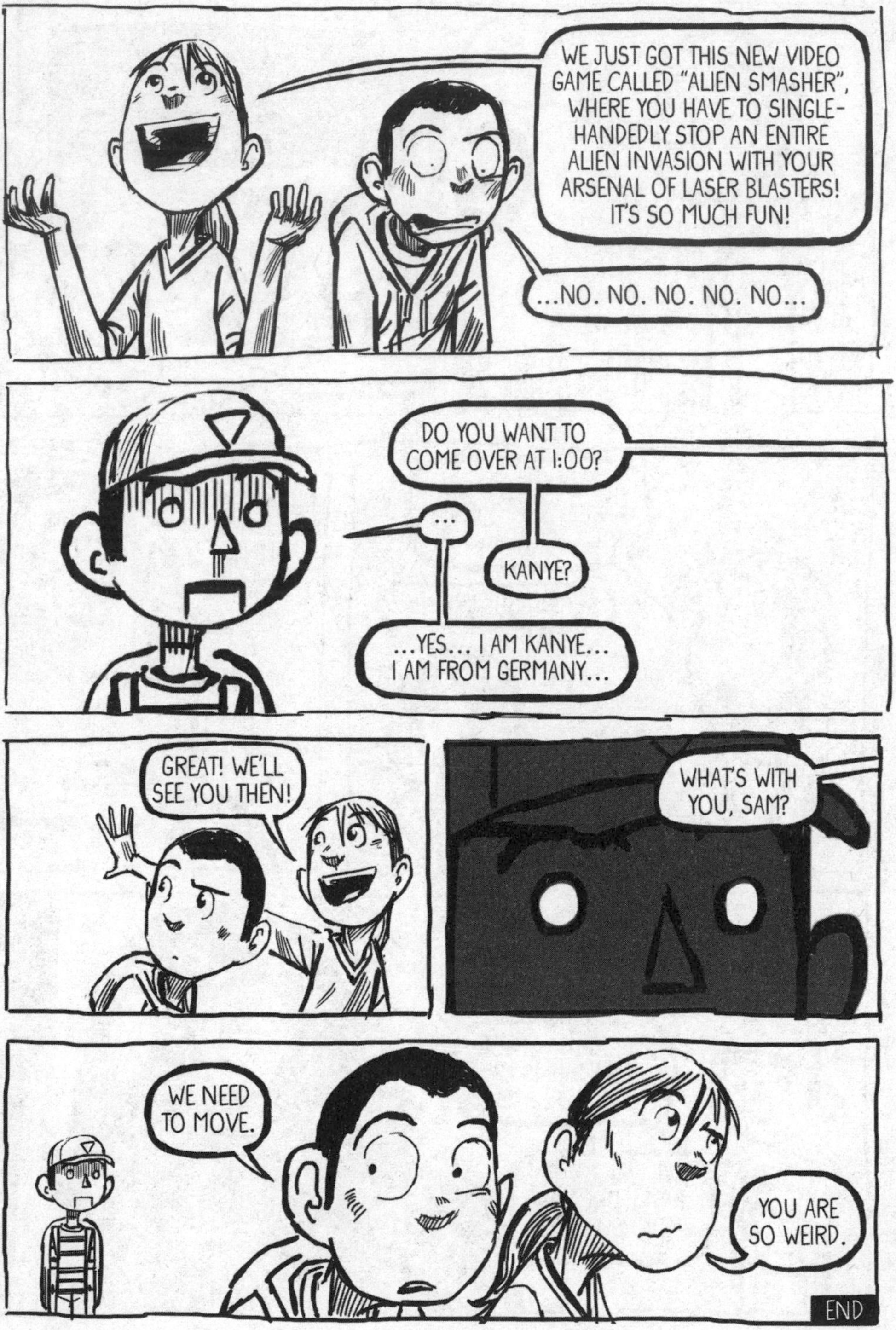
WE JUST GOT THIS NEW VIDEO GAME CALLED "ALIEN SMASHER", WHERE YOU HAVE TO SINGLE-HANDEDLY STOP AN ENTIRE ALIEN INVASION WITH YOUR ARSENAL OF LASER BLASTERS! IT'S SO MUCH FUN!
...NO. NO. NO. NO. NO...
DO YOU WANT TO COME OVER AT 1:00?
...
KANYE?
...YES... I AM KANYE... I AM FROM GERMANY...
GREAT! WE'LL SEE YOU THEN!
WHAT'S WITH YOU, SAM?
WE NEED TO MOVE.
YOU ARE SO WEIRD.
END

BY DANIEL NAYERI

"Home, Roddy, and don't spare the horses!"

"Erm. We ain't got no horses, Cap'n."

"I know, Roddy. *I know*. It's a play of the language."

"Fer bein' set to full sail 'n' the like?"

"Yes. Full speed ahead, Roddy. No time to waste."

"Aye aye, Cap'n."

"And Roddy?"

"Yes, Cap'n?"

"Could you, perhaps, loosen my chains a little?"

RESPONSE

BY KIRBY LARSON

"Home, Roddy, and don't spare the horses!"

"Erm. We ain't got no horses, Cap'n."

"I know, Roddy. *I know.* It's a play of the language."

"Fer bein' set to full sail 'n' the like?"

"Yes. Full speed ahead, Roddy. No time to waste."

"Aye aye, Cap'n."

"And Roddy?"

"Yes, Cap'n?"

"Could you, perhaps, loosen my chains a little?"

Roddy scratched under the kerchief covering his bald head. He cleared his throat. "You know, Cap'n, that I am a first mate of the most faithful persuasion."

"You have served me and the *Wicked William* fair and true, lo these many years," Captain Dervish agreed.

"And you ain't once seen me disobey yer orders, neither," Roddy continued.

Captain Dervish shifted to ease the pressure of the particularly heavy links around his ankles. "Nary a time. Not even when I ordered you to face down those Alberian swashbucklers all on your own." At that memory, the captain tried to wipe away a tender tear. But both hands were constrained. He held them up, hopeful of immediate release. "Roddy?" He jangled the chains to obtain his first mate's full attention, and to claim his compassion.

"Erm. Here's the rub." Roddy shuffled his booted feet along the quarterdeck. "I have orders from a higher power. I can't loosen yer bonds. Yet."

Captain Dervish rocked in anger, rattling his chains. "What higher power be there than me?"

"I swear by the Jolly Roger, I'll let you loose."

The captain exhaled in relief, holding out his hands. "Get to it, then, man."

A rueful smile slid across Roddy's mostly toothless mouth. "Soon!"

Resigned, the captain sighed. "All right, then. Can you at least hold up my sextant so that I might check our course?"

Roddy threw back his shoulders. "Aye-aye, Cap'n!" Happy to obey this order, he snatched up the sextant and held it to the captain's eye.

Captain Dervish took a careful sight. "What in the name of Blackbeard's ghost? This is not the course I ordered."

Several of the nearby crew suddenly busied themselves with meaningless tasks. One tar even polished the captain's spectacles, though he had but the one good eye.

"'Tis true, Cap'n," Roddy assured him. "We're sailing what yer might call the scenic route."

"I don't give a fig about the scenic route!" Captain Dervish struggled to stand, but got only a few inches off the deck before collapsing in a heap. Roddy was an expert at clapping a man in irons. "You are going to walk the plank!" the captain bellowed.

"That may well be," Roddy agreed with cheer. "But we *are* headed fer home." He sliced his finger through the air, crossing his heart. "More or less."

Captain Dervish closed his eyes. "Grog," he moaned.

"Why, that's the ticket, Cap'n!" Roddy summoned the cabin boy, who brought the captain's favorite bejeweled goblet. Captain Dervish drank it right off. "Fill 'er again," Roddy advised the cabin boy. "His humors might improve with a bit of shut-eye." Roddy reached out to pat Captain Dervish on the head, but his captain's glare made him think better of that. Instead, he rubbed his hands together. "Not much longer, sir."

After another goblet or two, Captain Dervish did fall asleep. For a good portion of the sail, he enjoyed sweet dreams about robbing rich merchants, and cannon battles against the queen's navy—he and his men emerged victorious, of course. He especially enjoyed the dream in which Roddy walked the plank. The sharks were an elegant touch. When he awoke, however, his good spirits quickly disappeared with a glance over the gunnels. There, moored in the harbor, bobbed *The Sea Hag*.

"No!" he roared. "Not that!"

Roddy patted the captain's shoulder as several swabs cast off the landing ropes, securing them to the pier. "It'll only hurt for a short bit," he reassured. Another pair of tars hefted the captain onto their shoulders, as if unloading a chest heavily laden with doubloons and the like.

"Put me down!" The captain threw himself this way and that, but the tars were skilled at off-loading all kinds of cargo, some quite lively, such as chimpanzees and kidnapped maidens. They held fast. "I'll have you all flogged!"

Roddy chuckled. "Yer getting yourself overwrought."

"I'll overwrought you!" Captain Dervish tried to kick Roddy in his good leg, but caught the wooden one instead.

It was quite the procession, over the gunnels, into the dinghies, and up onto dry land. Roddy couldn't be sure, but the captain may have been whimpering as they approached the rotting door of the Claw and Feather, an inn favored by pirates and brigands and such. Two hulking rogues, with mirror-image scars tracking down their faces, scowled as the group drew near.

"Yer late," said the one on the left.

"We said high noon on the dot," added the one on the right.

"We caught a bit of bad wind a few days back." Roddy gestured toward the captain. "But here's yer package, as promised."

The men sneered for good measure, then allowed the party to pass into the inn. The shabby interior was lit only by lanterns; strange shadows lurched and gyrated against each plastered wall. When a face *was* visible in the gloom, it was the stuff of nightmares: scars and tattoos and body parts replaced by hooks and peg legs. Had his arms not been chained, Captain Dervish would've covered his ears against the assaulting din of sea chanteys and other ballads. One would be hard-pressed to tell the difference between this "singing" and the sounds made by the giant howler monkeys of Skeleton Island.

When Captain Dervish's eyes adjusted to the dark, his blood ran cold.

There, at the head of a long table across the room, sat Rowan the Rampager. Many who sailed the seven seas never dared to even *mention* the name. The cut of Rowan's jib had sent more than one lily-liver to an early grave. And Rowan's odor alone could put the hungriest of sailors off their slops for days. A few of the greenhorns from the *Wicked William* began to edge their way to the door at the sight of this fearsome pirate. Roddy used his peg leg to encourage them to stay.

"Bring him here." Rowan slammed a scarred hand on the equally scarred tabletop. "Now."

"Aye-aye." Roddy reached into his pocket and pulled out a key, unlocking each padlock right smart.

Captain Dervish shook out his bloodless arms and legs, wobbling as he stood. "I'm close enough," he snarled back at Rowan.

"Come here!" Rowan roared again, this time smacking the table so hard all the mugs on it did a jig, sloshing grog this way and that. Men dove under the table for safety.

"And why should I?" The captain stood, his arms akimbo, matching fierce glares with the other pirate.

Roddy nudged him forward. "Best get it over with," he said.

Captain Dervish slowly reduced the space between himself and Rowan. When the captain was ten feet away, Rowan jumped up, leapt the table in one bound, and tackled him. They rolled around on the filthy floor, sending sailors and swabs scurrying. After breaking three chairs, two tables, and a handful of teeth, Rowan grabbed Captain Dervish in a grizzly bear hug. "You remembered!"

The captain wiped his bloody nose. "Well, what kind of son would forget his own mother's birthday?" With a glance at Roddy, he handed over a small packet—a gold-filigreed locket he'd removed from a marquise's neck in Portugal. "I hope you like it."

Rowan clasped it under her jowls. "It's just what I always wanted."

When all the cake had been eaten and the ale drunk, Roddy led a rousing rendition of "Happy Birthday to You." Then Rowan slapped Captain Dervish on the back. "See you next year, son!" she hollered before jumping on the table and challenging all comers to an arm-wrestling match.

Back on the ship, Captain Dervish snapped off orders. "Full speed ahead, Roddy!"

"Aye-aye, Cap'n!" Roddy passed the command along.

"And Roddy?"

"Cap'n?"

"Next year, could you use ropes instead of chains?"

"Aye-aye, Cap'n. Aye-aye."

PROMPT

BY CHRIS GRABENSTEIN

Here's a prompt adapted from a writing-aptitude test I took back in 1984. The executive creative director at J. Walter Thompson Advertising created a "Write If You Want Work" test, which ran as an ad in the *New York Times*. It's how I landed my first professional writing job. And the executive creative director? His name was James Patterson. That's right, THE James Patterson.

You are a songwriter for hitmaker Poppy Putrid. She's just had three recent number one hits. All love songs. For her next hit, Poppy wants a song about moldy pizza, rancid butter, and flat root beer. Her agent is convinced it should be another love song. Make it both. (Don't worry about the music, or write new lyrics to a simple tune you already know.)

YOU HAVE A COW?—
A LOVE SONG
BY KATE DICAMILLO

I feel dark.
I feel drear.
I feel fizz-less,
like flat
root beer.

Oh, I feel dark.
I feel cold.
I'm a slice of pizza
all slicked up
with mold.

I'm young.
I should sing!
I should dance!
But with you gone
there's no chance.

With you gone
there's no chance, boy.
There's no chance.

Oh, I feel dark.
I feel drear.
I moan; I mutter.
The whole world smells!
It does. It reeks
of old, rancid butter.

I'm young.
I should sing.
I should dance.
But you are gone, boy.
There is no chance, boy.

The world is dark, dreary, cold.
It is a moldy-pizza-rancid-butter-flat-root-beer
sad, dark place.
Without you.
Without you.

But wait.
I hear a knock.
It's you and you've brought the fizz!
You'll scrape away the mold!
And what's this? You have a cow?
Oh, the world is golden, yellow,
bright, bright, bright.
Let's make butter.
Butter, pizza, root beer.
It's all right here, boy.
It's all right here.

PROMPT

BY BOB SHEA

RESPONSE

GRANDPA MARIUS
BY TRAVIS JONKER

My family has a mystery. It's about my grandpa Marius. When he was young, he was lost at sea. He used to sail the small lakes near his home, but his first solo trip in the ocean was different. He disappeared. He was thirteen. They searched and searched. But as the months went by, hope faded. Finally the search was called off.

Then one day, to the shocked joy of everyone, he showed up.

So here's the mystery: *What happened?* To this day, Grandpa refuses to talk about it.

When we were visiting over the holidays, I was snooping in Grandpa Marius's desk (I know, I know) when I found something. An old notebook.

I opened it.

This is what I saw.

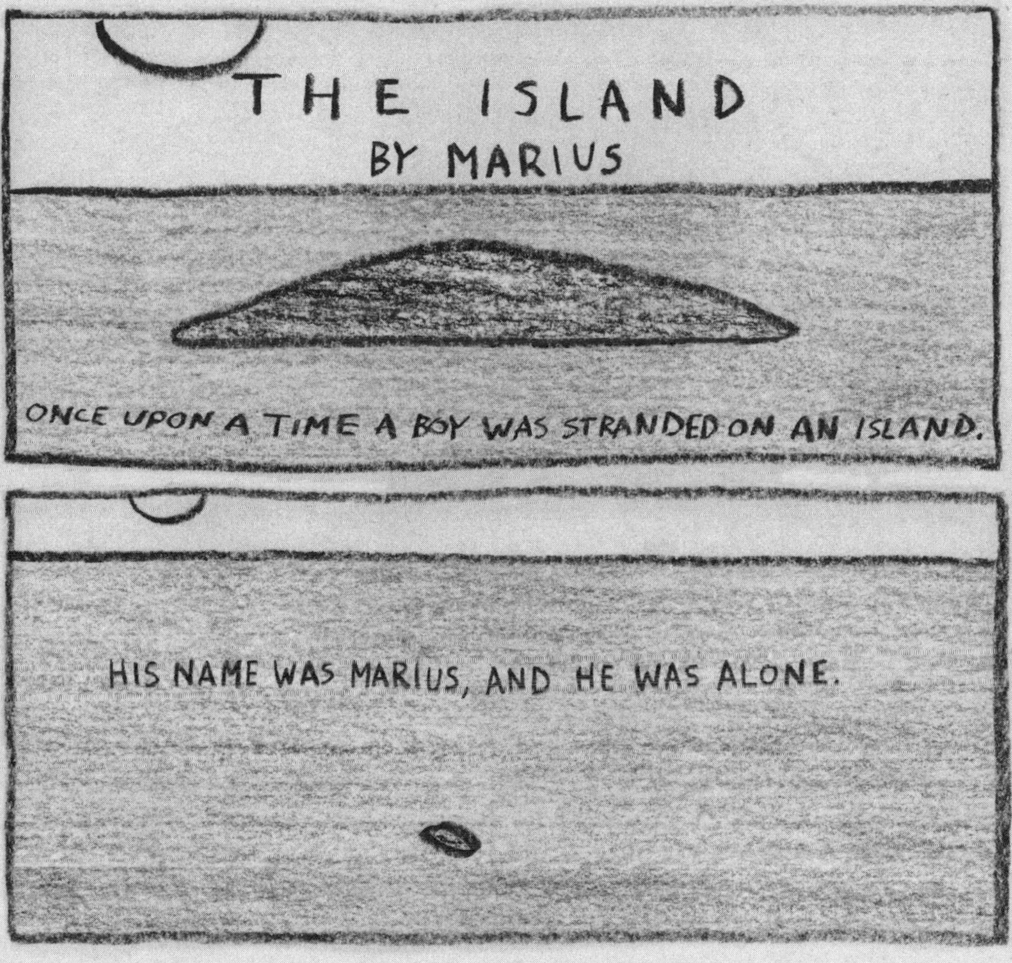
THE ISLAND
BY MARIUS
ONCE UPON A TIME A BOY WAS STRANDED ON AN ISLAND.
HIS NAME WAS MARIUS, AND HE WAS ALONE.

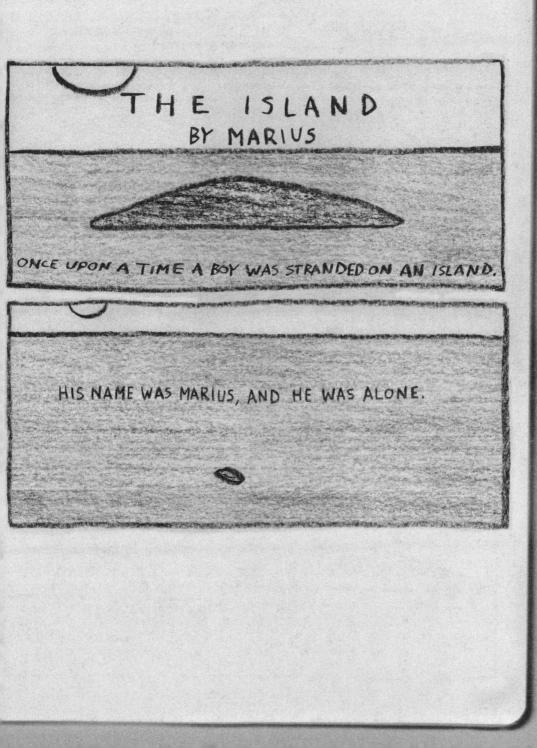

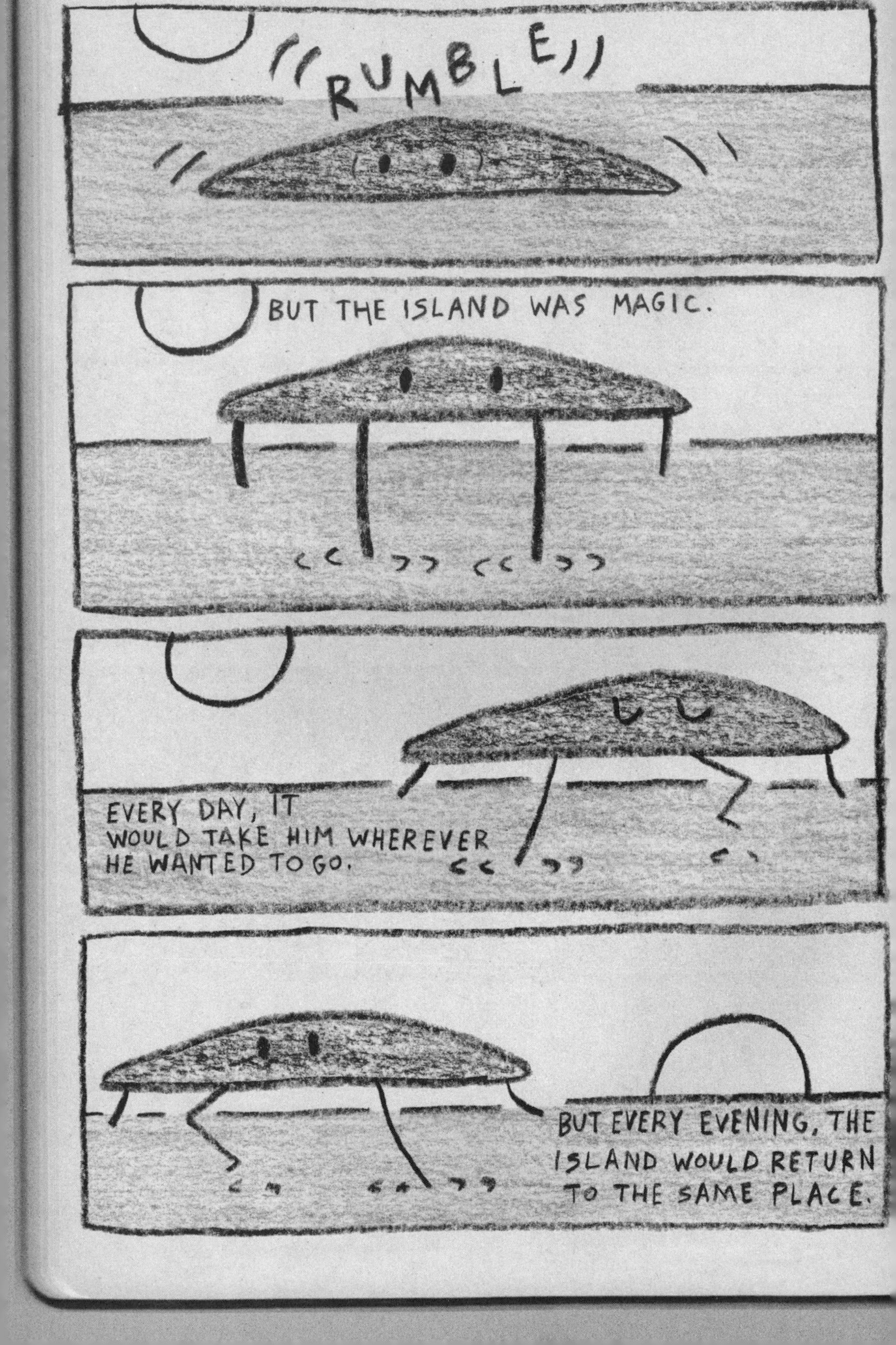
RUMBLE
BUT THE ISLAND WAS MAGIC.
EVERY DAY, IT WOULD TAKE HIM WHEREVER HE WANTED TO GO.
BUT EVERY EVENING, THE ISLAND WOULD RETURN TO THE SAME PLACE.

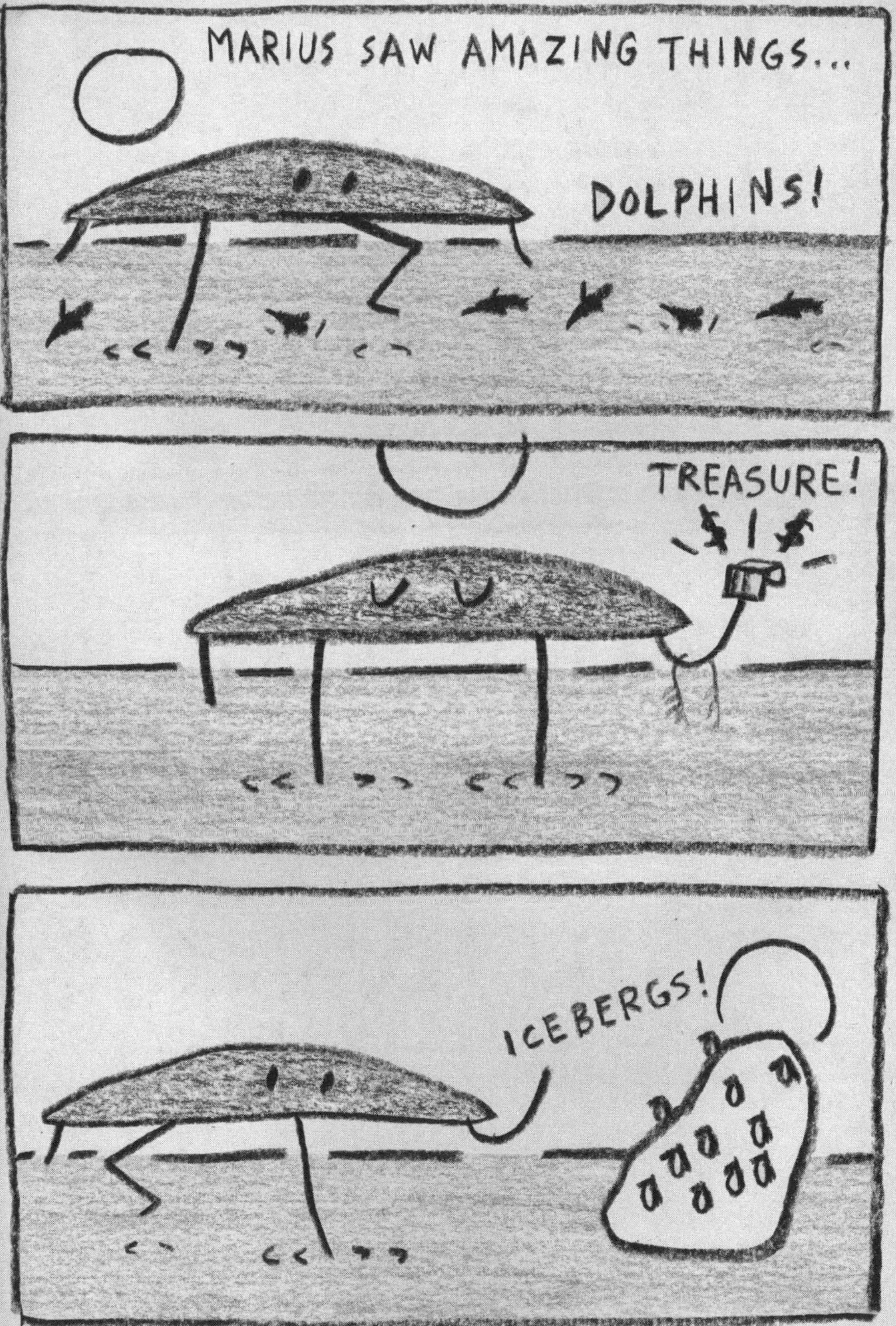
MARIUS SAW AMAZING THINGS...
DOLPHINS!
TREASURE!
ICEBERGS!

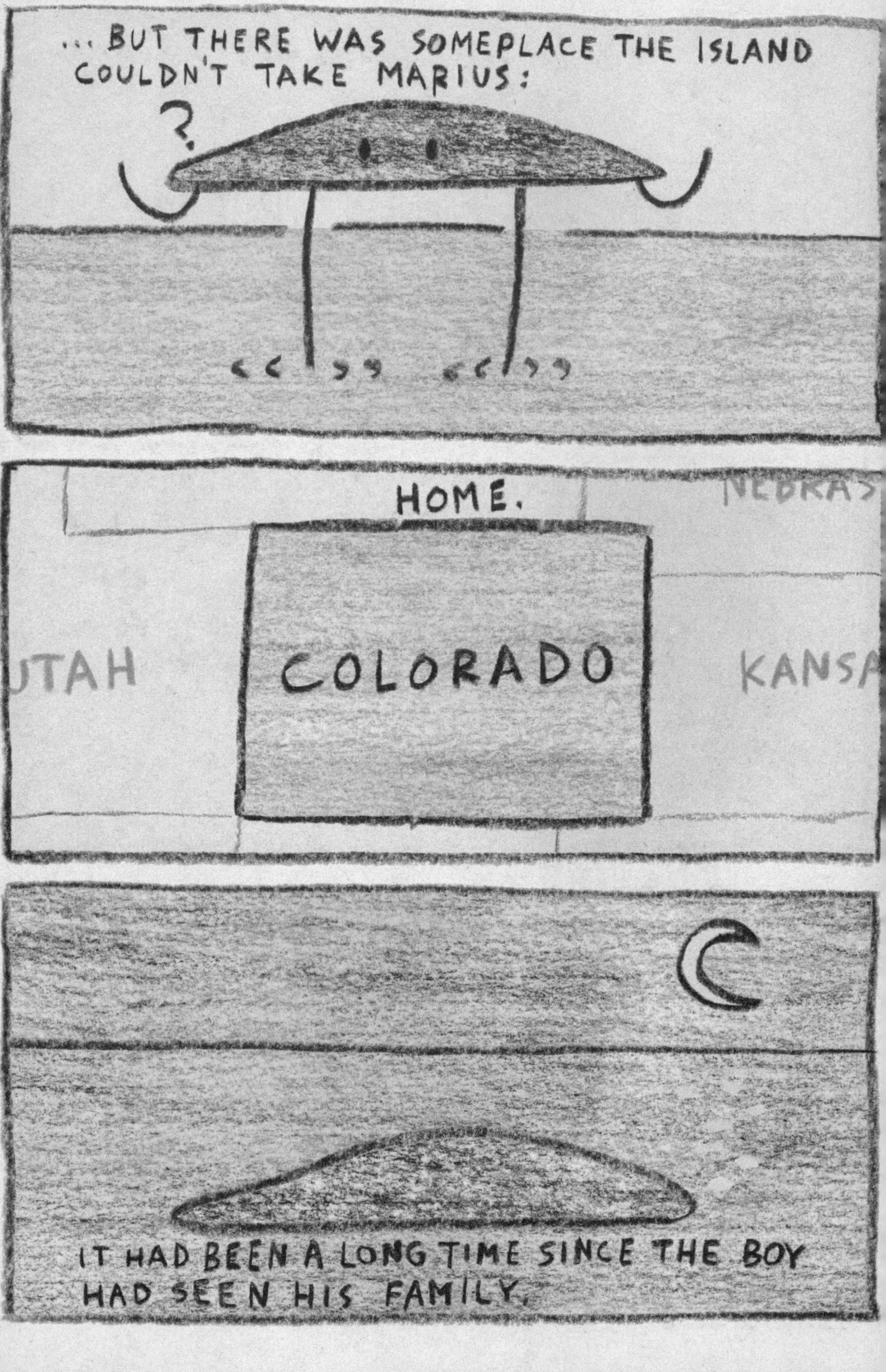

...BUT THERE WAS SOMEPLACE THE ISLAND COULDN'T TAKE MARIUS:
?
HOME.
UTAH
COLORADO
KANSA
IT HAD BEEN A LONG TIME SINCE THE BOY HAD SEEN HIS FAMILY.

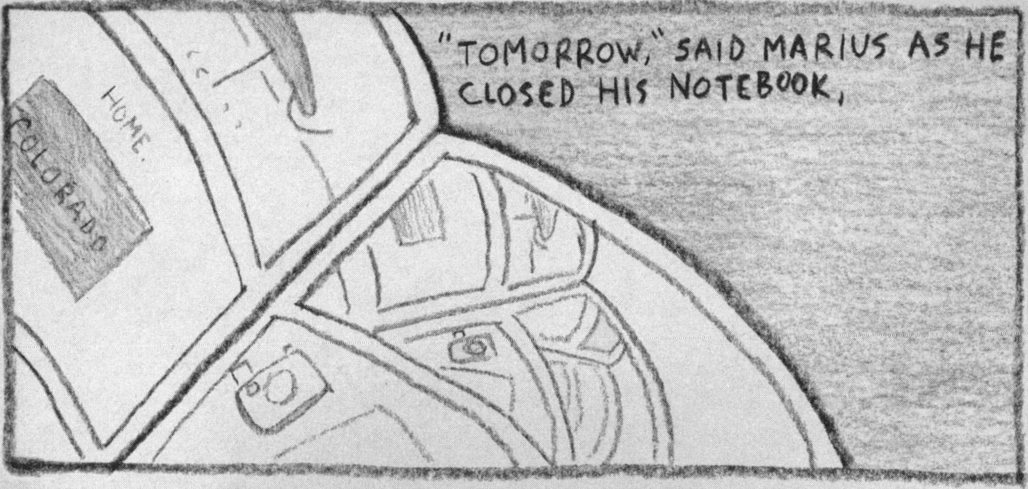
"TOMORROW," SAID MARIUS AS HE CLOSED HIS NOTEBOOK,
HOME.
COLORADO

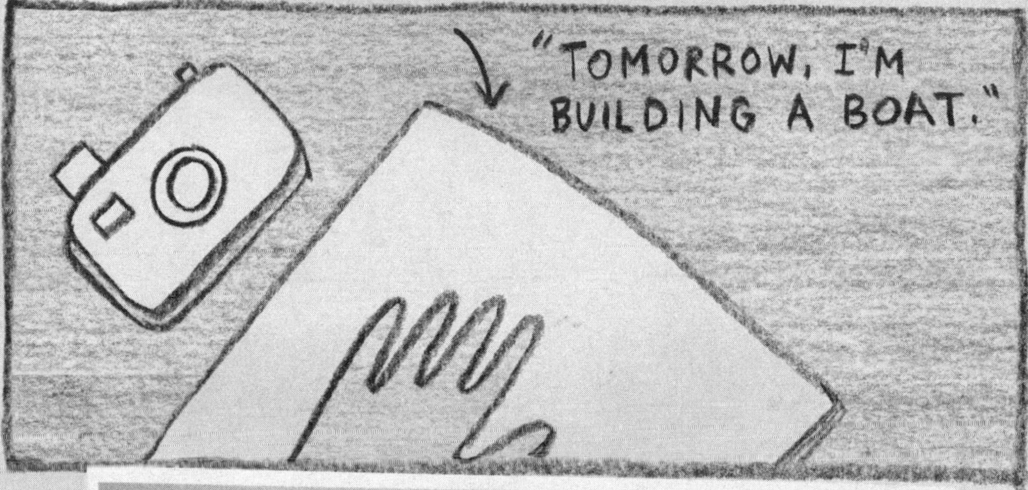
"TOMORROW, I'M BUILDING A BOAT."

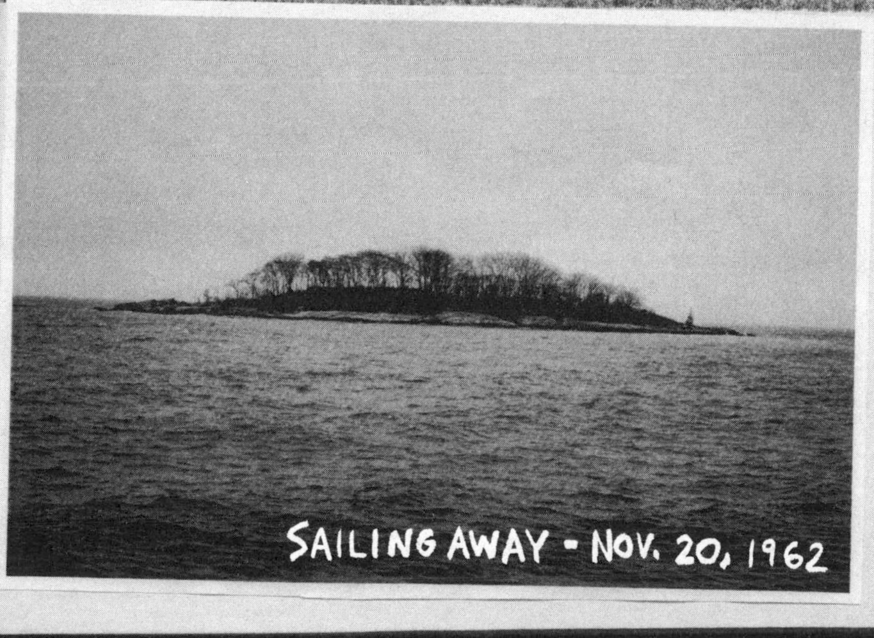
SAILING AWAY - NOV. 20, 1962

BY KIRBY LARSON

I buried Pa on that rise by the Douglas fir. My fingernails were still caked with dirt from digging the grave as I sat, sharing his view of the valley below. From my perch, I could see a Model T make its slow way along the road.

Aunt Olive.

I couldn't fault Pa for dying, but I was mighty irked that he'd set Aunt Olive on me. At thirteen, I would manage fine on my own.

The automobile would reach our shack soon. I stood, brushing grass from my skirt, calculating that I had about twenty minutes to pack my things to start a life with Pa's persnickety eldest sister.

Or, I could...

RESPONSE

BY JEWELL PARKER RHODES

Or, I could run. Far, fast, deeper, higher into the woods and mountains.

I take off—wishing I'd worn my overalls instead of a skirt. But it didn't seem right burying Pa in anything less than my Sunday best. (Though we didn't go to church.) Church, like town, was fifty miles away. Hiking was our church.

Step-by-step, me and Pa walked slowly picking up pinecones, snake skins, and pretty rocks. Today, I run. Fast like a deer runs trails. Or like a rabbit leaping toward home.

Sun warms my back; twigs scratch my legs. Still I run. Breathing deep, heart beating strong.

I stop, my back to bark, shoulders rising, lungs aching. "Pa," I yell. "Pa." Then, I start laughing.

Beneath the fir trees, I can feel Pa's spirit wrapping his arms around me.

"*The hollow never leaves you,*" I hear him whispering. "*You never leave the hollow.*"

This is home, I think. "That's right, Ellie, girl." Pa's going to be in the hollow forever. His body in the ground; his spirit in the air.

Where am I going to be with Aunt Olive?

I sniff, starting to feel sorry for myself.

"*Who?*"

I look up. A ghost owl. I can tell, because its face is white and heart-shaped and it hasn't any ears.

"*Who...ooo?*"

I start to climb the tree. Fir needles scrape my hands and calves, but I don't care. My arms and legs push me higher, up through the tree's Christmas smell.

"You're supposed to be sleeping," I say.

The owl's yellow eyes blink. Its face is the size of my hand.

I stare, amazed by its calm, amazed that the owl seems to see inside me. "*Who?*" it coos.

"You're beautiful." Soft white and gold feathers, layered like hair. I see its heart beating, like my heart beats. "*Who?*"

"Me," I say. "Ellie."

I lift my head, seeing cloudy sky between tree limbs. Sunlight streams high; down below, shade hovers like a gray sheen.

"I'm me" echoes through the air.

I look up. The ghost owl is gone. The limb bare.

◆

"Aunt Olive?"

Wearing a straw hat, white tights, and gloves, she rocks in the porch rocker. She looks like Pa, except younger, more pinch-faced. Here comes the scolding, I think.

"Is he buried?" she asks.

I scuff my shoe, spraying dirt.

"You're like your pa. Strong that you can do that. How'd you move the body?"

"Wheelbarrow."

Aunt Olive chuckles. "Resourceful. I wouldn't expect less from Robert's girl."

"Pa said, 'You're fussy.'"

Aunt Olive laughs again. "He would. Because I preferred town, dresses, and books. Still, he's a good brother. And I'm a good sister," she murmurs, softly, her eyes sparkling with tears.

"What do you mean?" I ask, wary.

She leans forward. The air sparks. "Who're you?"

"A hollow girl."

"That's why before your pa died, we both signed this hollow, these acres of land, over to you. To hunt, to farm…just to live, the choice is yours."

I fall to my knees, hugging Aunt Olive's waist. "I don't have to leave?"

"But you do. It just means the hollow is yours to come back to."

"I'm not leaving. I won't."

"What? A hollow girl not resourceful enough for adventures?"

Sullen, I don't answer.

I study the land, the valley and the horizon beyond, feeling that I'm being torn from my home. Hating that I'm a kid. Believing I'll have to run away again. Far from Aunt Olive, from the hollow. From everything.

"Mysteries abound. Just like an owl who decides to stay awake in the day."

Aunt Olive's eyes, just like the ghost owl's, are greenish-yellow with dark orbs.

"The hollow is inside me, too, Ellie. Just wanted to teach school. Live in town. Talk with people." Her eyes blink. "Your 'me' doesn't have to choose."

"I can be…do all those things?" I ask, awed.

"1910, you can do, be anything. Your pa and I were both set about that."

"Even drive a Model T?"

"Sure. The only thing your pa said wasn't 'persnickety' about me. Admired it."

I nod. Pa was teaching me to drive a tractor. "Are there owls in town?"

"Sure. Most important, there's an owl inside you. Asking 'who.'"

Trembling, beginning to dream of possibilities, I murmur, "'Ellie' doesn't have to mean one thing?"

"All kinds of possibilities for a modern girl."

"A hollow girl."

I look up the hillside. Pa's grave. It's not going anywhere. And I can come back again and again. Stay, leave as much as I want.

I squint. Something sits atop the dirt mound. "Do you see that?"

"What?"

Now it's gone. Was it an owl?

Aunt Olive hugs me tight. Standing side-by-side, I'm at ease with Pa's sister, my aunt. She kisses the top of my head just like Pa used to do.

"I packed some of your things. We can come back next week, the week after that, and pack more. Or have a picnic. A party."

"Hike?"

She nods, stepping toward the car, opening the green door. "Shall we go and find all there is for you to see, do, and be? Shall we, Ellie, girl?"

I feel Pa urging me. I hear the owl, inside me, cooing, "*Who?*"

It's my adventure to find out.

"Come on, now."

"Let's go," I holler while the engine sputters, chugs, then hums.

I spin backward, watching the hollow, our small house, and Pa's grave fade farther away. Then, I face forward, my hands in my lap. Sunset streaks the sky red, yellow, and gold.

I'm going to have adventures.

I smile at Aunt Olive. She smiles at me.

BY TRACEY BAPTISTE

People sometimes get angry when they are hurt. Think of a time you saw someone who was angry or upset. Write about what you think hurt them.

LITTLE HOUSE OF BLAME
BY NAOMI SHIHAB NYE

You had been in a spotlight
people recognized you
congratulated your good work
beam of buttery yellow attention
and then
then
it was a long road in the rain
foggy gray
stretching into future days
not enough coins jingling in your pocket
but fancy tastes and how to pay for
them—
how did you get here?
Where did they all go?
Of course
it had to be someone else's fault
since you were the smarter one
someone did you wrong
stepped on your toes
got in your way

shunned your idea
turned their back.
If blame were bricks
you would haul them
in a green wheelbarrow
and stack them up
cleanly
perfectly aligned
as only you knew how to do.
Building a little brick Blame House felt
    just right.
You would hide in it
and wait for them to bump into it some
    night
when they were on their own long road
in the rain.

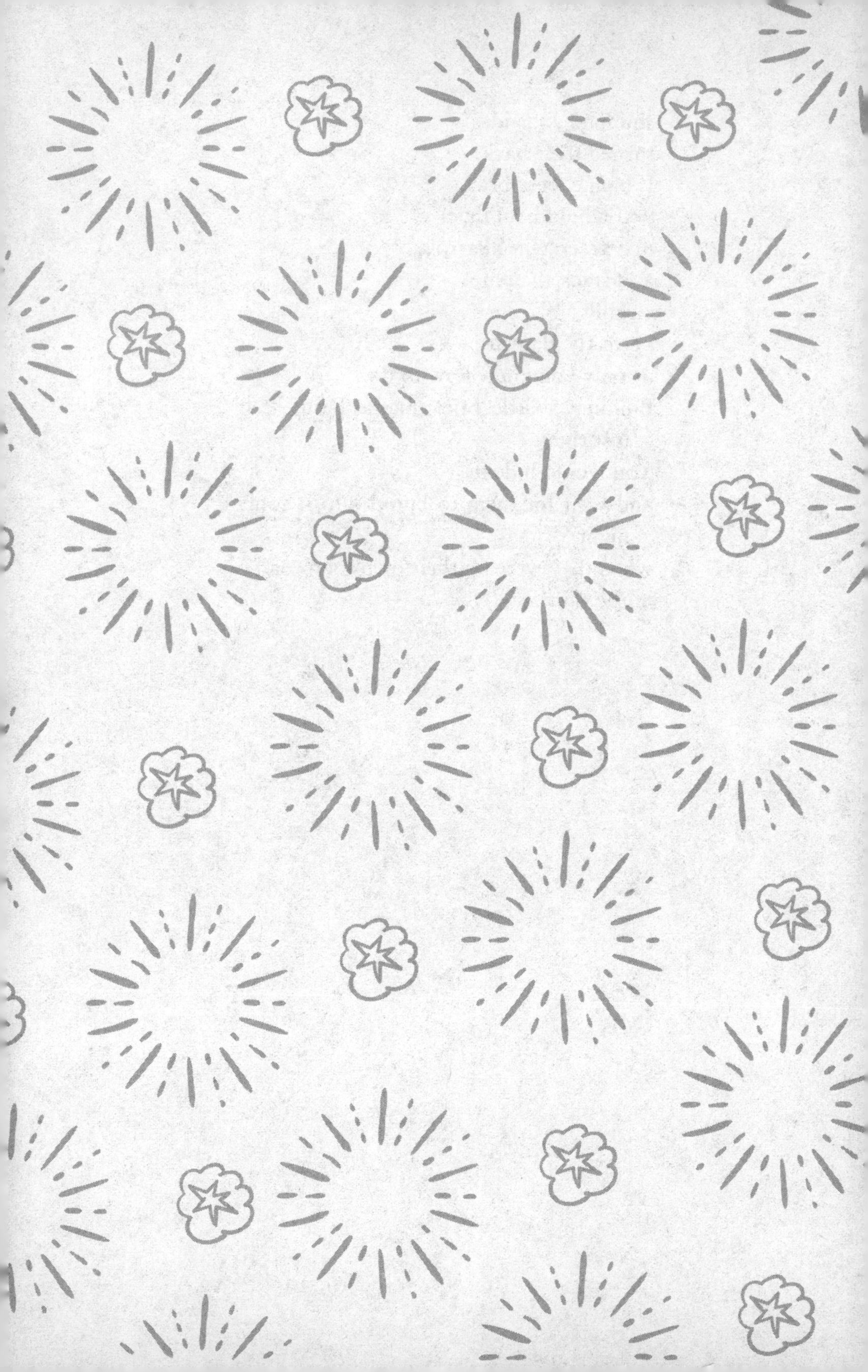

PROMPT

BY LAURIE KELLER

Draw an object (clock, baseball bat, banjo, pickle, etc.) as an animated character and give it an emotion or expression (happy, suspicious, sad, excited, angry, etc.). Then ask yourself why your character is feeling that way. For instance:

"Why is the umbrella scared?" Maybe she's never been used before and is worried she'll melt in the rain. Maybe she's afraid that she'll blow away in the wind. Or maybe she's terrified of thunder and lightning and just wants to stay indoors. The possibilities are endless! For an added challenge, try it with two or three characters and combine them to see what you come up with!

The same exercise works using people and animals, but inanimate objects can provide a whole new world to create and explore that you might not have considered before.

RESPONSE

BY BOB SHEA

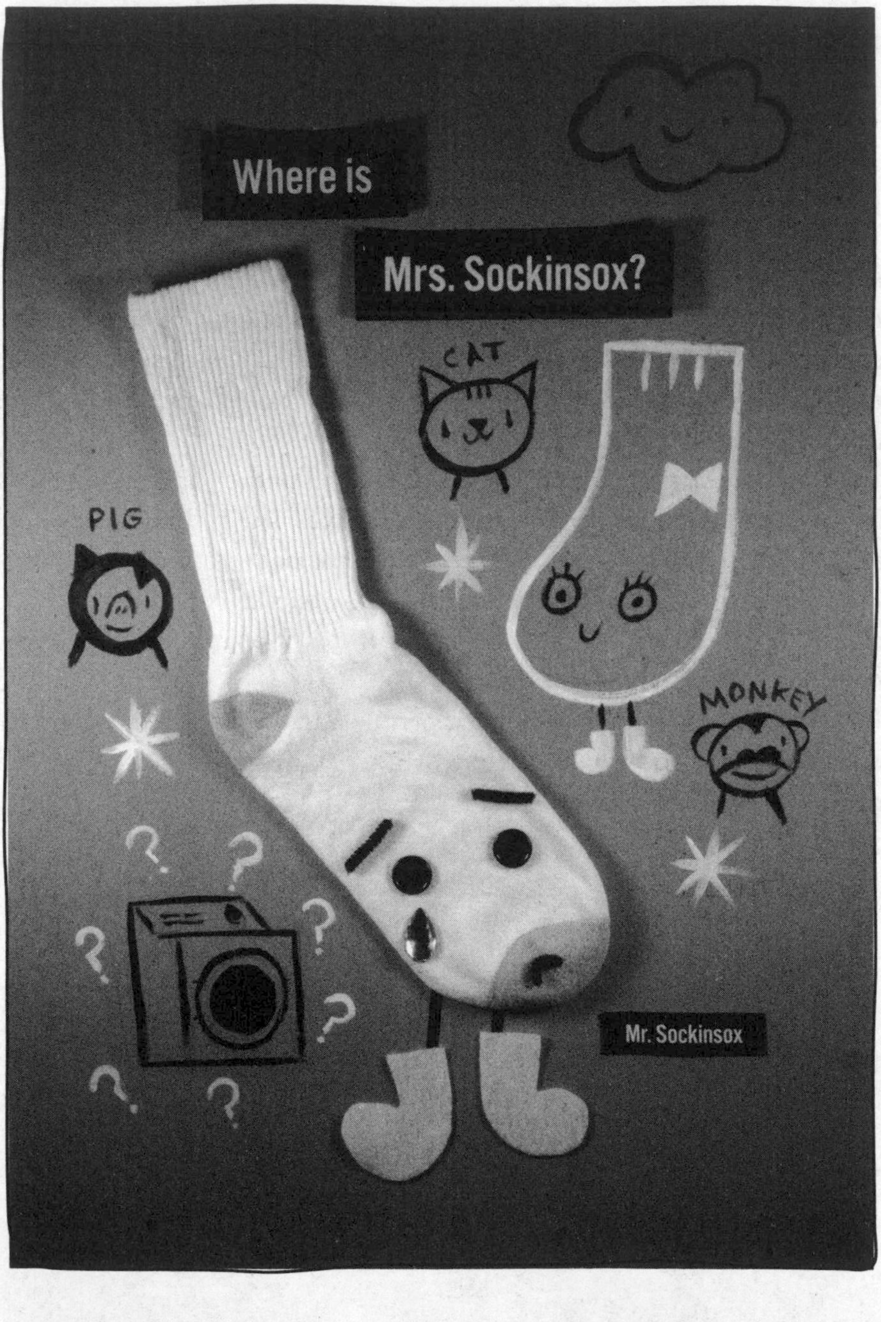

Where is
Mrs. Sockinsox?
CAT
PIG
MONKEY
Mr. Sockinsox

PROMPT

BY GARY D. SCHMIDT

Since sixth grade, when his family began to visit Lynn's family at the shore, Ronnie had imagined holding Lynn's hand. Three years of imagining her on the boardwalk, and him back in Greenville.

And then it just happened. They sat on the edge of the boardwalk and Lynn said, "I love the sea," and Ronnie said, "Me, too," and their hands sort of touched, and then she played with his fingers, and he played with hers, and then they stood up still holding hands, and that was it.

Worth the wait, thought Ronnie.

They walked down toward the rides as the sun set, and the neon lights came on, and the waves fell back into darkness, and Lynn said, "Let's try the Whirly-Gig," and they did. It spun them around and they never let go of each other's hands.

"Let's do it again," said Ronnie.

They did the Whirly-Gig six times, and by then it was full dark. They passed the cotton candy booth, and the orangeade stand, and then they stood in front of the Human Statue, completely painted in gold, who did not move as they watched for the tiniest blink of an eye.

Then, in the neon lights, Lynn saw a shell on the beach and she jumped down to get it. Ronnie watched her until he felt another hand—this one on his shoulder.

The hand of the Human Statue, who opened his golden mouth and said, "The last kid took three days to wash up."

RESPONSE

BY LINDA URBAN

Since sixth grade, when his family began to visit Lynn's family at the shore, Ronnie had imagined holding Lynn's hand. Three years of imagining her on the boardwalk, and him back in Greenville.

And then it just happened. They sat on the edge of the boardwalk and Lynn said, "I love the sea," and Ronnie said, "Me, too," and their hands sort of touched, and then she played with his fingers, and he played with hers, and then they stood up still holding hands and that was it.

Worth the wait, thought Ronnie.

They walked down toward the rides as the sun set, and the neon lights came on, and the waves fell back into darkness, and Lynn said, "Let's try the Whirly-Gig," and they did. It spun them around and they never let go of each other's hands.

"Let's do it again," said Ronnie.

They did the Whirly-Gig six times, and by then it was full dark. They passed the cotton candy booth, and the orangeade stand, and then they stood in front of the Human Statue, completely painted in gold, who did not move as they watched for the tiniest blink of an eye.

Then, in the neon lights, Lynn saw a shell on the beach and she jumped down to get it. Ronnie watched her until he felt another hand—this one on his shoulder.

The hand of the Human Statue, who opened his golden mouth and said, "The last kid took three days to wash up."

"Sorry, I don't have any change," Ronnie told the statue man.

Buskers were everywhere on the boardwalk. Crooners, jugglers, fortune-tellers, dancers. A lot of them were talented. Ronnie had surprised himself by dropping a hard-earned dollar in the case of a girl who had played the cello so ferociously it sounded more like a warning than a song. The statue people, though? All they did was stand around in their metallic face paint, pretending they had gears instead of guts. Was that supposed to be a talent, standing still, saying nothing? Heck, that's how Ronnie had gotten through middle school. If only he had put out a sign and asked for donations, maybe he'd have enough cash to buy Lynn an ice cream now.

And this guy? He wasn't even doing *that* right. He had grabbed Ronnie's shoulder. He had talked. He had said something weird. "What did you say?" asked Ronnie.

The Human Statue raised a golden eyebrow. He was back in robot mode. Standing erect, moving rigidly. Silently.

"Really, you can be yourself," said Ronnie. "There's nobody else around to hear, and I don't have a dollar. What did you say?"

Three of the statue's fingers closed into a fist. One extended. Slowly. Very slowly. Like three years of waiting slowly, he lifted his pretend-mechanical arm and pointed out to sea.

The tide had snuck in and waves were curling around Lynn's calves. She had twisted the hem of her long skirt and tucked it into her waistband so it hung no higher than her knees. Did she figure that trick out herself, Ronnie wondered. Or was it one of those things girls just seemed to know how to do? Like hair braiding and fast dancing and smiling in a way that makes a boy forget where he came from and who he's been? So the only parts of himself that he is sure about are the parts that have touched her. Fingertips. Wrist. The places where the wind had brushed her long hair against his face.

The golden man kept pointing.

"What did you say?" Ronnie asked again. Truth was, he didn't need the statue to repeat it. He had heard. *The last kid took three days to wash up.*

The moon lit the crests of waves as they roared toward the beach. He thought he heard a laugh of surprise. Ronnie saw Lynn knocked off balance, then recover.

"Let's go," he called, but she had turned her back to him. Like the golden man, she faced the sea.

Ronnie watched what she watched. Thought about calling her again. Imagined himself hopping down from the boardwalk, striding across the sand, sweeping her up and away from danger. He thought about how heroic that would be, to save Lynn from the sea. But if he were wrong, he'd look foolish and fearful and weak. He shifted his weight. Shielded his eyes as if the sun were in them.

Had she gone deeper into the water? Or had the tide risen to her waist? He thought he saw the pale of her arms above her head. Was she dancing? Was she playing? Another wave. She disappeared.

What happened next Ronnie saw more than felt, perfectly lit, like a movie or a memory. He saw himself leap from the boardwalk, rush to the water, dive, splash, search. He was not a strong swimmer, but he swam and called and swallowed sand and salt and called again.

Then he heard her voice and turned. She was behind him. Standing in the knee-deep water, laughing, waving him back to shore.

He was not a strong swimmer, he thought, aware now that he was narrating his own actions. He was not a strong swimmer, but he kept swimming, even at the point where he might have found footing and walked back to shore. If he stood up, he'd have to look her in the face and see his soggy, sandy self reflected back. He swam until his knees scraped sand, then stood.

She held out a hand. He took it. And it just happened, all over again. She laughed and he laughed. They climbed back up to the board-walk, still holding hands.

The Human Statue had moved and now he stood, as if waiting for them, at the top of the wooden stairs. He spoke no words of warning about kids and time and washing up, but his hand was extended, a flyer pinched between his fingers.

There was just enough light to make out a photo on the page—a glossy image of a family-size bar of soap. Underneath was a dollar-off coupon and the words *Sand in your shorts? Salt in your hair? Try Sea-Be-Gone. Wash up in no time!*

The Human Statue did not blink. Ronnie didn't, either. Not until Lynn tugged his soggy sleeve. She tugged his sleeve and squeezed his hand and Ronnie blinked and that was it.

That was it.

Author's note: This prompt was a challenge for me. It seemed to require that I finish the story, and I've not written any short stories since I was in middle school. That formal challenge was only half the battle, though. Unlike the "freewrites" I do in my notebooks, I was keenly aware that this story would be read by kids and teachers and by my writing peers. I didn't want to let them down.

That's a lot of pressure to put on a prompt response.

And so, in the end, I tried to forget all of that and just write something. Anything. I won't claim that I didn't revise it. I did. But what you are reading here is not very far away from that first-draft prompt response, because I want all the readers and writers who are looking at this anthology to understand that prompts like these are for play. They are for exploring and trying things out and seeing what skills you might have and where you might want to grow.

There are things I like about my prompt response and things that I'd like time to think about and change. It makes me a little nervous thinking that you will read this in its clumsy, not-quite-finished state and maybe judge it, or me, at least a little bit.

But that's not what we're here for, is it? The project isn't called the Perfection Project or the Judgment Project or the Published Authors Can Do No Wrong Project. It is the Creativity Project. I stretched my creativity a little here, to try to finish a short story. I'm going to call that a success. Now, how about you?

How about you give one of these prompts a try? Do it, and we'll call that a success, too.

BY JESSIXA BAGLEY

You go to visit a distant relative who lives in an old Victorian house. While everyone is downstairs having tea, you quietly sneak away and explore the rooms upstairs. While you are looking around, you come across a loose floorboard. When you inspect it, the board comes up and inside you find…

THE FAIRY UNDER THE FLOOR
BY LIESL SHURTLIFF

The old ladies were having tea again, and young people were not welcome. Being barely ten years old, Magdalena was instructed to keep quiet and out of sight.

"What am I to do?" Magdalena asked.

"Do?" said Aunt Olive. "I don't care what you do, as long as you don't destroy anything. Good heavens, what a silly question."

Magdalena thought it wasn't at all a silly question. The grand old house at 421 Gray Lane was not a place for children. The furniture was white and expensive. Breakable things were at every turn. The walls were covered with oil paintings of fruit and flowers and Aunt Olive's dearly departed dog Belinda. There was no television. No computer. No books except a dusty old set of encyclopedias that probably still marked Pluto as a planet. There was not a suggestion of youth or imagination. Great-aunt Olive had never married, never had any children, never desired them, and never welcomed them into her home. She certainly wasn't pleased when Magdalena showed up on her doorstep, suitcase in hand. But Magdalena was certain Aunt Olive's feelings were nothing compared to hers. It was one of the worst moments in her young life. As Aunt Olive would say, it quite did her in.

As the old ladies in hats and handbags came to the door, Magdalena went upstairs and wandered from room to room, exploring shelves and drawers and closets. She found an old chess set, the only evidence of play within the house, but then she had no one to play with. There were no children in the neighborhood. How she wished she had someone to keep her company besides Great-aunt Olive!

Magdalena took a step and the floor beneath her groaned. She paused, then bounced up and down a few times. Her foot seemed to sink into the floorboard, and the other end of the floorboard lifted up. She bent down and wedged her fingers under the board. A secret hiding space! Perhaps Great-aunt Olive had a stash of jewels, or a treasure map, or the remains of her deceased dog! How horrific. Her heart beat a little faster as she lifted the board, but when she looked inside there was nothing there. Just dust and mouse droppings. She replaced the floorboard and flopped down on the bed.

Something flapped in her face. Magdalena shrieked and swatted at it. She'd let a bird into the room! It flew to the ceiling, then to the window, then back to her. It was very fast, small, and colorful. Maybe a hummingbird? Whatever it was, Aunt Olive wouldn't be happy to find a bird in the house, especially if it did its business on the floor. She would have to catch it and let it out.

"You summoned me?" said a small voice.

Magdalena gasped and tumbled right off the bed, landing with a hard *thwack* on the floor.

A tinkling little laugh sounded right in her ear. "You are clumsy, aren't you?"

A tiny, humanlike creature hovered in the air just inches above her face. Her wings were an iridescent blue, her hair bright purple. A soft glow surrounded her little being, as though light were emanating from her.

"Are you a...a fairy?" Magdalena asked.

"Well, I'm not a beetle, am I?" said the creature in a haughty little voice.

"No, I didn't think so, except I didn't know fairies were real."

The fairy crossed her arms. "Humph! You humans don't have the brains to see a leprechaun."

"Leprechaun? Are they real, too?"

"Of course!" said the fairy, scrunching up her nose. "Nasty little tricksters."

Magdalena tried to take all this in and keep her head from falling off. What else could be hiding under her aunt Olive's floor? A dragon? The Easter Bunny?

"Well," said the fairy, "I'm here now. Why have you summoned me?"

"I summoned you?"

"You did."

"Oh," said Magdalena. "I didn't realize."

The fairy fluttered her wings in such a way that reminded Magdalena of an eye roll. "You aren't very intelligent, are you?"

Magdalena didn't think this was fair. She had always been told by all her teachers that she was very smart. She knew all her times tables and state capitals and could spell difficult words like *meticulous* and *vignette*, even if she wasn't sure exactly what they meant. But here, with a fairy before her, she was beginning to feel quite like a baby and the slightest bit annoyed.

"There's no need to be rude," said Magdalena. "You didn't have to come. I don't even know what to ask of you."

"Well, for starters I can change your hair color. Brown is rather bland, don't you think?" The fairy flew up high and flicked her wings so a silvery dust poured over Magdalena's head. Her scalp felt warm and tingly, and when she looked down, her long brown curls turned bubble-gum pink.

"There! Much better," said the fairy. "I could also teach you to fly. You'd probably be less clumsy that way." And before Magdalena could say whether or not she wanted to fly or go on a quest, the fairy had sprinkled shimmering dust onto her feet and she lifted off the ground.

"Oh!" Magdalena cried. She flew up to the ceiling so fast she hit her head and immediately dropped down onto the bed. She bounced once and then tumbled to the floor, landing with a great *thump*.

"I beg your pardon," said the fairy. "Your mass is quite a lot to work with, you know."

Magdalena sat up, rubbing her head, when she heard slow, heavy footsteps coming down the hall.

"Hide!" said Magdalena. The fairy fluttered up into the light fixture. Magdalena stood and tried to straighten herself up. She looked down. Her hair was still pink! She looked around. The footsteps drew nearer. She snatched the throw on the chair and threw it over her head. She pulled it down over her forehead and tight beneath her chin, just as the door clicked open.

"Magdalena?"

"Yes?"

Aunt Olive stepped inside. "What are you doing?"

"Just playing...a little dress-up?" She pulled the blanket tighter around her.

Aunt Olive's eyes narrowed. She peered around the room. "What was that noise?"

"I tripped over the bedpost when I was...dancing."

"Dancing." Aunt Olive sniffed as though she could smell the lie, or perhaps she didn't approve of dancing. "Have a care, child, and keep quiet."

"Yes, Aunt Olive."

Aunt Olive turned and shut the door. Her heavy footsteps went back down the hallway.

Magdalena took a deep breath and looked up at the light. "Hello? She's gone now. You can come down."

All was still and quiet. Magdalena began to think she had only imagined the fairy. Of course she had! But when she took off the blanket, her hair was still pink.

"Who was that?" Magdalena looked up. The fairy was floating down.

"That's my great-aunt Olive."

"Her hair would look much better if it were blue. I could arrange it."

"Don't!" said Magdalena. "I mean, I agree, it would look better, but Aunt Olive doesn't care for blue hair." Magdalena remembered the time she went to the grocery store with Aunt Olive. The woman at the register had a thin blue streak in the front of her hair. She had smiled and asked how they were, but Aunt Olive only scowled in response. Imagine what she'd do if she looked in the mirror and her own head of gray hair was blue!

The fairy sat cross-legged on the bed with her wings pressed down. She placed her elbows on her knees and her chin in her tiny hands. "Then what do you want from me? I'm beginning to think you don't fully appreciate the presence of a fairy."

"Oh, I'm sorry. I *do* appreciate you. This is the most fun I've had since I came to live with Aunt Olive. I've had absolutely no one to play with, no friends at all."

"How sad," said the fairy. "I haven't had anyone to play with, either. There are very few fairies around here, you know."

"No, I didn't know," said Magdalena.

"Yes," said the fairy. "Only a few, and none of them care for me." Her wings trembled. Magdalena thought she saw a tiny tear trickle down her cheek. Magdalena's heart broke a little.

"Perhaps I summoned you to be my friend," said Magdalena.

The fairy lifted her head. "Your friend?"

Magdalena nodded. "And I could be yours, too."

The fairy stood and spread her wings wide. "Fairies do make fantastic friends!" She flew up and spun around and shot out her silvery dust until the entire room was a rainbow of color and sparkle. It would put Aunt Olive in a rage.

Magdalena smiled. Having a fairy for a friend was going to be a lot of fun.

PROMPT

BY JENNIFER L. HOLM

RESPONSE

BY MINH LÊ

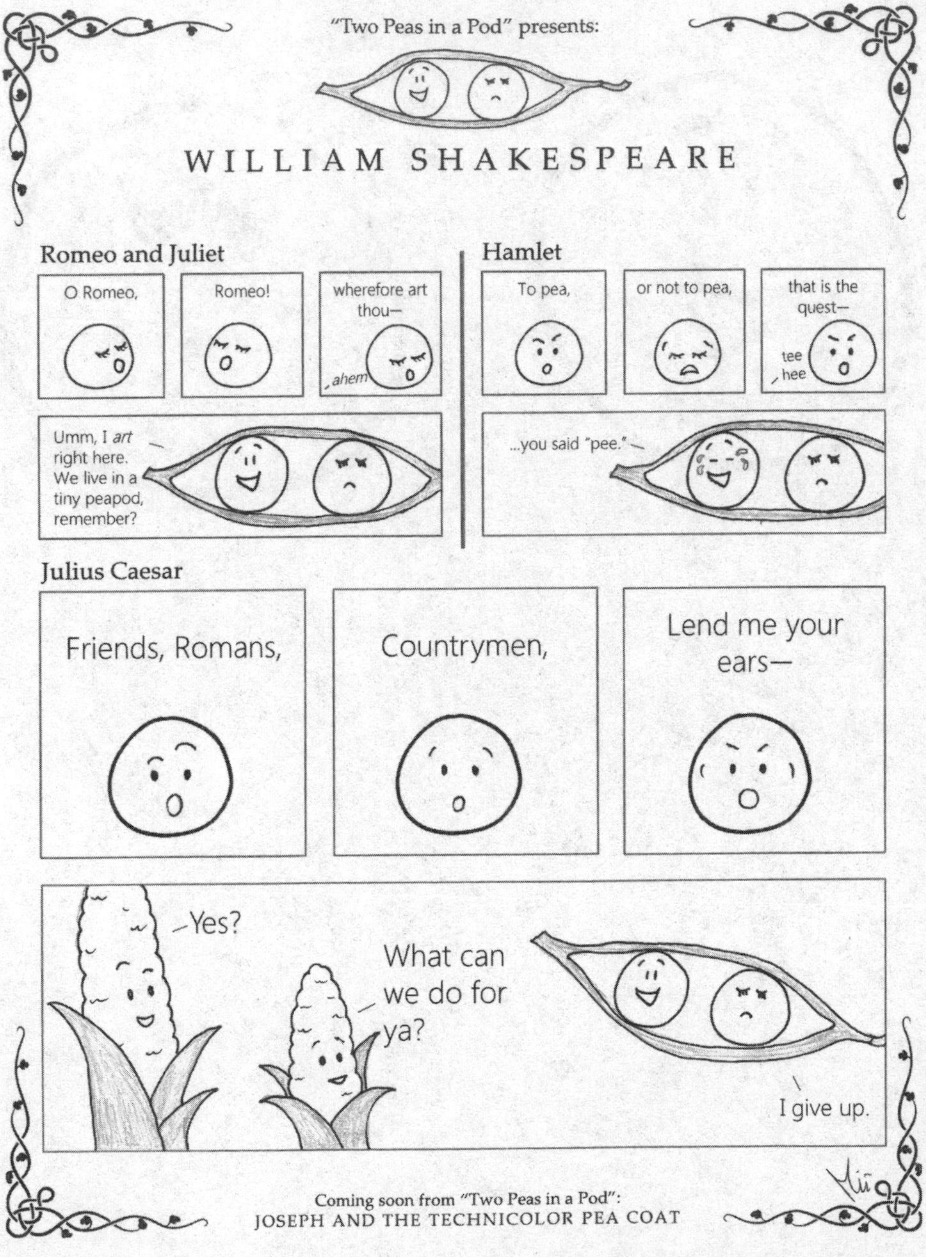

"Two Peas in a Pod" presents:
WILLIAM SHAKESPEARE
Romeo and Juliet
O Romeo,
Romeo!
wherefore art thou—
ahem
Umm, I *art* right here. We live in a tiny peapod, remember?
Hamlet
To pea,
or not to pea,
that is the quest—
tee hee
...you said "pee."
Julius Caesar
Friends, Romans,
Countrymen,
Lend me your ears—
Yes?
What can we do for ya?
I give up.
Coming soon from "Two Peas in a Pod":
JOSEPH AND THE TECHNICOLOR PEA COAT

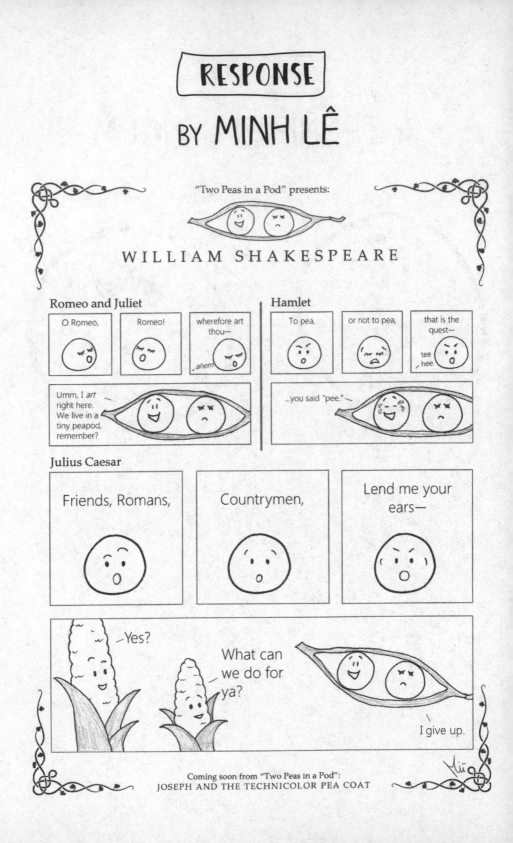

PROMPT

BY TOM ANGLEBERGER

This is something I have tried on literally hundreds of people. And then I read the results out loud, onstage. The audience chooses a winner by yelling...or making gagging and retching sounds.

You, however, do not have to have yours read out loud. Instead, it will be published in this book for people to see for years to come!

Please create something titled "The Worst Thing I Ever Smelled." Your challenge is to create it so well that the reader will think they smell it, too!

RESPONSE

BY FRANK VIVA

THE WORST SMELL:

A PRESENTATION BY PROFESSOR F. LUVIUM
[Loud applause]
"Thank you for the lovely introduction, Barb. As mentioned, my name is Professor F. Luvium, and as you probably already know, I am a professional smellologist. Today, I have been asked to present to you, and the esteemed panel sitting directly behind me, some fascinating insights into terrible smells.

"Let me just start by saying that smells are nothing more than a by-product of the olfactory bulb reacting to a cluster of chemicals that float in the air. The process, which takes place in the forebrain, occurs in a flash. When you think on it, a smell, however bad, is—once the chemicals, which are very small, have dispersed—nothing more than a memory. Even as one of the country's leading smellologists, I believe that far too much fuss is made over unpleasant smells."

[Pfft]
["What was that?"]
"What was what? To continue. After that, what are you left with? The memory of a stenchless nought; the fallible recollection of a whiffless diddly-squat. That's the thing about memory: It's fallible, which means you can't trust it, in that same way that you can't trust a pol-

itician who says, 'Trust me.' Like memory, nobody who truly under-
stands how their five (or more) senses work, including smell, could
ever—indeed, would ever—assume that they can be trusted. My question for this esteemed panel and audience: Why all the fuss about
bad smells? They are a commonplace everyday occurrence. In general
terms, people should just…get over it! I mean, unless you've been living in a bubble—and I admit that a small fraction of the population do
indeed live in a bubble—let it go. Move on. Stop griping. Get a life. In
scientific terms, bad smells are not even moored in reality. It is just a
chemical process."

[Poot]

["Good God."]

"Getting back to my talk. Think about it: If you can't trust your
sense of smell or your memory, how can you possibly trust your memory of a smell? I'd like you to turn your attention to the screen to see
a lovely animation. It was created by my students and illustrates the
smelling process. As you can see, ordinary substances make their way
into the nasal cavity. From there they find their way into the olfactory
bulb. Finally, they arrive in the limbic system. I know exactly what
you're wondering. You want to know what is housed in the limbic
system? Emotion. Yes, folks, emotion. I ask you this: Can you trust
your emotions? Can I? Can anyone? My friends, I think not. In fact, I
believe that it can be very dangerous to allow your emotions to control
your behavior. There is nary a day that goes by when this fact isn't
painfully obvious on Twitter and other social media outlets. Even the
dullest and most thoughtless among us would have to concede to this
unfortunate reality."

[Polite applause]

[Brraaapp]

["Professor! Are you all right?"]

"Panel! Please save your questions until I conclude!

"Even if you could trust your sense of smell—and we all now know
that this is scientifically impossible—why in heaven's name would
you consider smells to be objectionable? How could you? Let's take
the common household fart. As we all know, the gases that make up

flatulence include nitrogen, oxygen, and methane. It is only when sulfates are added to the mix that the molecules react in a meaningful way with the olfactory bulb. Other than some controversial 'science' about these chemicals harming the ozone layer, it is agreed among experts in the field—experts, mind you—that these chemicals are completely and utterly harmless to human beings. Logically, if you are offended by these everyday odors, you must ask yourself this simple question: Am I a human? And by extension, am I acting in a humane way if I show disdain when my fellow human lets slip a few molecules of these harmless gases?"

[Mild applause]

[Frrrrr]

["Professor Luvium!"]

"To continue. The human fart is probably the most relatable smell in the entire world. In fact, I can say with a high degree of certainty that everyone in this audience—and the panel to my rear—have participated in the act as well as been on the receiving end. In preparation for this talk, I asked a panel of leading linguists if there were any clues to be had in names that we commonly give to the act of farting. Specifically, words that might help provide meaningful clues when it comes to the degree of tolerance and/or kindness that we extend (or do not extend) to our fellow travelers. Some of the more popular euphemisms for the act include breaking wind, butt sneezing, the back draft, cutting the cheese, the gas attack, 'bumson' burner, scud missile, the fizzler, the quacker, the trouser cough, the slider... and, of course, the pop tart. What do *all* these terms have in common, dear listeners? That's right, they are all cute. The terms are jaunty and nonthreatening. One might even say...friendly. So, I say this to all of you in the audience, and to my colleagues at the rear: Let him who is without fart cast the first aspersion."

[A smattering of applause]

[Ssssst]

["This is intolerable! I'm leaving."]

"As it must now be clear, the linguistic encoding of olfaction and the related subject of odor injustice are near and dear to my heart. I can say categorically that the social implications of this area of study have been neglected and forever misunderstood. To quote my long-suffering wife, 'It does not pass the smell test.'"

[*A single clap*]

[*Boount*]

[*"Repulsive."*]

"In conclusion, my lifetime goal is to get to the bottom of these inquiries. I intend to start a movement of sorts. And I humbly ask that all you here today join me in this noble endeavor. Help me to sniff out the denizens of fetid alleyways and noxious bedroom communities who routinely and without thought stifle free and healthy expression. Join me in spreading the word, won't you? Hello? Hello?"

[*Phffff!*]

BY ADAM GIDWITZ

Write an encyclopedia entry about an undiscovered animal. Tell us where it lives, what it eats, what its personality is like, is it good as a pet, and any other interesting information you can think of (be sure to include an image).

RESPONSE

BY JESS KEATING

Excerpted from *Madame Petunia Glasswing's Encyclopedia of Insect Oddities*

Kingdom: Animalia
Phylum: Arthropoda
Class: Insecta
Order: Lepidoptera
Family: Saturniidae
Genus: Ingenium
Species name: *Ingenium luna*
Common name: Genius moon moth

If you have ever seen this peculiar creature, consider yourself a lucky duck! The genius moon moth (*Ingenium luna*) is very tricky to find, and it reveals itself only to viewers willing to look beyond what they see with their eyes. They are found in every color of the rainbow, including gold, red, indigo, green, and even iridescent shades of purple, orange, or silver. Strangely, these moths might also be unassuming or downright boring in color, with brown, cream, or gray wings. These wings, spanning six inches or more, can carry the genius moon moth across entire continents or oceans in a single night. But do not let their looks fool you; pretty wings or not, the most fascinating detail about this creature is not its appearance but rather, how it *survives*.

Genius moon moths do not eat solid food. They have no mouthparts and no digestive system. How do they survive? Genius moon moths are *ideavores*: They feed off the creative energy of those around them, particularly that of young children. To ensure a supply of food, this moth has a special trick up its sleeve, or rather, its *wing*. When a genius moon moth flies nearby, it sparks brilliant ideas in those around it, encouraging them to write, draw, or build their idea in real life. In exchange for providing the inspiration, the moth feeds off some of the resulting creative energy whenever a human creates something new. Genius moon moths are responsible for providing inspiration for several famous works of art, but they have also played a role in the human invention of electricity, progress in modern medicine, and even cheese making.

You might be wondering, do the more vibrantly colored and bright moths bring greater ideas or inspiration? Research shows that this is not so. In fact, some of our greatest creative ideas arrive after visits from incredibly dull-looking moths. For this reason, moon moth experts recommend acting on every creative impulse you have.

Genius moon moths are found all over the world in every climate, yet they are often seen in schools, where they linger near the bookshelves in libraries, science laboratories, and art rooms. If you feel a sudden inspiration to write a story, draw a picture, or create something new, you can be sure that you have been visited by a genius moon moth. However, a word of warning: If you are inspired to create something new and do *not* act on it, this moth will not stick around. Instead, it will disappear in search of another human. Often, it takes its inspiration with it!

The genius moon moth is not suitable as a pet—it will disappear if you try to trap it! But if you would like to entice one of these extraordinary animals into your home, there are several ways to pique their interest. Genius moon moths love the written word, and a fresh supply of books at home is an excellent way to make them feel comfortable. They also enjoy the smell of clay, pencil shavings, and paint, and especially love the sound of all types of music. A surefire way to attract a genius moon moth is to keep a journal. They love reading your secrets and doodles, and will flit through the pages when you are not looking! Pay attention, reader, for a Genius moon moth might be on your shoulder right now.

PROMPT

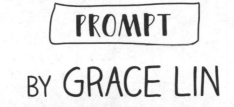

BY GRACE LIN

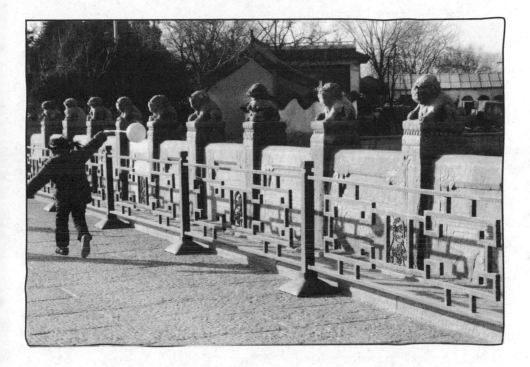

A PUPPY'S BEST FRIEND
BY MARGARITA ENGLE

As soon as I saw the running girl
race so boldly past rows of lions
I knew that I would follow her faithfully,
my paw-beats matched to her arm-swings
and foot-leaps,
together
our six legs
moving
as one.

My tail dances, and my voice
Sings—tall garden walls can't stop us
when we roam far beyond daydreams.

My nose meets her fingers
each greeting
an adventure
treasured.

PROMPT
BY JESS KEATING

The whistle is small enough to fit in your hand. It's silver and worn, with an intricate design carved into the side. A faded yellow note is attached:

Only one creature can hear this whistle.
It will come to you when called.

Use with caution.

You lift the whistle to your mouth, and blow.
What creature answers the call?

RESPONSE

BY PETER BROWN

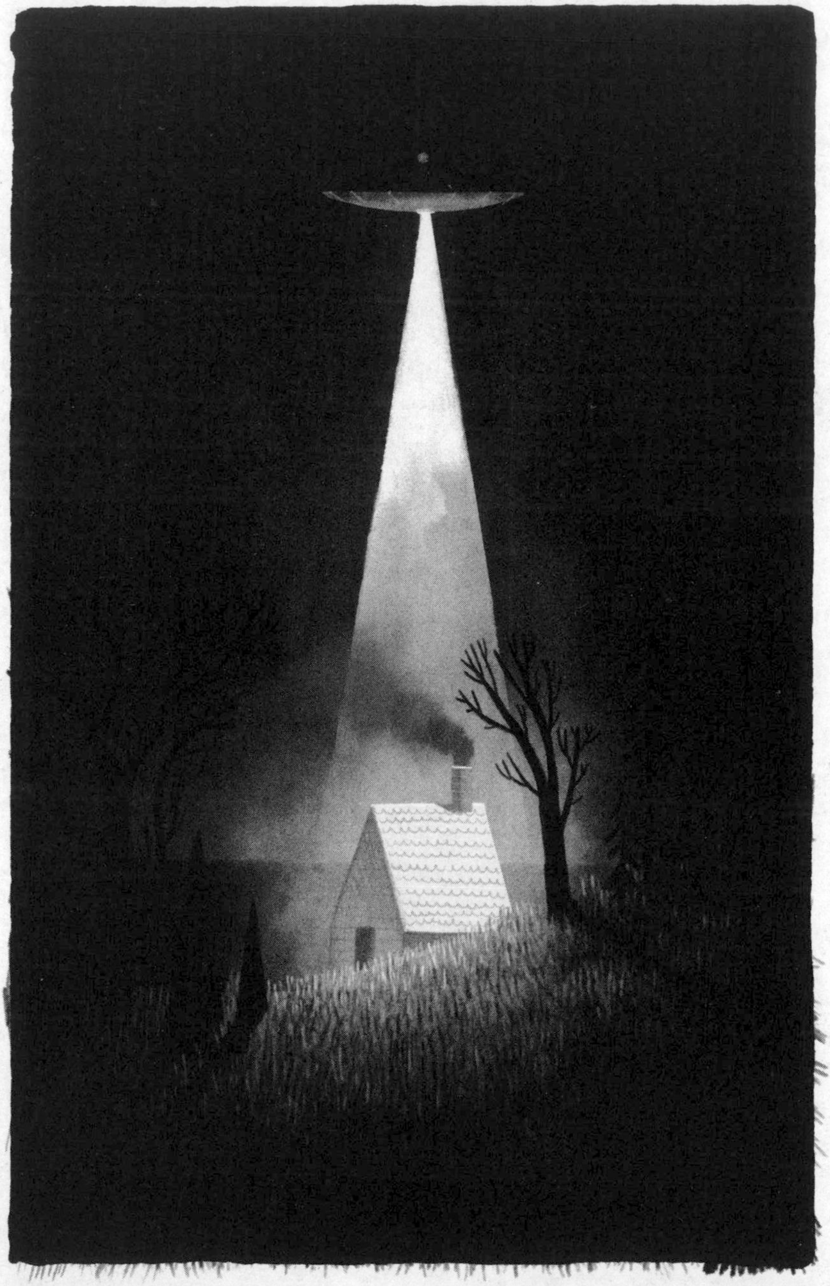

PROMPT

BY COLBY SHARP

I had everything I needed in my pockets: twenty-five dollars, Chap-Stick, a map, and _____.

COME, COME, COME, COME
BY GARY D. SCHMIDT

I had everything I needed in my pockets: twenty-five dollars, Chap-Stick, a map, and the address.

The twenty-five bucks was for bus fare.

The ChapStick is pretty obvious: It was January.

And the map and address are pretty obvious, too. I mean, when you're getting instructions from someone who's dead, you can't exactly count on him for perfect directions. It's more like, "Come to my grave in Fairfield Cemetery, Damian Whitaker. Tell no one. Come by yourself. Come on the first night of the second full moon. And do not listen to the Dead—but listen to the dead! Come, Damian Whitaker, or all who care about you will come to grief."

Yeah. It doesn't even make sense.

And no address.

But you know what it's like to stretch out in bed and hear the same voice every night for seven nights, and to not know whether it's a dream or not?

You know what it's like to open your locker and hear that same voice while everyone else in the seventh-grade hall is walking by and not hearing anything except the PA announcements?

You know what it's like to stand in the shower and suddenly the water goes ice cold and you hear that same voice?

You know what it's like to watch *How to Train Your Dragon* with your brothers and sisters and suddenly you hear that same voice coming from Hiccup's mouth and your dog perks up her ears because she hears it too but your brothers and sisters don't and you know that Fluffy the cocker spaniel doesn't represent a whole lot of comfort?

And you know what it's like to never hear the voice's name—but to somehow know it anyway?

And it's your name? Damian Whitaker.

I failed the algebra quiz that week. Guess why. I forgot the language arts composition on "Did Young Goodman Brown Have a Dream or Not?" I couldn't decline *être* to save my life. And in life sciences, I forgot the three characteristics that have to be true of something to call it alive—probably because I wasn't exactly dealing with those right now.

"Come, Damian Whitaker. Come. Come. Tell no one. Come."

The first night of the second full moon was on a Saturday.

I decided I'd better go to Fairfield Cemetery—and tell no one.

You would, too.

But I'm not a complete jerk. I mean, I wasn't going to show up at midnight when mysterious lights are hovering over gravestones so old that their names are worn away. If you're getting haunted by someone with your own name, you need to go with every advantage you can find—and arriving in daylight is one.

So on Saturday, when I went to buy the ticket for the two o'clock bus, I asked the teller when the bus would get to Fairfield. "The ninth hour," he said.

"What?"

"Three o'clock," he said, "but thou shouldst not go thither," and he pulled the shade down on the ticket window.

Really.

I went to another window and bought the stupid ticket.

So, an hour to get to Fairfield. Maybe a half hour to find Fairfield Cemetery. Plenty of time to get there, do whatever I had to do, and get back home on the five o'clock bus. I'd be home for supper. My parents wouldn't even miss me.

I climbed on board at 2:00. "The Fairfield bus, right?" I asked the driver.

"Truly, it is so, Damian Whitaker," he said, "but thou shouldst not go thither."

I looked at him.

"It's a little creepy, you saying my name like that."

"I know your destinations, Damian Whitaker, but you must stay here, for warm and cozy is the grave," said the bus driver.

"Okay, that was pretty creepy, too," I said.

I got off and looked for another bus. There was one with a not-creepy driver, and I got on. "Is this the bus for Fairfield?"

"As you will." He held his hand out toward the seats. It was kind of pale. "Wheresoever you wish."

So I was wrong about the not-creepy driver. But there wasn't any other bus.

I decided to find a seat near the back. It was colder than it should have been, and the windows in the back were frosted. But it was farther away from you-know-who. I put on some ChapStick.

It took a while for the rest of the passengers to sort of glide on. They all had hoods and long cloaks wrapped tightly around themselves, which I guess they knew they needed, since the bus got colder and colder. Some of the passengers looked my way and nodded. One kid—she also had a long cloak wrapped around her, so completely that I couldn't see anything but her pale face—pointed at me until her mother guided her onto a seat.

Then the bus doors closed, and all sound vanished, and the bus left the station for Fairfield.

I pulled my legs up underneath me—that's how cold it was—and fell asleep, which I hadn't been doing all that much the last week. It's hard to sleep when you've got a voice telling you to come, come, come, come.

I woke up in Fairfield when the bus stopped. One by one, the hooded passengers stood, looked at me, and said, "Go home, Damian Whitaker," until only the bus driver and I were on board.

He watched me come up the aisle.

"Thou shouldst..."

"Thanks," I said, and got off just before he closed the doors.

It was warmer outside the bus, but the wind howled at me along the main street, where one by one I looked into the shops, and it was always the same: In Annabelle's Bakery, the owner looked up from the counter and smiled sadly. In Usher's Shears, the barbers looked up and shook their heads. In the Raven Yarn Store, a customer holding a black ball of yarn looked at me and began to cry.

After three blocks of this, I found a sign pointing to Fairfield Cemetery. I looked at my watch. It had stopped.

I decided I'd better make this really quick.

The road to the cemetery meandered along bluffs beside the ocean, and the wind was really howling here. The gray water broke into white rolls, and the wind was whipping off their froth. Above all that, I could hear the bells in an old stone church along the way begin to toll four o'clock.

"Come," they tolled.

"Come."

"Come."

"Come."

"I'm coming already," I said to no one—or maybe to the guy with the scythe who was walking by the gray water, or maybe to the five guys in dark hoods who danced past me on the road and pointed back toward town.

Whatever.

It was still a long walk to the cemetery—a really long walk—and the road rose higher and higher, and then it suddenly turned away from the gray water and there was Fairfield Cemetery.

The gates were chained closed, so I had to climb over the wrought-iron fence and hope no one saw me. But I dropped to the ground and was finally in the cemetery—and yeah, it was as creepy as you'd expect, with a howling wind and wintry night now starting to come on and dead people all around you.

I followed the row of stones closest to the iron fence, where there were no trees and I could still read the inscriptions in the waning light, except that most of the stones were so decayed I could make out only a few words: "Mortal Remains," "Beloved Relict of," "Heed This, Mortal Man." Stuff like that.

I wasn't even halfway through the cemetery when the sun went down and the darkness came on and the air went still and the waves down below the bluff went quiet. I knelt down by a stone and couldn't see anything.

But in all that quiet, I could hear this: "Come, Damian Whitaker. Come. Come. Come."

When I stood up, I could see him, slouching by a crypt.

Of course he was slouching by a crypt.

And of course the door to the crypt was open.

And of course it looked like darkness was coming out of it.

"Come. Come. Come. Come."

I came.

In the darkness, I could barely make out the marble columns, the granite sides, the tiny windows with fancy ironwork over them, the stone angel—or maybe it was a gargoyle—looking down.

"Come. Come. Come. Come."

It was suddenly really cold.

I put on some ChapStick again. It couldn't hurt.

And then I was there, and the second full moon came up, and the guy limped away from the door of the crypt, and I could see him.

It was me.

I think.

Same clothes and everything, except his were all burned and in pieces. His hands were shriveled and burned, and his chest, and his face was dark with smoke and ash. He dragged a ruined leg behind him.

But it was me.

And then he held out his hand—his burned hand—and I knew what he wanted.

I gave him the ChapStick.

"Now," he said—and his voice was dry like late October leaves— "go home, Damian Whitaker. Now you're safe." He turned and limped into the crypt, and the door closed behind him.

That was it!

That was it?

The moon rose higher, and the cemetery filled with light, and I headed home.

Along the way, I hardly saw anyone. No hooded guys dancing down the street. No guy with the scythe. The bus was empty except for a mother with a couple of kids. No creepy bus driver. Hardly anyone all the way home.

Until I got close.

When I turned the corner to my street, a horrible glow wavered from our yard where our house had once stood. The whole house had crashed in, and the beams were still flickering red, and smoke filled the air. Our neighbors stood across the street, holding my mother and father, and my brothers and sisters, who were all crying, until suddenly Fluffy saw me and started barking her "Where have you been?" bark and everyone turned and someone shouted and they all saw me and ran toward me and my mother and father and brothers and sisters all shouted "Where have you been?" and "You're alive!" and "We thought you were in the house!"

And I saw, on the other side of the crowd, the guy with the scythe, shaking his head, then fading into the dark night.

PROMPT

BY JARRETT J. KROSOCZKA

HIDE-AND-SEEK
BY COLBY SHARP

"Kyle! It's time to wake up," my mom calls to me. "You don't want to be late."

"Five more minutes," I say as I roll onto my back. I've been awake for at least an hour, but I'm not ready to get out of bed. I'm not a fan of all that comes with the last day of school: cleaning out desks, sentimental teachers, and girls crying over how much they are going to miss their teacher. Blah.

The minute I start walking downstairs, my mom says, "Good morning, Sunshine!" I love my mom, but I don't understand how she can always be so happy and so positive before the sun comes up.

"Hi, Mom," I say. I give her a hug, and then sit down at the counter. I'm not really a hugger, but my mom likes it. I gave up fighting the morning hug last year. It's easier to just do it and get it over with.

"It seems like it was just yesterday that I was carrying you kicking and screaming to your first day of kindergarten." She waits for me to say something. I instead fill my mouth with a giant spoonful of cereal, hoping she'll take that as a sign I'd rather not talk. "You only have minutes before you have to meet Kendall," she says as she begins to load the dishwasher. Watching my mom move so fast this early in the morning makes me want to take a nap.

Kendall and I have walked to school together almost every day since she moved here at the end of first grade. She is my best friend. We are JUST friends. A bunch of kids in class started teasing us about being boyfriend and girlfriend a few months ago. We tried ignoring them, but that didn't help, so now we just tolerate it. I don't understand why people think that just because we are friends, we are madly in love with each other. Sigh.

"Thanks for breakfast, Mom. I'm going to go pick up Kendall. I'll see you after school," I say as I place my empty bowl of cereal in the dishwasher.

My mom grabs me by the shoulders, looks into my eyes (I can tell she is trying not to cry), and says, "Kyle, I am so proud of you. I can't believe that when you come home today, you will be a middle schooler. You'll be so grown up! Things are never going to be the same." An annoying tear sneaks out of her eye as she kisses my forehead and opens the door.

Kendall's dad is waiting with her at the end of their driveway. "Hey, Kendall. Hi, Mr. Greenway," I say.

"I just can't believe you guys are almost middle schoolers. You do know that things will never be the same after today, don't you?" Why do people keep saying that?

"We're playing hide-and-seek after school, so I'll be home late," Kendall says.

How could I forget the end-of-the-year game of hide-and-seek? We started this tradition in second grade. Our school is located right next to a forest, and all the neighborhood kids in our grade rush there after the last day of school to play. The winner gets bragging rights for the entire year. I guess this means that the winner of today's game gets bragging rights for the rest of eternity. Winning would be pretty cool, but what I love most about the game is getting to spend a few more minutes with my friends before getting home to my mom and all the big plans I'm sure she is going to have to fill up my summer.

"Have a great day, you two," Mr. Greenway says as he heads to his car.

215

"Kyle! This is it. We are almost middle schoolers. Can you believe it?" Kendall says, hopping down the sidewalk. Kendall is the only person I know who has more energy than my mom. She doesn't wait for me to answer. "I can't wait to play hide-and-seek. I think I've found the best hiding spot this year. You know that giant oak tree that was struck by lightning? I'm going to hide under it. Nobody will EVER find me." She looks at me sort of funny. She smiles kind of funny. I've never seen that smile from her before. Her mouth looks like her everyday smile, but something is up with her eyes, like she's trying to study my pupils. Weird. And she really shouldn't be telling me her hiding spot!

"Today is going to be great, Kendall," I say. "Do you think it's odd that everyone keeps telling us that nothing is going to be the same after today? First my mom. Now your dad. South Parma Middle School is less than a mile from the Village Elementary School. How different could things really be?"

"I just so happen to agree with them, Kyle. Middle school is a big deal." Kendall smiles again, this time with her everyday smile, and we turn the corner and head toward the Village Elementary School for the very last time as elementary students.

◆

Tick. Tock. Tick. Tock. Two minutes to go. Summer vacation is so close. This is the last time I'll ever have to sit on this hard gym floor and listen to Principal Gilpin. "I'm so proud of all of you. I can remember when you were all little five-year-old kindergartners walking into this school for the very first time. When you walk out of here today, things will never be the same. I can't wait to see the people you all become. Class dismissed!"

The gym erupts, and we all spring to our feet. I give my friends quick high fives and head to the front door to meet Kendall. I have to maneuver my way through the crowds of parents and crying first graders. Kendall pops into view as she weaves her way around a second-grade teacher locked in a hug with a gaggle of students. Our eyes meet.

She is so happy as she skips toward me. I throw my hand up for a high five like I gave my other friends. She surprises me when she comes in for the hug. I stumble back a bit and just barely avoid falling on a little kid. "We did it!" I shout.

"We sure did," she says, with that odd smile she gave me earlier today. "Are you ready to play hide-and-seek?" I nod, and we dart to the woods.

My classmates and I make the trek across the playground to the woods. It looks like everyone is the happiest they have ever been in their lives. Even the kids with puffy crying eyes look like they are happy.

"Hey, guys! Everyone come on over to the big maple, and let's get this game started," Jackson says. Nobody in the world loves hide-and-seek as much as Jackson. He has taken it upon himself to be the leader of our annual game. "Today marks the last game of hide-and-seek of our elementary lives. I've created a trophy for today's winner."

"That's awesome, Jackson," someone says. It *is* pretty awesome. The trophy appears to be made out of Popsicle sticks. It stands about three feet tall, and it is spray-painted orange.

"Thank you. I call it the Leaning Tower of Hide-and-Seek. The winner of today's game gets to keep her *forever*. The rules for today's game are simple. When you're found, you're out. The last person to be found is the winner. The hide-and-seek champion!" Everyone is getting super excited. "I've cut these straws different links. Each of you will grab a straw out of my hands. The person with the shortest straw is it."

Kendall jumps to Jackson and grabs a straw. We all inch closer and tentatively grab a straw. Nobody wants to be "it," because everyone wants to win the trophy. I grab my straw with my eyes closed. I open them and see a teeny-tiny straw and a big dorky smirk on Jackson's face. "Kyle is it," he shouts. Then he whispers to me, "No cheating. You better not let your girlfriend win."

"She's not my girlfriend," I say back. He raises his eyebrows like a jerk, and then starts running.

Here we go. I look around and then say, "I'm counting to fifty, and then I'm going to find all you suckers in less than two minutes. "One...two...three..." I can hear everyone scurry away. As much as I

217

love winning, I'm kind of glad that I'm it. It will be cool to see where everyone is hiding, and I never win anyway.

◈

I open my eyes and look around in a full circle. The woods aren't that big. I can still sort of see the school through the trees, and I can see the cornfield at the opposite end of the woods. It feels weird to stand alone in the middle of the woods knowing that a bunch of my friends are less than one hundred yards away.

"Forty-eight, forty-nine, and fifty. Ready or not, here I come!" I shout at the top of my lungs. I can't see any of them, but I feel all their eyes on me. I decide to head toward the cornfield. That's where I'd hide if I wasn't it. Within two steps of my journey, I hear a giggle. I freeze, then turn my head toward the noise. Baxter, who was my third-grade math partner, is about five feet off the ground in a tree. "Good try, Baxter, but I found you. No trophy for you," I say. "Have a good summer."

"FREEDOM!" Baxter yells as he climbs out of the tree. He dashes out of the woods, and his summer vacation begins.

Soon I am picking kids off left and right. Jill and Jane were hiding together in a bush. Roger wasn't hiding at all. He was just walking around the edge of the woods near the cornfield. The twins, Shelby and Lindsay, managed to climb about thirty feet up in a maple tree.

Eventually, I'm down to only two people hiding: Kendall and Jackson. I know that if I find Jackson first, I'll spend the summer trying to convince him this wasn't a conspiracy. He'll refuse to accept the fact that Kendall isn't my girlfriend. Basically, he'll be a thorn in my side the entire summer. If I find Kendall first, she'll laugh and we'll go back to her house and have some fruit snacks and orange juice. I've got to find Kendall.

I head to the tree Kendall was telling me about earlier in the day. It isn't hard to find. The tree was the biggest one in the forest, so it caused quite a bit of destruction when it fell down during a giant storm back in the spring. When I get to the tree, everything is silent. It is almost creepy. I climb up onto the fallen-over trunk and start walking across it like it is the world's longest balance beam. "I know you're here, Kendall," I say to the woods. "You can't fool me. I know you way too well." I jump off my wooden balance beam and begin searching under the trunk. Nothing. I look everywhere around that dumb tree, and Kendall is nowhere to be found. She tricked me.

Finding Kendall shouldn't be this hard. Where the heck is she? I'm about to head to a different part of the woods when I feel like something is behind me. I nervously turn around. Kendall is standing right in front of me. She's wearing that funny smile that she had on her face when I picked her up this morning. She tucks a loose strand of hair behind her ear. Oh. My. Goodness. She is beautiful. Wait. I don't think girls are beautiful. I try to snap out of it and yell, "I found you!" but nothing comes out. Instead, my body leans in, and I kiss her.

ON. THE. LIPS.

Kendall smiles. A big smile. I can't move. Kendall breaks the silence by shouting, "Hey, Jackson! Kyle found me. You win." Kendall starts running home. I have no idea what to do. I can't move. Kendall turns and waves me toward her. My body unfreezes, and I follow her out of the woods.

Things are never going to be the same.

PROMPTS FOR YOU

NOW IT'S YOUR TURN. PICK A PROMPT
AND MAKE SOMETHING AWESOME!

SHERMAN ALEXIE

"I am stuck! I am stuck! I am the worst writer in the history of the world! What do I do? Where do I begin?" Relax—just randomly grab two books. Open the first book to any page and use the first sentence on that page as the first sentence of your story. Then open the second book to any page and use the first sentence on that page as the last sentence of your story. Now, start writing to make those sentences fit together.

TOM ANGLEBERGER

This creative exercise costs two dollars, plus tax. I call it the Circle of Life.

Go to the dollar store.

Buy two toys. The toys must be dolls, action figures, animals, etc.... things that have bodies and heads.

Return to the privacy of your own home and CAREFULLY behead both toys. Sometimes the heads will pop right off; other times, force will be required. (Don't hurt yourself! Remember, a handsaw may be safer than a knife for this job. Ask an adult to help.)

Now swap the heads and glue them back on.

You've created two new creatures! Now make them hug! They are best friends!

Submit a black-and-white photograph of these new friends with a caption to illuminate the image.

JESSIXA BAGLEY

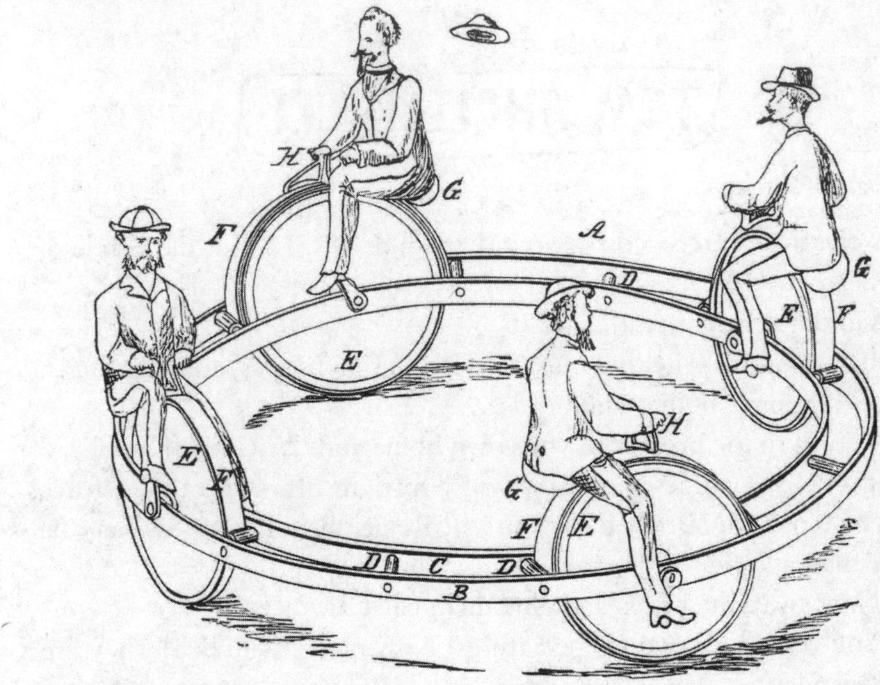
H
G
F
A
D
G
E
F
E
H
E
F
G
F
E
D
C
D
B

Sturdy & Young, of Providence, R. I. Velocipede. No. 89,700. Patented May 4, 1869.

TRACEY BAPTISTE

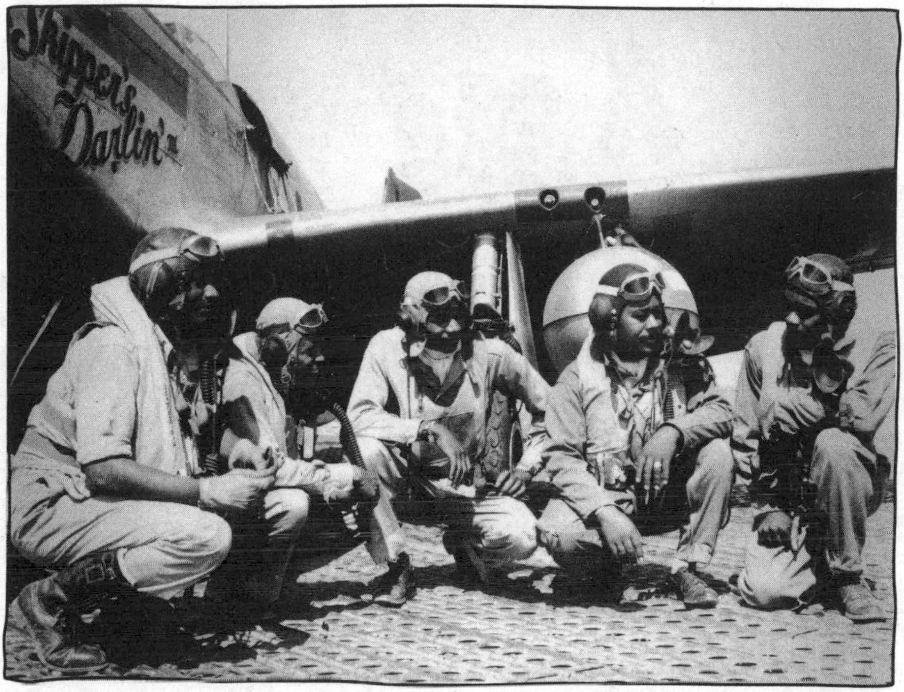
Skipper's Darlin'

SOPHIE BLACKALL

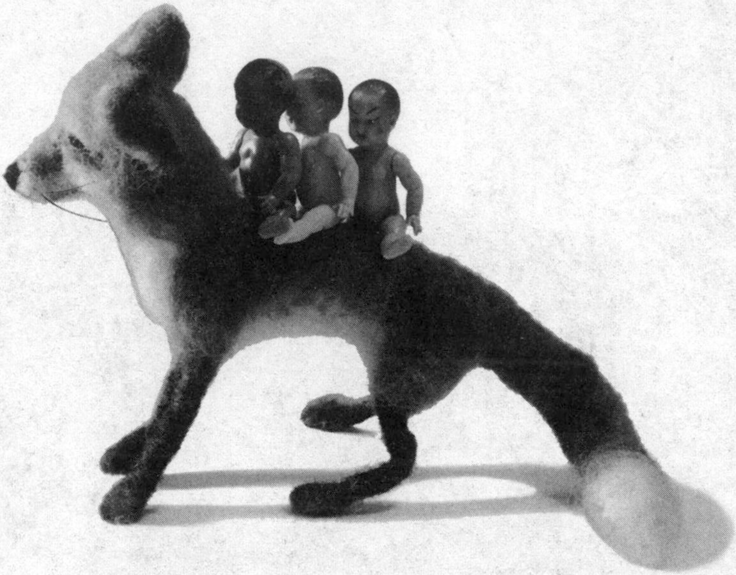

LISA BROWN

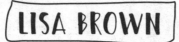

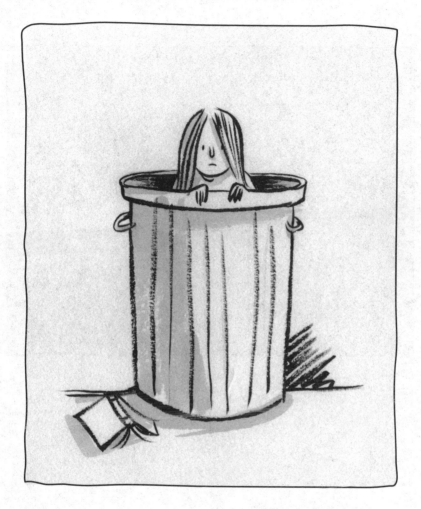

PETER BROWN

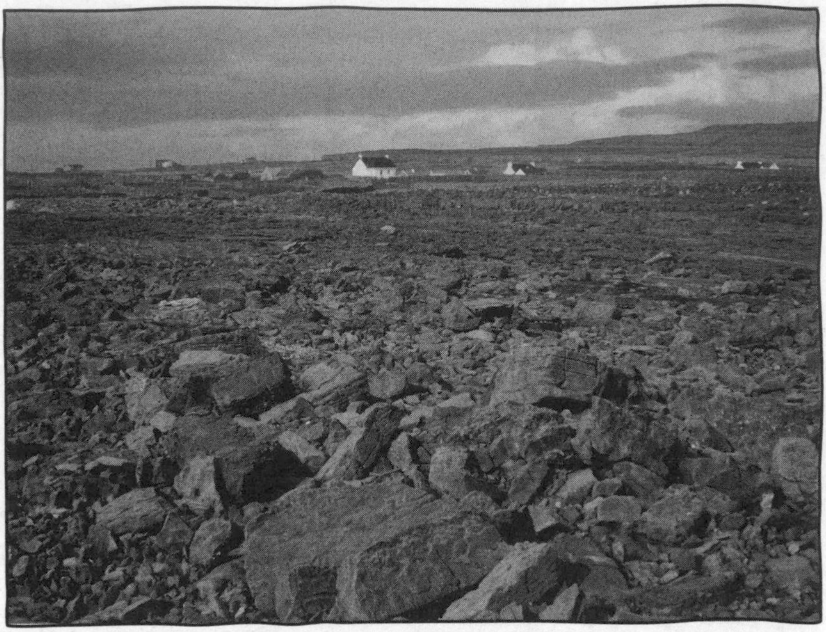

LAUREN CASTILLO

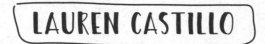

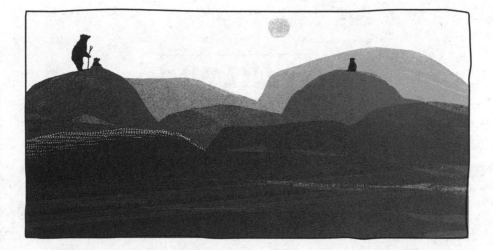

KATE DICAMILLO

Find someone who is over eighty years old and ask them to tell you their clearest memory from childhood. Retell this memory in the third person and add one fictional flourish.

MARGARITA ENGLE

hummingbird frenzy
each whir of wings helps me feel
earthbound and dazzled

DEBORAH FREEDMAN

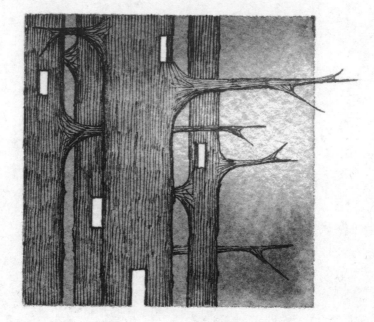

ADAM GIDWITZ

End a story with this sentence: "And when the dragon began to cry, I knew that I had won."

CHRIS GRABENSTEIN

Create a five-hundred-word story inspired by this photo. The last sentence has to be: "By the end of the week," said the leopard, "I taught her how to wear a funny hat and wave a baton!"

Make sure everything builds to that last line—even if you have to think and write backwards for your first draft.

JENNIFER L. HOLM

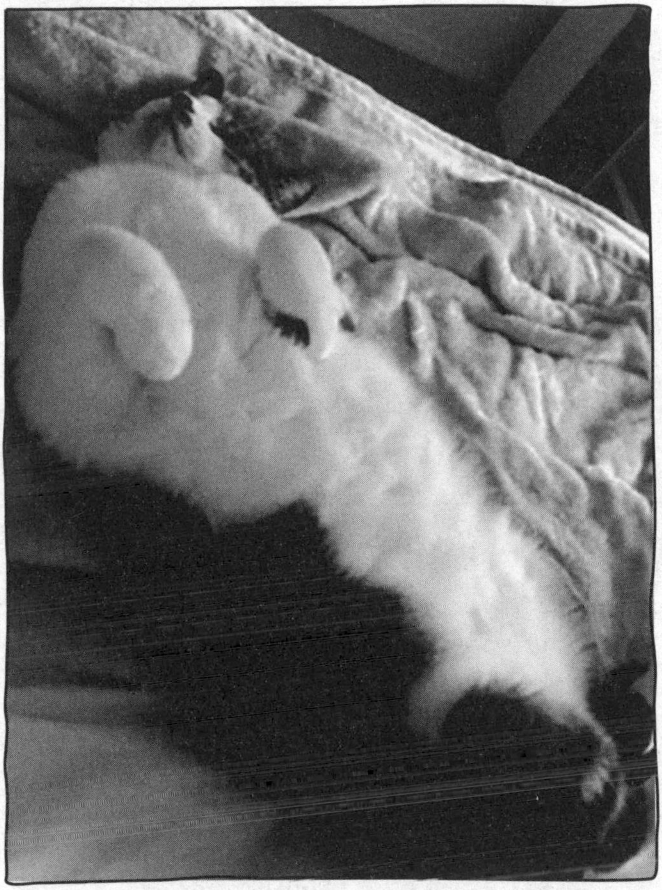

VICTORIA JAMIESON

With your eyes closed, run your finger along each column of text, picking out one word from each column. When you're done, you should have one word from column A, one from column B, and one from column C.

COLUMN A	COLUMN B	COLUMN C
bunny	grumpy	dancer
robot	bossy	soccer player
sloth	loud	new kid
hedgehog	shy	cousin
bear	nervous	spelling bee competitor

Those three words make up your new character!

TRAVIS JONKER

An (Unfinished) Argument with Myself: Who Will Win?

Me: *Sigh*.

Me: Why do you keep doing that?

Me: I can't help it.

Me: You *can* help it! It's weird. And rude.

Me: It's also fun!

Me: IT IS NOT SUPPOSED TO BE FUN!

Me:

Me:

Me:

Me:

Me:

JESS KEATING

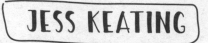

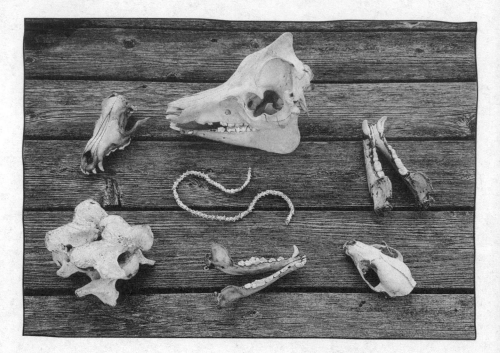

LAURIE KELLER

Did you know that there are lots of words hidden within other words? Choose a word (or words) that you like and mix up its letters to find words to use in a story—the more letters in your word, the better (there are lots of word scramble generators online to help you). For instance, HIBERNATE contains the words BEAR, TREE, BARN, TRAIN, TRIBE, BERET, BATH, TEEN, HEART, EARTH, and HAIRNET, to name a few. TRAMPOLINE contains PLANE, ANTLER, PILOT, OPERA, PIRATE, LEMON, LIMP, PEARL, EMAIL, PAINTER, and TOENAIL. Some words may seem unrelated to one another, but using them together could give you a zany, fun idea that you wouldn't have thought of otherwise!

A variation would be to pick three or four of the words to create a wacky title, then write a story based on it.

JARRETT J. KROSOCZKA

ZERO ADJUSTMENT
ENERAL ELECTRIC
MADE IN U.S.A

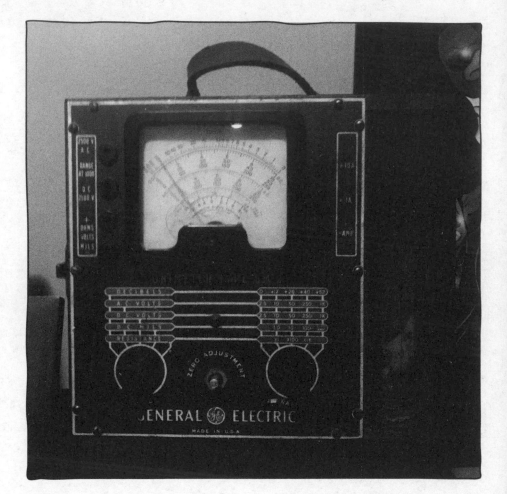

KIRBY LARSON

It's a school morning and you come downstairs for breakfast as usual but to a quiet kitchen, which is definitely not usual. You look around for your family and spy a letter leaning against the box of Cheerios. You open it, and this is what you read:

MINH LÊ

Speech! Speech! Speech!

What would it be like if Matilda gave a graduation speech? Or if Nana from *Last Stop on Market Street* gave a TED Talk? How would Max from *Where the Wild Things Are* address his school if he were running for student body president?

Instructions: Write a short speech from the perspective of one of your favorite fictional characters. It could be anything: a graduation speech, a wedding toast, a pep talk before the World Championships of Thumb Wrestling...totally up to you!

You have just met a girl named Hanrui. In Chinese, her name means "a bud just ready to bloom."

KATE MESSNER

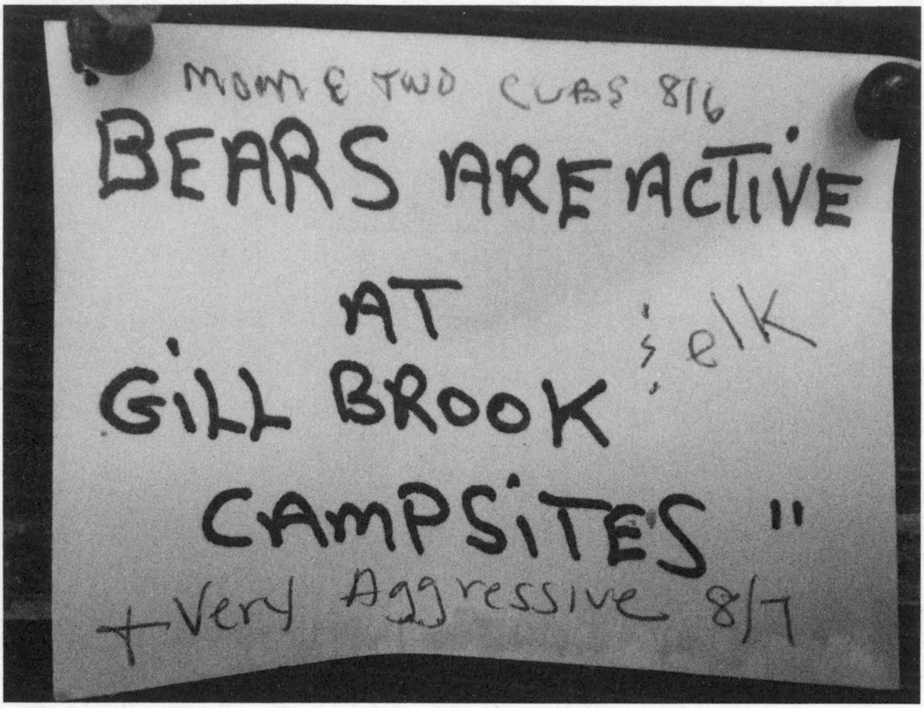
MOM & TWO CUBS 8/6
BEARS ARE ACTIVE
AT
GILL BROOK
CAMPSITES
& elk
+ Very Aggressive 8/7

DANIEL NAYERI

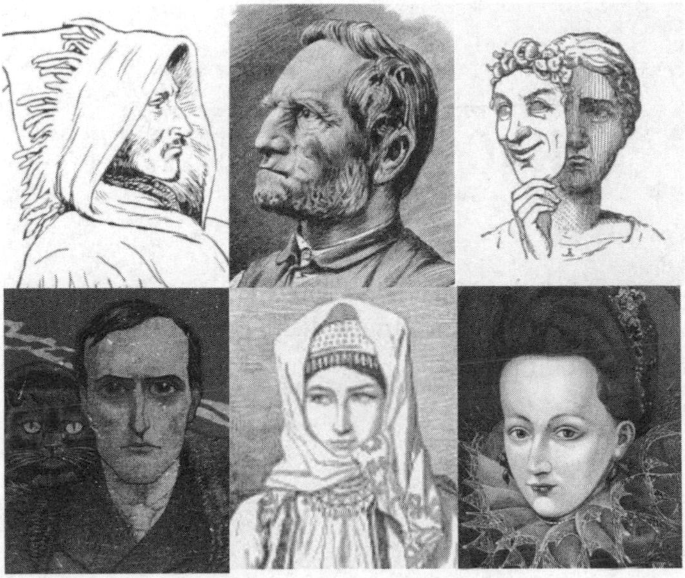

These are the weirdos I met at summer camp. By the end of the summer, one of them would become my best friend. One my mortal enemy. One would go home early. And one would wind up dead.

NAOMI SHIHAB NYE

Write a list of ten things you are NOT (not an astronaut, a perfectionist, a wool spinner, a butterfly, a name-caller). Then pick your favorite lines and develop, or embellish, them, adding metaphors, more description, whatever you like.

DEBBIE RIDPATH OHI

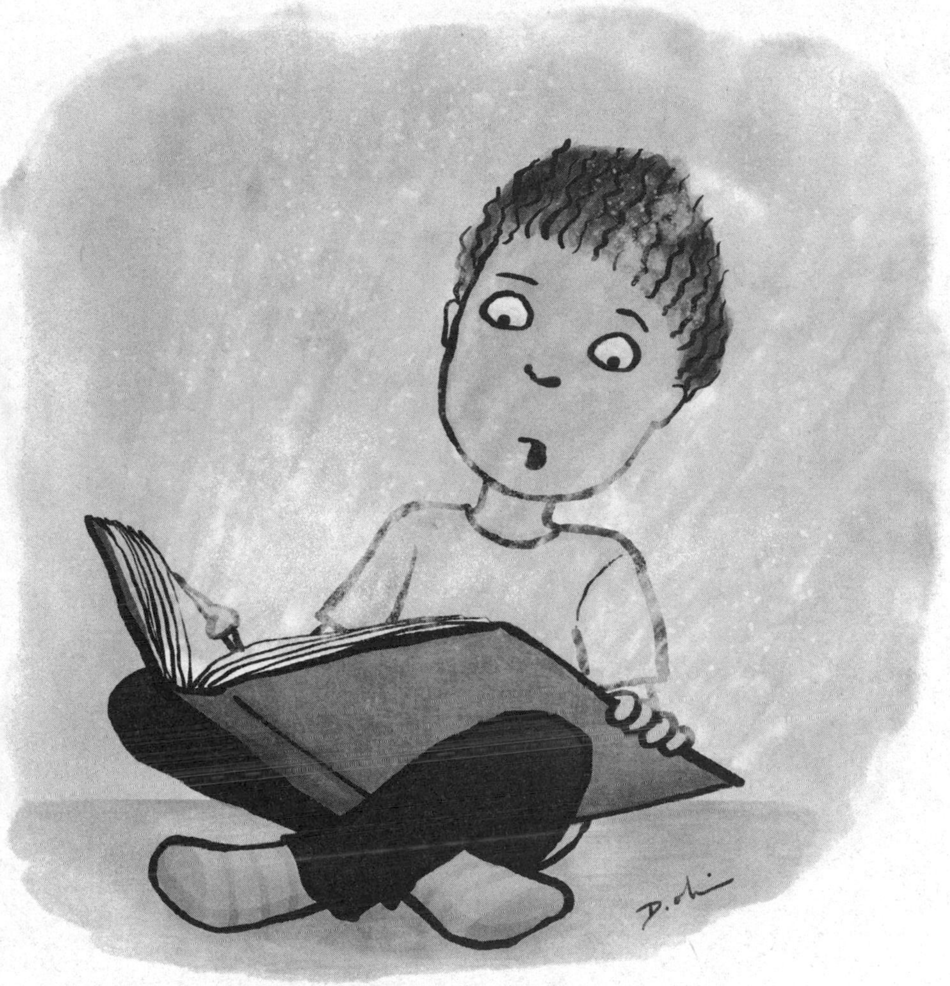
D. Ohi

R. J. PALACIO

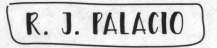

I bark, therefore I am.

LINDA SUE PARK

My friend didn't steal money from my sister.
My friend didn't *steal* money from my sister.
My friend didn't steal *money* from my sister.

DAV PILKEY

PLEASE DO NOT CHANGE THE LETTERS AROUND ON THIS SIGN!

PROMPT: Rearrange the letters on this sign to spell out
something funny or poetic. You don't have to use all the letters,
but you MUST use only the letters on the sign.
Here's an example: *Underpants taste so good in a tree!*

ANDREA DAVIS PINKNEY

Another morning of fishing into my purse to find some lipstick. I dug deep, felt the jingle of my keys, the hard plastic of my sunglasses, the crinkly foil of a discarded chewing gum wrapper. My hand then touched something warm, soft, furry—unfamiliar, but friendly, and definitely alive.

JEWELL PARKER RHODES

Describe a room you could imagine happily living in, without ever leaving, for the rest of your life.

DAN SANTAT

GARY SCHMIDT

Since they'd converted the basement to a bedroom, Ethan had put his stuff exactly where he wanted it. Now he could tape *his* posters up, leave *his* clothes where he wanted to, and stack *his* hockey stuff in *his* corner without Travis messing around with everything.

But definitely he missed windows. It was hard to wake up without the sun.

That's what his mother had gotten him the alarm clock for—and it was ringing now, telling him he had to get up for hockey practice. On a Saturday. Which stunk.

He shut off the alarm clock. He dressed, his eyes closed. He stuffed his hockey stuff in his bag and slung it over his shoulder. He grabbed his stick and skates, climbed the stairs, and walked into the kitchen.

"Morning, Ethan," said his father.

"You'd better hurry," said his mother.

Ethan looked out the window. It was still pitch black.

"Did I get up too early?" he said.

His mother looked at her watch. "We leave in ten minutes," she said.

"The sun isn't even up yet," Ethan said.

His parents looked at him. "Son? You mean Travis?"

Ethan dropped his bag and skates and leaned his stick against the refrigerator. He opened the cupboard to look for Cheerios.

"The sun. You know: that huge ball of fire that Earth orbits. The one that gives light and warmth to our planet so that life can exist. That sun."

He sorted through the cereals. No Cheerios.

When he turned back, his parents were still looking at him. "What are you talking about?" said his father.

Ethan looked at the clock on the stove. 9:05. He looked outside. Pitch black.

"What's going on?" he said.

"Eight minutes," said his mother.

JOHN SCHU

"Ezra, your word is *genuine*," Ms. Pollard calls out.

"Can you use it in a sentence, please?" I ask, sweating.

COLBY SHARP

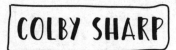

It was all my fault.

BOB SHEA

New hat, shiny shoes, and a fresh, new, positive attitude.
"Let's see them call me a pig now!" said Pig.

LIESL SHURTLIFF

You are walking along the beach when you come upon a small box, no bigger than a shoe box, half-buried in the sand. It's covered in barnacles and seaweed, but the lock is broken. You open it up and...

LEMONY SNICKET

I learned two words yesterday: "frog-march," which is to force someone to walk while holding their arms behind them, and "rantipole," which is a rough and reckless person. Surely they should be used in something.

LAUREL SNYDER

You can create anything you want, anything at all! The only catch is that you need to mention:

1. A type of fruit
2. An animal
3. Something musical
4. Some sort of machine
5. A historical figure

Now, go crazy, but be sure to include them all.

JAVAKA STEPTOE

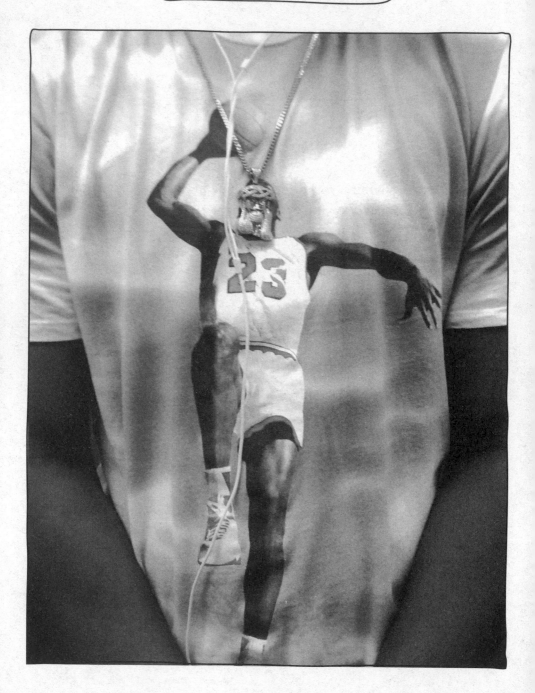

MARIKO TAMAKI

Somewhere between 11:36 PM and 11:59 PM, New Year's Eve.

LINDA URBAN

The only thing she left behind, the only clue to what she was thinking, was her to-do list. Most of it had been checked off, but three items remained undone.

FRANK VIVA

"Atop her bushy red hair she wore a box-shaped paper hat made from folded newsprint—the kind worn by pressmen in the first half of the last century."

KAT YEH

You sit down in class and realize you've forgotten to bring a pen. There's one lying on the desk, so you pick it up and doodle a quick stick figure to see if it has any ink.

It does. But the figure you just drew looks up at you and then jumps off the page.

CONTRIBUTOR BIOGRAPHIES

SHERMAN ALEXIE is a poet, short story writer, novelist, screenwriter, and performer. He has published twenty-six books including his upcoming memoir, *You Don't Have to Say You Love Me*.

A Spokane/Coeur d'Alene Indian, Alexie grew up in Wellpinit, Washington, on the Spokane Indian Reservation. Alexie has been an urban Indian since 1994 and lives in Seattle with his family.

TOM ANGLEBERGER is the author of the Origami Yoda, Inspector Flytrap, Qwikpick, and Rocket and Groot series. Serieses? Seriess? Definitely not series's, right? Angleberger thinks learning is important and often wishes he'd done more of it.

JESSIXA BAGLEY is a Seattle-based picture book author and illustrator. Jessixa loves hamburgers and drawing anthropomorphic woodland critters—something that is inspired by her growing up in the Pacific Northwest. She invited some of her forest animals into the woods of the Creativity Project, and they got lost.

TRACEY BAPTISTE, M.Ed., is the author of several books for children, including *Rise of the Jumbies*, *The Jumbies*, and *The Totally Gross History of Ancient Egypt*. She volunteers with We Need Diverse Books and the Brown Bookshelf, and she teaches in Lesley University's creative writing MFA program.

SOPHIE BLACKALL has illustrated more than thirty-five books for children, including the Ivy and Bean series and, most recently, *The Witches of Benevento*. She won the 2016 Caldecott Medal for *Finding Winnie* and has received four *New York Times* Best Illustrated Awards. Originally from Australia, she lives in Brooklyn and shares a studio in an old factory with four other illustrators and teetering piles of books.

LISA BROWN is an illustrator, author, and cartoonist. Her books include *The Airport Book*, *Mummy Cat* by Marcus Ewert, *Emily's Blue Period* by Cathleen Daly, and *Goldfish Ghost* by Lemony Snicket, to whom she is allegedly married. She lives in San Francisco and is fairly quiet.

PETER BROWN lives in Brooklyn, where he writes and illustrates books for children. His picture books include *The Curious Garden*, *Children Make Terrible Pets*, *Creepy Carrots!*, and *Mr. Tiger Goes Wild*. His first novel for children is entitled *The Wild Robot*. Peter's website is peterbrownstudio.com.

LAUREN CASTILLO is the creator of many books for young children, including the Caldecott Honor–winning *Nana in the City* and *The Troublemaker*, as well as the illustrator of *Twenty Yawns*, written by Jane Smiley, and *Yard Sale*, written by Eve Bunting. She currently draws and dreams in Pennsylvania.

KATE DICAMILLO is one of America's most beloved storytellers. She was the National Ambassador for Young People's Literature and is a two-time Newbery Medalist. Born in Philadelphia, she grew up in Florida and now lives in Minneapolis, where she faithfully writes two pages a day, five days a week.

MARGARITA ENGLE is the Cuban American author of verse novels such as *The Surrender Tree*, a Newbery Honor winner, and *The Lightning Dreamer*, a PEN USA Award winner. Her verse memoir, *Enchanted Air*, received a Pura Belpré Medal and many other awards. *Drum Dream Girl* received the Charlotte Zolotow Award for best picture book text. Her next verse novel is *Forest World*, forthcoming from Atheneum.

DEBORAH FREEDMAN was an architect once upon a time, but now she loves to build worlds in picture books. She is the author and illustrator of, most recently, *Shy* and *This House, Once*. She lives in Connecticut, in a colorful house full of books, art, and stuffed animals. Learn more about Deborah at deborahfreedman.net.

ADAM GIDWITZ is the bestselling author of *The Inquisitor's Tale*, as well as *A Tale Dark and Grimm* and its companions.

CHRIS GRABENSTEIN is the number one *New York Times* bestselling author of the Lemoncello Library series, the Wonderland series, and *The Island of Dr. Libris*. He is also the coauthor of several fun page-turners with James Patterson: *I Funny*, *Treasure Hunters*, *House of Robots*, *Jacky Ha-Ha*, and *Word of Mouse*.

JENNIFER L. HOLM is a *New York Times* bestselling children's author and the recipient of three Newbery Honors. Jennifer collaborates with her brother, Matthew Holm, on three graphic novel series—the Eisner Award–winning Babymouse series, the bestselling Squish series, and the My First Comics series. Her new book is *Babymouse: Lights, Camera, Middle School*.

VICTORIA JAMIESON is an author and illustrator of books for children. Her graphic novel *Roller Girl* was awarded a 2016 Newbery Honor. She is also a professor of illustration at Pacific Northwest College of Art, where she teaches both undergraduate and continuing education courses. She lives with her family in Portland, Oregon.

How Well Do You Know **TRAVIS JONKER**?
    Travis is a _____ (please select A or B).
    A. husband, father, Michigander, elementary school librarian, writer, podcaster, children's literature and peanut butter enthusiast.
    B. horse trainer and sometime prank player.
    Answer: B.

JESS KEATING is an author, zoologist, and Plasticine illustrator. Her award-winning books include the hilarious My Life Is a Zoo trilogy, The World of Weird Animals series, and *Shark Lady*. She loves helping young writers and artists find their creative voices. Visit her online at jesskeating.com or on Twitter @Jess_Keating.

LAURIE KELLER is the author and illustrator of *The Scrambled States of America*, *Do unto Otters*, *Arnie the Doughnut*, and *We Are Growing!*, winner of the 2017 Theodor Seuss Geisel Award. In her spare time she travels, hikes, plays the banjo, and rescues ladybugs from the waves in Lake Michigan.

JARRETT J. KROSOCZKA writes and illustrates picture books (*Punk Farm*, *Baghead*), graphic novels (the Lunch Lady series), and middle grade novels (the Platypus Police Squad series). He has also delivered two TED Talks, which have collectively accrued more than two million views online. Krosoczka has been featured on NPR and can be heard weekly on SiriusXM's Kids Place Live.

KIRBY LARSON went from history-phobe to history fanatic while writing the Newbery Honor Book *Hattie Big Sky*. Other titles include *The Friendship Doll*, *Duke*, *Dash*, *Liberty*, and the Audacity Jones series. Kirby and her husband share a home in Washington State with Winston the Wonder Dog. She owns a tiara and is not afraid to use it. Follow on Twitter @kirbylarson. Learn more about all her books: kirbylarson.com.

MINH LÊ is the author of *Let Me Finish!*, illustrated by Isabel Roxas, and *Drawn Together*, illustrated by Dan Santat (both published by Disney-Hyperion). He also writes about children's literature for a number of publications, including the *New York Times*, the *Horn Book*, NPR, and *HuffPost*.

GRACE LIN is a *New York Times* bestselling author-illustrator of picture books, early readers, and novels. A Newbery and Geisel Honor winner, as well as a National Book Award Finalist, Grace was recognized by the White House as a Champion of Change for Asian American and Pacific Islander Art and Storytelling in 2016.

KATE MESSNER is passionately curious and writes books that encourage kids to wonder, too. Her award-winning titles include *Capture the Flag*, *All the Answers*, *The Seventh Wish*, and the popular Ranger in Time chapter book series. Kate lives on Lake Champlain with her family. She's on Twitter @KateMessner.

DANIEL NAYERI is the director of children's books at Workman Publishing. He was born in Iran and came to the United States as a refugee when he was eight. He is the author of *The Most Dangerous Book*, *How to Tell a Story*, and *Straw House, Wood House, Brick House, Blow*.

NAOMI SHIHAB NYE lives with her photographer husband in an old house with high ceilings a block from the San Antonio River. They have a fluffy cat, Soxy Durango, and a sixteen-year-old turtle named Neon, who lives outside in the yard and sleeps in a red tub of water. For fifteen years they thought Neon was a boy; then she laid six eggs. Naomi likes to write by hand in little notebooks and trim the vines.

DEBBIE RIDPATH OHI is the author and illustrator of *Where Are My Books?* and *Sam & Eva* (Simon & Schuster). Her illustrations also appear in children's books such as the *New York Times* Notable Children's Book *I'm Bored* by Michael Ian Black and Atheneum's reissued Judy Blume titles. Find out more and visit Debbie at DebbieOhi.com, on Twitter @inkyelbows, and on Instagram @inkygirl.

R. J. PALACIO was born and raised in New York City. Before writing *Wonder*, she was a graphic designer and art director. R.J. is also the author of *Auggie & Me: Three Wonder Stories*, *365 Days of Wonder: Mr. Browne's Book of Precepts*, and *We're All Wonders*. Learn more at rjpalacio.com or on Twitter @RJPalacio.

LINDA SUE PARK is the author of *A Single Shard* (the 2002 Newbery Medal winner), *A Long Walk to Water*, the Wing & Claw series, and many other books. Her first love as a young writer was poetry, and although today she is best known for her fiction, she still loves reading and writing poems.

DAV PILKEY is the author and illustrator of more than sixty books for children, including the Captain Underpants series, and the new graphic novel series Dog Man. His 1996 book *The Paperboy* was named a Caldecott Honor Book.

ANDREA DAVIS PINKNEY is the *New York Times* bestselling and award-winning author of numerous books for children and young adults, including picture books, novels, works of poetry, historical fiction, and nonfiction. She lives in New York City with her husband and frequent collaborator, illustrator Brian Pinkney.

JEWELL PARKER RHODES is the author of the children's books *Ghost Boys, Towers Falling,* and the Louisiana Girls trilogy, as well as six adult novels, two writing guides, and a memoir. She lives in San Jose with her husband and dogs.

DAN SANTAT is the author-illustrator of many books, including *Are We There Yet?*, *Sidekicks*, and *The Cookie Fiasco*. He is also the recipient of the 2015 Randolph Caldecott Medal for his book *The Adventures of Beekle: The Unimaginary Friend*. He lives in Los Angeles with his wife and two kids. Visit him at dantat.com.

GARY D. SCHMIDT is a professor of English at Calvin College; he also teaches in the MFA in Writing for Children program at Hamline University, and at the Handlon Correctional Facility in Ionia, Michigan. He is the author of *The Wednesday Wars* and *Okay for Now*; his most recent novel is *Orbiting Jupiter*, and his *So Tall Within: A Story of Sojourner Truth* will soon be his latest picture book.

JOHN SCHU is an advocate for all kids, a blogger, a part-time lecturer at Rutgers University, and the Ambassador of School Libraries for Scholastic Book Fairs.

COLBY SHARP is a fifth-grade teacher in Parma, Michigan. He is the cofounder of the Nerdy Book Club with Donalyn Miller.

BOB SHEA wrote and drew *The Happiest Book Ever*, the Ballet Cat series, *Unicorn Thinks He's Pretty Great*, and the Dinosaur Vs. series. He is taller and smarter than he appears. He's fun to be around for a while, but all that complaining gets old real fast, you know?

LIESL SHURTLIFF is the *New York Times* bestselling author of *Rump: The True Story of Rumpelstiltskin* and other "fairly true" tales. Her books have received many awards, including an IRA Children's and Young Adult Book Award. She lives with her husband and three kids in Chicago.

LEMONY SNICKET is the author of many books. He can be found on the web and was once also briefly discovered in person.

LAUREL SNYDER is the author of many books for kids, most recently an early chapter book called *Charlie & Mouse* and a middle grade novel, *Orphan Island*. Find her online at laurelsnyder.com.

JAVAKA STEPTOE's picture book debut, *In Daddy's Arms I Am Tall: African Americans Celebrating Fathers* (Lee & Low Books), earned him a Coretta Scott King Illustrator Award and a 1998 NAACP Image Award nomination. Since that time, Steptoe has illustrated and/or written more than a dozen books, including the 2017 Caldecott Medal and Coretta Scott King Illustrator Award winner *Radiant Child: The Story of Young Artist Jean-Michel Basquiat* (Little, Brown).

MARIKO TAMAKI's works include *New York Times* bestseller *This One Summer* and *Skim*, with Jillian Tamaki, and the YA novel *Saving Montgomery Sole*. *This One Summer* received Printz and Caldecott Honors, an Ignatz Award, and an Eisner Award for Best Graphic Album (New). Mariko also writes *Supergirl: Being Super*, with Joëlle Jones, for DC Comics, and *Hulk: Deconstructed*, with Nico Leon, for Marvel Comics.

LINDA URBAN writes picture books, chapter books, and middle grade novels. Her works include *A Crooked Kind of Perfect*, *Hound Dog True*, *The Center of Everything*, *Milo Speck, Accidental Agent*, *Mouse Was Mad*, and, most recently, *Weekends with Max and His Dad*, winner of the Center for Children's Books 2017 Gryphon Award.

FRANK VIVA is an author, illustrator, and designer. His illustrations have appeared on the cover of the *New Yorker* and many other places. His first picture book, *Along a Long Road*, was a *New York Times* Best Illustrated Book. Making books is his favorite thing to do.

KAT YEH is the award-winning author of middle grade novels *The Truth about Twinkie Pie* and *The Way to Bea*, published by Little, Brown Books for Young Readers, as well as a picture book, *The Friend Ship*, from Disney-Hyperion. Kat currently lives on Long Island with her family.

INDEX